THE
GHOSTS
OF
HAVELOCK

THE GHOSTS OF HAVELOCK

OF

PART ONE

MARK A. JEEVES

THE GHOSTS OF HAVELOCK
PART ONE

iUniverse books may be ordered through booksellers or by contacting:

iUniverse
1663 Liberty Drive
Bloomington, IN 47403
www.iuniverse.com
1-800-Authors (1-800-288-4677)

Because of the dynamic nature of the Internet, any web addresses or links contained in this book may have changed since publication and may no longer be valid. The views expressed in this work are solely those of the author and do not necessarily reflect the views of the publisher, and the publisher hereby disclaims any responsibility for them.

Any people depicted in stock imagery provided by Thinkstock are models, and such images are being used for illustrative purposes only. Certain stock imagery © Thinkstock.

ISBN: 978-1-4917-9303-9 (sc)
ISBN: 978-1-4917-9302-2 (hc)
ISBN: 978-1-4917-9304-6 (e)

Library of Congress Control Number: 2016904773

Print information available on the last page.

iUniverse rev. date: 06/07/2016

The three silhouettes appeared from behind a tree and moved swiftly across the road. A few street lamps, plus the quarter moon on this clear night, were providing a small amount of light; however, it was dark enough and quiet enough that the figures were moving unnoticed.

At 1.30 a.m. in this exclusive residential area, the only sound that could be heard was a fox screeching out into the still night. All the dwellings here were large, detached, and unique, and most of them were hidden behind large gates set well back from the quiet road. This wasn't Beverly Hills, this was south-east England, but it could only be described as a very upmarket area; it was inhabited only by the rich and successful.

The human shapes were dark, but it was obvious from their gait that they were three adult males. The trio stopped tight up against the boundary wall of one particular property. Instantly, one crouched down and formed a cup by linking his hands together to act as a support, and the other two, in turn, placed a foot in the cup and effortlessly scaled the wall.

The drop the other side was not long – the same ten foot or so they had just scaled – but as they hit the ground one after the other, they landed on stones, scattering them noisily. One of the men, looking sinister in his balaclava, motioned to the other to stop. Both men froze in their stances, as if they were playing the children's game of statues. However, after ten seconds of no sounds or any lights coming on, the same man waved his arm in the direction of the house, and they both set off across the gravel. Meanwhile, on the other side of the wall, the third man, the human ladder, remained tight up against the brickwork, hidden in the shadows.

The largish house was about twenty years old, with the stony driveway area leading to a double garage away to the left, which created an *L* shape with the main building. The front door was about twenty yards away, directly across from the place where the men had dropped from the wall. The house was a two-storey structure that, judging by the size, probably had five or six bedrooms. It was brick-built, with a few potted plants dotted around this area for decoration, the only vegetation at the front of the property. There was probably a sizeable rear garden, but in this light it was impossible to see. The intruders headed behind the garage at the left edge of the plot, moved round to the side of the house, and soon found themselves at a back door; this was fully hidden from view by the garage structure and the property's side wall. The men seemed to know exactly where to go.

The second man, also in a balaclava, then set to work on the lock of the back door, which would presumably lead into a kitchen or utility room. He crouched down by the door handle, pulled out a couple of tools from his back pocket, and within what seemed just a few seconds, the door was open. This was clearly not beginner's luck. The modern kitchen door with two locks proved no barrier to this seasoned burglar. There was a split-second pause as the two men stared at each other, waiting for an alarm to start blaring. The relief was visible in the men's eyes when all remained silent. As had been promised to them, there was no alarm.

The men stepped into a deserted kitchen, not quite pitch black but dark all the same. It felt cold, due to the floor tiles and the fact that the heating had probably been off now for a few hours. Again the first man, who seemed to be the leader, instructed his expert burglar companion to wait by the kitchen door simply by holding up his right hand and motioning him to keep still. The man did as he was told.

The leader, a large, well-built man, then stepped out of the kitchen into an empty hallway, gently lit by the moonlight coming in through the two panels of glass in the front door.

"The front door," he thought. The man now had his bearings and knew exactly where in the house he was. More importantly, he knew where he needed to go next. With just the mechanical tick-tock of a small wall clock for company, he noticed the time, 1.35 a.m., and then continued his quiet journey. He walked past two doors, one fully closed and the other wide open – through which he could see a large sofa in a sizeable lounge. He was, however, heading to the end of the hall, towards a third door, one which was slightly ajar.

He very slowly and gingerly pushed the door open to reveal a small room, which was clearly being used as an office. This room was a mess. The man thought to himself that if he could get out of the property unnoticed with the prize he had come to steal, it could actually be some time before the owner was even able to report a robbery. There were bits of paper everywhere: across the desk, on the floor, and also pinned to the wall on several cork notice boards. There were shelves on two sides of the room, and these were literally bursting with books, folders, and document holders in no apparent sequence or logical order. The kitchen and the hallway had seemed spotlessly clean and tidy; however, this room was a complete shambles; dusty and disorganised. This villain was going to have a harder job than he'd imagined finding what he was looking for.

He reached into his dark, lightweight jacket and pulled out a small torch, instantly flicking it on. The extra light it produced showed that the room was in an even worse state than the original negative impression he'd formed by the half light. Had someone already ransacked the room and beaten him to his prize? Had he been double-crossed somewhere, leaving his master plan in tatters? He knew the answer to both of those questions was definitely no, but he did feel slightly less confident of success than he had three minutes ago when he and his companion had so effortlessly gained entry to the property.

He walked over to the desk in the far corner of the room, on which stood a computer, switched off and dusty. He pointed the torch at the desk to reveal the sea of papers and discarded envelopes. There were utility bills, bank statements, and even some good old-fashioned letters, a throwback to the pre-email era. He picked up a small picture from the desk. It showed an elderly man and woman being greeted by a dignitary of some kind. Maybe it was the mayor of their town? Who cared? The man knew the elderly couple were the owners of the property, and he also knew for certain they were upstairs – hopefully fast asleep. Under the balaclava, an evil smirk crossed his face.

He suddenly lifted his gaze towards the door of the study – and froze. A figure stood there. He let out a huge breath of relief as soon as he realised that it was his co-intruder, the master burglar, who had ignored his orders and left the kitchen. The shape stood in the doorway, tapping his wrist as if pointing at a watch, reminding his leader that the operation was taking too long. There was certainly no time to be looking at family photographs.

The leader nodded, put the picture back on the desk, and held up his hand and index finger as if to signal one more minute. After all, he had just spotted what he was looking for. He walked over to the bookcase on the wall to his right, pointed his torch at a shelf, and removed a glass container. He slowly lifted the lid and removed a flat A4 card folder. This was definitely it – he recognised it immediately. He shone the torch on the folder. It read "Battler's Theory: 17 July, 2004". He put the lid back on and placed the empty glass box back on the shelf.

The thief drew a large intake of breath. He knew the only reason why this priceless folder was so poorly protected was that the current custodian thought there wasn't a single person in the world who actually knew it existed, let alone what it contained. He tucked the folder under his arm, motioned to his accomplice to go, and they both headed out of the room, across the hall, and back into the kitchen. It all seemed too easy.

Back in the kitchen, the master burglar picked up a kitchen chair to enable the pair to easily scale the property's perimeter wall again. He then headed for the door. The leader followed him to the door but then unexpectedly stopped, turned, and unleashed another evil grin from inside the mask.

For reasons not yet known to his companion, he flicked the kitchen light on and started to look around the room. Just outside the back door now, the other burglar held his arms out wide, suggesting he was bewildered as to what was going on. The leader simply turned, picked up a large vase from the kitchen work surface and hurled it at the kitchen window, smashing both the glass pane and the vase. The crash of crockery and splintering glass was predictably loud and instantly bought audible movement from upstairs. A neighbour's dog started barking frantically at the same time.

The puzzled look on the eyes of the burglar turned to one of panic, and both men then dashed away from the house and back across the gravel driveway to the wall. They placed the kitchen chair down beside it, and the burglar climbed over the wall first. A quick glance back at the house showed him that several upstairs lights had now come on. An elderly male face could be seen at one of the windows, clearly petrified as he looked down on his driveway to see two masked men leaving his property – two masked men who had clearly just been inside his house.

The lady of the house made the emergency 999 phone call instantly, and as she was speaking to the police, all the elderly man was able to do was stare out of the window. From on top of the wall, the second man turned his head around and looked up at the occupied window to the scared male face. He rolled down the bottom of his balaclava to expose his mouth and expose his sinister smile. With that, he jumped down the other side and joined his two companions, and the three of them ran off into the night. Already a whiter shade of pale, the ageing, frail gentleman collapsed.

Running at a steady pace, the third man put his thumbs up as if to question how the mission had gone. The intruder holding the folder, the leader, gave a thumbs-up in response, but the door-entry expert ripped off his balaclava in disgust and, speaking with a strong French accent, said, "Yeah, everything was perfect until Einstein 'ere deliberately woke ze neighbour'ood," nodding his head in the direction of the leader.

"Look, I know what I'm doing," the leader said sternly and abruptly, despite gasping for breath from the running. "Just stick to the plan. We just need to get back to the hostel in the next five minutes, and we are home and dry," he added in an equally aggressive manner.

"What did you—?" the first man said, coming to a halt and removing his own balaclava, but he was cut short by an "enough" gesture by the leader.

"Five more minutes of running, and we are there," he said, this time with a slightly sympathetic tone, as if realising that with some people, even burglars, aggression may not always be suitable and that a reassuring stance might lead this team of criminals to success tonight.

"And both of you put your masks back on, or the whole plan is ruined," he finished as the trio broke into a run again. Their destination was now in view.

Their masks were all back on as the three men jogged up the steps of a small hostel in the centre of town and let themselves in, to the sounds of an ambulance siren and a police car off in the distance. They were in.

2

Detective Sergeant David Johnson had been on duty since 10 p.m. when the call came in. This shift was somewhat unoriginally known as the "graveyard shift" because once the pubs had emptied things generally quietened down until the day shift took over.

"Reported break-in, Linfield House, Sandy Lane, south side of Arleswood," announced the duty sergeant, Sergeant Hughes. "Shall I send a squad car?"

Johnson thought for a moment. "Isn't that where old Freddie Leston lives?"

"That's right, Detective Sergeant," added Hughes. "His wife has just reported the burglary, and she has also called for an ambulance."

"That puts a different complexion on things," thought Johnson, concluding that if an ambulance was needed, there might have been violence. "No, I'll go myself. We'd better have some forensic backup also," he said. "And please alert Inspector Hartnell."

"No need for that," said a voice from the doorway. "I'm already here."

Inspector Roger Hartnell and Sergeant Johnson were firm friends, although they were careful to maintain the formality of their ranks when on duty. As they were both in their early forties, and with experience of policing many tough London estates, they found they had a lot in common.

Hartnell, the senior man, was the taller of the two, with the sort of cultured voice that went down well with the wealthy local residents. He had a kind, friendly, handsome face and was respected and trusted in most situations. He was no pushover, though. Underneath the quiet exterior was a steely career policeman, and more than one hardened criminal had made the mistake of taking him for an easy touch. Although not required to wear a uniform in his investigative role, Inspector Hartnell was always immaculately dressed, preferring trousers and a shirt over smart jeans, and today was no different. He had young twin boys and always maintained that they should never see him anything other than looking his best, so he would set a strong example for them.

Sergeant Johnson was also a committed police officer. He was very competent but had never been able to progress beyond his current rank. He was of average height and, although slightly overweight, was fit and healthy. However, he often felt that, despite his exemplary record, he had been overlooked for promotion because of his physical appearance. Hartnell and Johnson had worked together for several years in London and again now in leafy suburbia, and each was totally loyal to the other. They made an excellent team. Hartnell had a reputation for putting gut instinct ahead of routine police work, and Johnson on most occasions ensured his superior office and friend didn't get too carried away.

Within minutes the two officers were on their way to Sandy Lane.

"It's rather worrying that an ambulance has been called to a break-in," mused Hartnell. "I hope neither of the Lestons are badly injured."

"According to Hughes, it was Mrs Leston who reported the break-in," replied his companion, "which suggests that her husband may be the one needing medical help."

"Indeed, Dave," replied Hartnell, calling his colleague by his first name now that they were alone. "It's a shame that he's a doctor in the academic field and not the medical one, or he'd be able to give himself the best possible help."

As the police car approached Linfield House, the officers could see that the gates were open and an ambulance was already on the driveway. A man was standing by the open front door; his coat appeared to have been hastily put on over his dressing gown, which gave him a rather dishevelled look. He looked relieved when he saw the policemen arrive, and he stepped out to greet them.

"Thank goodness you are here," he said breathlessly. "The paramedics are upstairs with Fred."

The inspector went straight into the house and up the stairs. Johnson turned to the man. "You are, sir?" he enquired.

"Andrew Williams. I live next door. I heard a loud smashing sound and general commotion, which set my dog off, so I rushed over to see what was the matter. Mrs Leston let me in."

"OK, Mr Williams," replied the Sergeant. "You did exactly the right thing. If you would like to come in with me now, your presence may be reassuring to the Lestons."

Together the two men went up the stairs, where they joined Inspector Hartnell on the landing. An elderly, frail-looking gentleman was sitting propped up against the wall, with a young paramedic leaning over him. It appeared the old man was just concluding a phone call, to the slight frustration of the medic. A petite grey-haired lady was looking on anxiously, and a second paramedic, a young lady, was comforting her.

"What is your name, sir?" the paramedic asked the frail gentleman the moment he'd finished his phone call.

"Leston. Frederick Leston," replied the gentleman in a rather weak voice.

In reality, the young medic already knew the answer, as his patient was quite well known in the area; he had even been his maths teacher just a few years ago at the local grammar school. In fact, it had been Dr Leston who had encouraged him to follow his dream of having a medical career of some sort. He felt a real concern here, knowing his former mentor had been burgled and had subsequently collapsed, but his gut was telling him that the old gentleman was going to be fine.

Indeed, after a few short checks and questions, the paramedic was able to conclude that no treatment was required and that the police could start to interview him and his wife. He stood up and went over to the officers.

"He's had a shock and fainted, but everything is fine now," he said. "He was even on the phone when I arrived. I recommend that the GP be contacted in the morning and asked to visit, just to make sure there are no delayed reactions."

"I can take care of that," interjected the neighbour. "I have the same doctor."

"Thank you, sir," replied the young man, and then he turned back to Inspector Hartnell. "I'll stay for a while just to make sure he is OK, but I know you need to start your investigation."

"Right, thank you," replied the inspector, shaking the young paramedic's hand firmly. He then turned to the patient, who was looking immeasurably better than he had a few minutes before.

"Dr Leston, if you feel well enough, we should go downstairs. Perhaps Mrs Leston could make us some tea?" he asked, looking enquiringly at the lady.

"Yes, of course," she said immediately. "I'll put the kettle on," and she made her way down the stairs. Her husband followed slowly, leaning on the young medic, leaving the other three men on the landing.

Inspector Hartnell now took charge and turned to the neighbour, Andrew Williams. "Thank you for your help, sir. I'm sure that Mr and Mrs Leston were pleased to have a familiar face here. Please give your details to Sergeant Johnson here, and then you may go home. An officer will come to interview you tomorrow." They all then followed the Lestons down to the ground floor.

The backup forensic team was just arriving at the house, and Inspector Hartnell quickly briefed them on events so far. The SOCOs headed straight for the kitchen door. An experienced team like the Scenes of Crime Officers needed no time at all to deduce the point of entry and went immediately to work dusting for prints and examining the lock.

In the kitchen, the kettle was boiling, and Mrs Leston was busy taking cups and saucers from the cupboard, clearly relieved to have something useful to do.

Seeing that their patient was clearly on the mend, the paramedics departed and left the police to their work. Andrew Williams put his head round the door to say goodbye to his neighbours and assure them he would look in the next day.

"You are lucky to have a neighbour like that," said Hartnell. "A lot of people just wouldn't want to get involved."

"Andrew has always been good to us," replied Mrs Leston. "In the bad weather he even gets our shopping in. Last winter he cleared the snow off our drive."

Although Inspector Hartnell wanted to get on with his investigation, he let the elderly lady talk, knowing that with each passing minute her husband was getting stronger and the colour was coming back to his face. Finally the tea was made, and Sergeant Johnson joined them. "There's nothing like a nice cup of tea," he said, again rather unoriginally.

"Mrs Leston," said Hartnell softly, taking a small sip of tea straight afterwards. "What I need you to do now is to go around your house, room by room, and see if you can spot what has been stolen. You mentioned to my colleague when you phoned that it isn't obvious. Sergeant Johnson will go with you. Your husband and I will be fine here, and we can have a little chat." He had been looking around the room and had noticed the broken window above the sink and the shattered remains of the vase, which of course, he found rather puzzling.

"Well, there's a chair missing from in here, for a start," said an elderly male voice. This was the first time Dr Frederick Leston had spoken apart from giving his name to the paramedics. He spoke in a quiet, hushed tone but with a degree of authority. It was an extremely eloquent delivery. Hartnell, a very well-spoken man himself, had always thought that Frederick Leston spoke with an upper-class tone a bit to the extreme, making it almost a parody of such a voice.

Hartnell looked at him in surprise. "Could it have been taken to another room? By your wife, perhaps?"

His eyes met those of the householder. Dr Leston, dressed in a dark-blue dressing gown, was a small man, about five foot five inches tall, with plenty of white, wispy hair and a moustache. He was 70 years old but could pass for older than that, especially tonight, considering the visible shock on his face at having his house broken into by men in balaclavas. Hartnell knew something of this man; he was, after all, well known in the community. You couldn't really call him a celebrity, as that was the last thing this shy, reclusive man would want, but he was certainly one of the town's better-known residents. As a world-renowned and award-winning mathematician, who later in his career had taught maths at the nearby school, Dr Frederick Leston was known by everyone in Arleswood.

"I don't think so," he said. "But we'll soon see, won't we?" With that he got to his feet and shuffled over to the sink and the remains of the vase. He looked at the broken pieces and the shards of glass lying around and shook his head.

"The vase was over there where you are sitting, Officer," said Leston, "and therefore didn't end up over here by accident."

"Meaning?" enquired Hartnell.

"I mean the vase wasn't knocked over and broken during a hasty dash to the door," added Leston in a somewhat condescending tone.

"Well, I did notice the broken window as well, Dr Leston. I was just hoping you might be able to make some sense of this."

Leston shook his head. "No, sir, I can't." He then slowly walked back across the kitchen floor and headed for the door to the hallway, where he met Sergeant Johnson coming back in.

"Something very odd, sir," Johnson said. "It looks as though nothing at all has been taken."

"Except a kitchen chair," thought Hartnell, sniggering to himself.

Everyone then left the kitchen, and after a walk around each room on the ground floor, Mr Leston confirmed his wife's conclusion that nothing appeared to have been taken. The TV and DVD player were in place, as were the other major electrical items. There had been a small amount of cash in a drawer, but it was still there. The safe in the small study at the far end of the downstairs corridor was still locked, and although the room gave the appearance of having been ransacked, both Lestons agreed it always looked like that and had done so for years. The computer and printer were still on the desk, and the mess was not the result of the burglary. Mrs Leston had already checked her jewellery before the police arrived and so was able to inform them that it was all accounted for.

Dr Leston seemed reluctant to leave the room, so the two officers walked back to the kitchen together.

"There's something very odd here, Rodge," remarked Johnson. "Two men break into a property and steal nothing?"

"This often happens when break-ins are disturbed, *Sergeant*," replied Hartnell, gently warning his friend not to get too familiar while they were on duty.

"Yes, sir, but the Lestons are saying that what woke both them, and the dog next door, was the smashing of the window, which was caused by a vase being thrown from inside the house," continued Johnson.

"Go on," encouraged Hartnell.

"So, either the burglars broke into the house simply to throw a vase into a window and run off again …" replied Johnson.

"Yes?" said Hartnell.

"Or one of our esteemed couple is not telling us everything about the chain of events," concluded the sergeant.

"Or there is a third possibility, sir," said one of the forensic officers, putting his head around the kitchen door. "Dr Leston has now realised what has been stolen."

3

The entrance hall of the hostel was brightly lit by two bulbs hanging from the ceiling, the light not tempered by a lampshade in either case. As the three men entered, they were all forced to squint slightly when they removed their black, sinister masks. They then moved beyond another internal door and into the main building. As the reception wasn't manned twenty-four hours, each resident was given a key to let himself in should he return late. It's not likely the management quite had offering refuge to criminal gangs in their business model, however!

It made sense for the men to be staying here. It was a no-frills establishment just off the high street. Small and unassuming, the attached two-storey Victorian terraced property was sandwiched between an estate agent's and a charity shop, fairly standard these days in the British town centre. It was not well advertised from the street as a hostel at all, and only a small sign right by the front door would tell any potential client that they were in the right place. To any passer-by it would simply look like a house quietly invading commercial space.

The corridor beyond the entrance hall was about fifteen meters long, with several doors leading off it and a set of stairs at the far end leading to the first floor. At the near end there was a small office to the side, visible through a glass sliding window, which also clearly operated as the hostel's reception.

"Right," said the first man, still clutching tightly the folder he had stolen. "Go straight t'dorm, and go straight t'bed," he added in a broad Northern English accent, and he pointed at the last door on the right before the stairs.

"Be very quiet, and I'll be two minutes." He held his finger up to his lips, mimicking a *shh* sound. One of the men nodded, and the other gave a small wink in agreement. The two-mile run they'd just performed, including a strange detour into the high street, seemed easy for them both as they took deep breaths and crept down the bright corridor. The leader, however, opened the first door and headed into the office-cum-reception room.

He was a fairly tall man, comfortably over six feet, with a muscular but medium build. He was about 30 years old and clearly very fit. Although he wasn't scarred, his face had an aggressive look about it, pained and unshaven. It was far from a beard, though; it just looked untidy, as did his jet-black hair, presumably as a result of spending the last thirty minutes or so under a balaclava.

He switched the light on. This room was in a much better state than the office he had just robbed. Everything was in order, from the files on the wall to the desk which housed the large guest book just below the glass panel window. He put his prize folder down on the clean desk and turned and removed a pre-placed pile of individually written sheets of paper from the top of a small head-high unit.

Smiling to himself, he then opened the dark-blue folder he had just stolen and removed all of the contents, putting them to one side. He placed the papers he had just taken from the unit into the stolen folder and closed it again. Reaching into the top drawer of the desk, he took out a large brown envelope, an address already written on it. He inserted the original contents from Leston's folder into the envelope, sealed it by ripping off the protective strip with one swift movement, and placed the envelope gently into the Post Out tray at the far end of the desk.

With that, he turned, picked up the dark-blue folder, which of course now housed different contents, and turned off the office light. He headed back into the well-lit corridor to join the others in their room, just as promised.

"It should be about two hours," he thought to himself as he turned the handle on the dormitory door.

4

"Please find it!" cried Dr Frederick Leston. "Please—use all the resources you have, whatever it takes!" He was sounding hysterical. "They are still here in Arleswood; they can't have got far."

He slumped into the chair at the desk of his untidy office, and for the second time that evening, his face lost its colour.

The small room was very crowded. Dr Leston was hunched over the desk, his elderly wife by his side, hovering over him. Hartnell, Johnson, and two forensic officers were also there, on the other side of the desk, starving the already cluttered room of any space.

Hartnell spoke next. "Dr Leston, I think you need to leave the house at first light and go and stay with relatives. Get away from here whilst we do our work." This suggestion set off a small murmur of agreement from around the room.

Leston clearly had other ideas, however, and held his hand up and ushered the room to silence. "I will not leave this house until my memoirs are back in my possession," he said through clenched teeth, determined despite his frail state. "And only then are we off, and off we shall go," he added, turning his head round and looking up at his wife.

Mrs Leston seemingly had to nod whether she wanted to or not. She looked very confused, as if she had little idea what her husband was referring to, something the sharp-eyed Sergeant Johnson noticed. He then watched her mouth the word *memoirs* silently, still with the same confused, screwed-up face.

"So, this folder, Dr Leston," said Inspector Hartnell. "Please describe it and what it contains, and please try to tell us why you think anyone would want to steal it."

"Or even be aware of it," chirped Johnson with a smirk, making the comment because he now believed that even Mrs Leston wasn't privy to the existence of the stolen article.

"Yes," said Leston, "but can't you get after the intruders immediately? Can't you go after them now? They can't have got far. Please, please." He was sounding agitated again, and his speech was getting faster and faster.

"Mr Leston," said Hartnell softly and slowly, with a warm smile, trying to calm the frantic man down. "Please understand. There are many house burglaries every month, all over this area. Usually they aren't reported until the following morning when the occupants wake up, or they take place during the day whilst people are at school and work. It is quite an unusual situation we find ourselves in, in that we are only here because the burglary was disturbed and you called us immediately. It is only standard procedure to dispatch a police car this soon if an ambulance is requested to a break-in."

Johnson interrupted. "In case it is more than just burglary we are investigating, perhaps assault as well. Or worse."

"What we are trying to say," continued Hartnell, "is that we do not go tearing off into the night, sirens blazing in search of burglars. We do an investigation, and usually, within just a few days we have apprehended the villains."

There was a pause.

"Are you with me, sir?" Hartnell asked, still speaking in a very sympathetic tone.

Leston still appeared agitated, bordering on frustration. "Can we go into the lounge?" he asked. "It is more comfortable in there, and I want to tell you why I want my work back tonight."

Everybody then made as if to leave, but Frederick Leston ushered everyone to a stop. "I meant just me and Inspector Hartnell," he said assertively.

Sergeant Johnson had suspected that the comment was coming. He had already realised that whatever Leston wanted to share with the Inspector, his own wife didn't even know about it, and he no doubt wanted it to stay that way.

"Very well, Doctor," said Hartnell. "Lead the way."

"Sergeant Johnson," he said abruptly after taking just a few steps. "Please look after Mrs Leston, and also see if the SOCOs have come up with anything."

"Very well, sir," replied Johnson, and he caught a glimpse of the inspector's face as he disappeared into the lounge with Frederick Leston.

He could see that Hartnell also sensed the strange chemistry between husband and wife in the office.

The sitting room in the Lestons' house was a large one, stretching from the hallway all the way to the back of the house. It had a giant L-shaped sofa in the centre of the room, strategically placed to allow maximum viewing pleasure of a huge sixty-inch flat-screen television. A two-seat sofa sat further away, on the other side of the room. Just to the left of the TV was a sizeable fireplace which, given the age of the house, was obviously not fully operational in the traditional sense but did give the room a comforting old-fashioned ambience. At the far end of the room were a set of double patio doors which led out to a conservatory and then out onto the back lawn.

With the door to the room closed, Inspector Hartnell and Frederick Leston seated themselves at opposite ends of the enormous sofa and began to talk.

"So, this folder of yours," said Hartnell. "These memoirs. They are *your* memories, sir, and yours only. Nobody can take that from you. They are worthless to anyone else."

He paused, offering Leston the opportunity to speak. He did not, so Hartnell continued. "And in my experience of burglaries, worthless items are usually discarded by the thieves. Firstly, and most importantly, people don't want to be found in possession of such items, because it becomes quite easy to prove their guilt, and secondly for the very fact that they have no value!"

Still Leston sat motionless, as if waiting for a verbal invitation to speak. In reality, he was waiting for the Inspector to finish his point and make the obvious suggestion that the police would spring into action only once the sun was up. So still Hartnell carried on.

"But one thing puzzles me, and I'm sure it puzzles you too, Frederick. It seems a strange thing for a couple of burglars to gain entry to a house, leave only with a folder that can simply be of zero value to them, and then wake you up on their way out."

He nodded his head in an attempt to get Leston to agree that this was indeed odd, and the old man duly obliged.

"So, can you tell me anything at all," added Hartnell with a sarcastic tone as he leant forward, "as to why this strange case of events has happened? We need to know why these men stole your memoirs and nothing else, and most importantly of all, why they wanted you to know they took them." The inspector then sat back in his seat and invited Leston to speak. He wasn't losing sympathy for the victim, but the oddness of the circumstances surrounding this crime were beginning to influence his professional composure.

Leston spoke quietly but surely. "Inspector, I do not know the answer to some of your questions. I don't know why the folder was taken. I don't know why these men didn't steal anything else, and I can't even begin to think why they disturbed their own burglary."

"Perhaps they thought they were stealing something else?" interrupted Hartnell. "Maybe they believed they were taking an item of value after all?" he queried, with a new sense of enthusiasm and empathy on his face. "You are, after all, very well known, sir – I hope you don't mind my saying. It seems clear that the men did part of their homework. They knew the house very well; this was not a random burglary. You, my friend, were definitely targeted. But perhaps they got their intelligence wrong as to what they wanted to steal. I have seen it many times in my career."

Inspector Hartnell's words didn't comfort Leston at all at first. He was fearing the worst and couldn't think of any scenario other than the horrific one he had in his head. However, hearing the words from the calm policeman and thinking about the situation with a relaxed mind, he realised it was possible he was being foolish. Perhaps he hadn't seen who he thought he had. Maybe it had been someone else. *He* was dead. And apart from *him*, there wasn't a single person on the planet who knew what the folder contained. And even though these men had it now, they would soon realise it wasn't what they were looking for, that it was nothing more than some useless ramblings from an old man, and would simply discard it. He was certain he would get it back.

Hartnell tried to fill him with more joy. "And as to why the fools smashed your window on the way out," he said, smiling, "many criminals are vain. What is the point of being brilliant if nobody knows you are brilliant? They wanted you to see them as they left. Some people get a kick out of things like that. It is the same mentality as when terrorist groups announce responsibility soon after a bomb blast. It is a kind of "look at me, look at what I can do" attitude. If they sneak out quietly, they miss their moment of glory. You see, sir?"

It seemed to Hartnell that Leston wasn't really concentrating at that point. He was, in fact, fiddling with his mobile phone, to the annoyance of the inspector. He finished whatever he was doing, put his phone down, and looked up at the police officer with an understanding nod and smile, as if to apologise for his rudeness. Hartnell forgave him inside. He had received an awful shock and a jolt this early morning, but he had dealt with it well after the initial fall. He had taken a lot of knocks in his life, and this latest episode, Hartnell felt, was just the price a man like Leston has to pay for being successful, rich, and well known.

Frederick Leston then proceeded to give the inspector a detailed description of the two men he had seen, as well as describing the outer appearance of the stolen folder. He also gave a passionate speech as to the sentimental value of the items it contained: photographs, letters, certificates, and short accounts of episodes of his life, which he had written. He was writing his memoirs, his autobiography, and had collected everything he wanted to include so far into this one A4 folder. Although well known, not just in this town but also globally in the realm of mathematics, he was a recluse, and very little was known about him.

"Plenty of people would be interested in reading about the life and times of Frederick Leston," he told Hartnell with a smile, finally showing just a little vanity himself.

It was already nearly 3.00 a.m. by the time the two men emerged from the lounge, joining Mrs Leston and Sergeant Johnson back in the kitchen. Frederick Leston sat down on one of the three remaining kitchen chairs, but Hartnell didn't sit. Instead, he beckoned Johnson back out of the room with a slight jerk of the head, nodding towards the doorway. Johnson didn't need any more of an invitation, as he had been itching to share his findings from his conversation with Mrs Leston as soon as he could. However, he let Hartnell recollect his chat with Frederick first.

The inspector proceeded to tell his colleague how he had calmed the old man down by misleading him with talk of the robbers erroneously removing the wrong item as well as his yarn about criminal vanity to explain the mysterious smashing of the window. Hartnell was as confused as ever about the behaviour of the intruders, but he'd needed a way to appease the hysterical Mr Leston. What Sergeant Johnson was about to tell him was not going to shed any light on things, either.

"Two things, sir," Johnson said. "Firstly, as I think we both suspected, Mrs Leston had no idea that her husband was writing any kind of autobiography or memoir of his life and career. I agree, that may not be too unusual. Many couples have secrets. But she said that Leston hadn't been in that room for nearly a year – in fact, not since the BBC were here filming that documentary about him, which was finally shown on TV last month."

"Which suggests that this little project of Leston's is not at all high up on his list of priorities, despite his passionate plea," concluded Hartnell, and his partner nodded in agreement.

"And the second point?" the inspector asked.

Johnson continued. "Mrs Leston told me what happened at the window tonight as the burglars were escaping. There were three, by the way. She said she saw *three* men running away, not two, as we previously thought. Another man joined them further up the road. He had presumably helped the two who entered the house to first climb the wall. Anyway, she said that although they were very shocked and frightened, having already been through a lot in their lives, this was not the scare for them that it might have been for other couples their age. I even then commented on how calm and relaxed I'd felt she had been this evening.

"But," Johnson continued, "she said her husband collapsed only after he saw the second of the two intruders that he saw was scaling the wall. She told me this intruder rolled up his balaclava and smiled up to Frederick at the window. Only then did her husband fall."

"What could that mean?" asked Hartnell.

"So, sir, we can't be certain, but I think Leston recognised the intruder."

"Yes, great work, Sergeant," replied Hartnell, before adding some wisdom of his own. "But even more importantly, therefore, the intruder wanted to be recognised. That is why he woke up Leston by smashing the vase. He couldn't just sneak off into the darkness. He wanted Leston to be looking out of the window so he could see him!"

"Now we just need to know why!" said Johnson with a sigh.

Inspector Hartnell and Sergeant Johnson left Mr and Mrs Leston with a junior female police constable and got into their car. They had again urged the couple to go and stay with relatives as soon they felt well enough to drive and to leave all contact details with the policewoman.

"I hate to say it, David, my friend," said Hartnell, "But I don't think we are going to get much sleep tomorrow. I think we need to spend the day shift working on this investigation."

"I agree – don't worry," responded Johnson. "Something very strange is going on here. We need to catch up with our intruders, as I think we can only speculate until we do so."

"And the sooner we do that, the sooner our inquisitive little minds can rest!" chirped Hartnell as he turned and smiled at his companion from the driver's seat.

"The break-in happened just after one thirty; that is just over ninety minutes ago," Hartnell added whilst looking at his watch. "They quite literally could be anywhere in the south-east by now."

"Indeed," said Johnson. "But maybe the boys back at the station can help us with that. Whilst you were talking to Leston, I radioed in with detailed descriptions of the men and also the direction Mrs Leston saw them running off in. She didn't see them appear in front of the gates after they dropped from the wall, so they could only have headed off in one direction. I was also able to give a very accurate time of the offence to the boys."

"CCTV!" exclaimed Hartnell as he turned the key in the ignition and idled the engine.

"Exactly, Rodge!" said Johnson. "These streets, this area, this town – it is simply crawling with surveillance cameras. There will be a few blind spots, for sure, but I have got the chaps back at the station trawling through as many of the town's cameras as possible. Each holds about forty-eight hours of recording on a hard drive until it overwrites itself. There is no spooling through reels of tape anymore, matey. This can be done from behind a comfortable desk with a mouse and a computer!"

Hartnell looked impressed. He had been too caught up with trying to calm down the elderly victim tonight and had lost sight of the fact that with each passing minute the chances of making a swift arrest were dwindling. His partner, however, always less likely to get sidetracked by the emotions of cases, was several steps ahead. At the very least, they might see the intruders climbing into a getaway vehicle, which could then be further tracked through road-traffic cameras. Maybe the three men would let their guard down in some other way and provide them with a more detailed look at their faces. Maybe they had taken refuge nearby, and the CCTV would lead the police straight to the location. Maybe, for once, the police and technology would be one step ahead of the criminals, which Hartnell had to accept was often not the case.

There was a new enthusiasm in Inspector Hartnell. Every policeman wanted to solve crimes and get to the bottom of mysteries, and this officer was no different. So many thoughts were racing through his head, none of which seemed to make a great deal of sense to him: What was really in the stolen folder? Why did the men want to be recognised by the homeowner and therefore have the police alerted, when they could have been a thousand miles away before anyone even noticed? Why was being seen by Leston even more important than disappearing unnoticed and undetected? They now knew the police would be hunting them, and that was an unnecessary distraction, surely?

Hartnell's instincts had usually served him well in the past, but in this case he was genuinely lost. His instincts were providing him with very little insight tonight. His investigative experience, therefore, had to take over, and it was telling him that only by finding the culprits quickly would he have any chance here. It was his own curiosity, however, that he mostly needed to satisfy.

A loud crackle on the police radio broke the inspector's thoughts.

"Inspector Hartnell, Sergeant Johnson, do you copy?" asked a male voice from the car dashboard.

"Copy," the men said in unison.

"Sir! I understand you have finished for the evening at the scene of the burglary," the operator added. "You must get back to the station as soon as you can. We believe we know exactly where the intruders are, sir."

"On our way!" said Hartnell excitedly, and with that they sped out of the gates of Linfield House and headed at top speed the three miles or so back to the police station. There was no need for a siren at this time of the morning. In fact, they only passed one other vehicle on the four-minute journey, but they were not hanging around. They didn't wait to hear any more details of the specific location the officer on the radio had mentioned. They both assumed it might be quite some drive from the town, but at least they were on the scent. This was time for some good old-fashioned police work, they thought.

Hartnell drove the car off the high street and into the small compound behind the station. It looked more like a post office than a police station, with a street front in the form of a long glass window and a small metal door accessed by three steps dropping down to the roadside path. There was an entrance for the disabled to the left of the front door, which zigzagged from the doorstep, turning ninety degrees down to the path, with a metal banister for company. Although it was only a small station – nothing more than an outpost, really, for the regional force – it was actually manned twenty-four hours a day and was well equipped with interview rooms and a couple of holding cells. These were usually used for detaining people involved in drunken brawls overnight, before reprimand and release the next day. There was even what was referred to as a "control room", an advanced command centre with state-of-the-art technology for directing operations. It was strongly rumoured, but fiercely denied by the authorities, that this station received subsidies from the rich local residents.

The men jumped out of the car and ran around to the front of the building and up the short flight of steps. The door sprang open before the men touched it, as if they were being watched from within. There was no time for pleasantries as they ran through the reception area. Two police constables were on duty, manning the reception area, but all they could do was wave as their more senior colleagues rushed through, pushed a second door, and headed down another corridor towards their destination.

The control room was quite dark. It had no external windows, and the light that was there was deliberately dimmed. There were about six computers, all in a line on a long desk, with a chair in front of each one. Only one of the chairs was occupied this evening. A young man who could only have been about 18 years old was the occupant. He had dark, thick hair and was wearing black-rimmed glasses and what appeared to be a white lab coat. Standing up at the front of the room was an older uniformed policeman who was completely bald, about five foot ten inches tall, and around 55 years old.

"Hello again, Sergeant Hughes," said Hartnell as he shook the man's hand. "You sounded anxious on the radio, my friend. What have we got?"

"Young Steve, here," said Hughes, directing his head at the person behind the desk, "has been able to pretty much trace the movements of your three crooks since they left the house."

Stephen Mortimer was indeed just 18 years old and was taking a gap year after finishing school before going to university. He was actually employed by Arleswood Town Council to monitor their CCTV surveillance cameras on Friday and Saturday evenings. It was a joint venture set up between the council and the Three Shires Police Force, as part of an overall crime-reduction initiative. Stephen's job was to monitor the pictures being beamed from the various cameras. He could control them remotely if he noticed something he felt was of interest; they had the ability to zoom in on faces, if required, turn the cameras to pick up events happening just off screen, and also to save significant events to a permanent file to ensure potential vital evidence wasn't automatically overwritten. This "big brother" scheme was housed in the police station, as camera operators were often the first people to notice potential trouble or incidents. They could then inform the police immediately, also giving live updates of situations whilst officers were en route. Tonight Stephen hadn't been on duty but had been summoned, as no one knew how to operate the system as quickly as he could. He didn't disappoint.

The young student cleared his throat. "We first picked up the three men from the camera here on Lacey Drive, the road next to Sandy Lane, where the burglary took place," he said, and he showed Hartnell and Johnson a moving image of three masked men running down the street.

"I can then tell from the direction they are running which camera I need to review next," he added, "and so here they are again, running along Culverhouse Road. Unfortunately, this is a fixed shot, and I can't zoom in or turn the camera to see where they head next. So I then lose them for thirty seconds or so. I had to check the feeds from three or four different cameras to try to pick them up after that, as I knew roughly the direction they were running. But as I knew the exact time I was searching for, examining the files was really quite simple, actually. And here they are, running down London Road, approaching the high street. They are still wearing their balaclavas, so it is impossible to get a useful facial view, I'm afraid."

Both Hartnell and Johnson were smiling with anticipation. When they had started their careers, technology like this simply hadn't been available. Now it seemed that people could be tracked wherever they went – tracked forever.

Stephen's grin faded to a puzzled look, though. "But now, officers, something very strange happens," he informed them.

"Everything is strange this morning," said Johnson with a grin. "So try us!"

"Well, I already thought it was strange that the men were running down the high street in balaclavas. I know it was around 2 a.m., but if there was going to be anyone around, it was likely to be there, do you agree?"

"Yes," said Hartnell with a nod. "And it's near the police station too!"

"Quite. But now watch what happens," added Mortimer without making any further clicks on his mouse. Everyone in the room stared open-mouthed at the monitor as the same three masked men came running back past the same CCTV camera from the opposite direction.

"They must have run a little way further, just beyond the reach of this camera, and just turned around; hence, we see them again. We can see them doing it from a different camera, albeit from slightly further away," he added, and he played a video from exactly the same time, taken from a spot further down the high street on the other side of the road.

"So what are they playing at?" asked Hughes.

"And where did they go next?" Hartnell asked, butting in.

"Well, I can answer that, sir," said Mortimer. "After the U-turn in the high street, I pick the three of them up again at the next camera along the road at the bottom. This is my final shot, officers. The burglars are clearly seen here entering Burgin's Hostel less than a quarter of a mile from this very building."

On the monitor now was a shot taken from a camera fixed in the high street but pointing up a small road off to the side. The three masked men, one of whom was clearly holding a folder, could be seen running up to the front of the building and disappearing inside.

"That was at 2.06 a.m., just over an hour ago. I have scanned the images from this camera right up until this moment, and we still have a live feed on it, and no one has entered or left the building in the meantime. I have done something similar to other nearby cameras, and there is no sign of any more movement."

The policemen were all impressed. "Not bad for a councillor!" said Sergeant Hughes jokingly.

The young student seemed very pleased with himself and his detective work. After the analysis he had just showed, his final comment wasn't really required, as it was obvious to everyone, but he said it anyway. "It is a good bet the men are still in there."

Inspector Hartnell was puzzled. Something was not right here, and it frustrated him that his instincts were still giving him very little. Instead of being relieved that there was no need for a wild chase across the country following clues and leads, given that an 18-year-old with a computer and basic skills had already tracked down his villains for him, it was the ease of this that bothered him.

He could tell from his observations at the scene of the crime, from the skilled entry through the back door, and the fact there had been no fingerprints found that he was dealing with experienced criminals here. So why had they woken up the household to even start this investigation? And what the hell were they doing running around the town centre like this? He scratched his chin and turned to the three men in the room.

"Sergeant Hughes," he said, "I need four men to accompany me and Sergeant Johnson to Burgin's. I need them here in five minutes. Can that be done?"

"Yes, sir," said Hughes. "Three are here already, and we can soon call in a fourth. But don't you want to call a specialised squad? They can be here in thirty minutes. Turning up at a hostel at three o'clock in the morning and arresting a criminal gang could be dangerous. They could be armed, for example. This isn't normal procedure."

Hartnell stood there and smiled. "In usual circumstances, I would agree with you, my old friend, but there is nothing 'normal' about this at all. What young Stephen, here, has shown us just now has confirmed a hunch I've had for a while now."

The other men all stood and stared at Inspector Hartnell.

"These men want to be caught!"

6

There was no time for Hartnell to explain his thoughts to Sergeant Hughes. He simply repeated the order for the personnel he required for the short trip to the hostel that stood just two streets from where he and his gobsmacked colleagues currently were.

"What's the plan then, Inspector?" asked Johnson after Hughes had left the room. "I'm not sure that six officers turning up in the early hours of the morning at a small family-run hostel to arrest three small-time burglars is a good idea. We can monitor the camera to make sure they don't leave and simply take them in the morning."

"Yes, we could do that," responded Hartnell. "But if we get there and they have somehow vanished, or have hidden or destroyed Leston's folder, then we look foolish, given we know exactly where they are right now. It would be a PR disaster for us, bearing in mind who the victim is. I don't want to make these arrests for the glory of apprehending the villains who robbed the great Frederick Leston. But, equally, I do not want all the negative bullshit we'd get if we failed to act, the article were destroyed, and so on."

Johnson gave a small nod, but it was Hartnell who continued to speak. "And besides, my friend, as I just mentioned to you all, I think these guys want us to find them. It is a small gamble, I know, but I think these chaps will come quietly. I think six of us should be enough. That is a nice ratio of two officers per burglar! I think we'll be OK!"

Sergeant Johnson would never be a man to act against the book purely on hunches if left to his own devices, but he was always happy to follow along behind his inspector and friend, who would, of course, carry the can should anything go wrong. Johnson was always sure to make Hartnell fully think about his impulsive actions, occasionally bringing the senior man back to a more textbook decision. He tried again.

"It's a lot of maybes, Inspector," he said quietly. "You *think* they want to be caught. You *think* the men will come quietly. And yet, have you ever known behaviour like this before?"

Hartnell turned his head slightly for two seconds as he thought about it. With a smile and a friendly wink after the short pause, he said, "Nope!"

The two men then left the control room and headed back to the station's main reception area, where Hughes had gathered the constables. Stephen Mortimer was still at his post, monitoring the camera pointing at the hostel. He had zoomed right in as far as he could in anticipation of the impending action. He had never felt so important. Usually all he did was watch and record drunken scuffles around the town centre and inform the police where they needed to head. This was very different, and he really felt a sense of achievement, especially considering he was completely unqualified for the work he was currently undertaking!

In the reception area of Arleswood Police Station, Inspector Hartnell gave a brief synopsis of the events thus far to the gathering of policemen and issued instructions. A phone call to the hostel was ruled out on the grounds that no one would answer it at this hour. They would have to force their entry. The outer door, with its simple latch mechanism to allow residents quick and easy entry, should be only a minor inconvenience for trained officers to open quietly. The layout of the building was quite well known to the police, as were most of the commercial properties in the town, and the male dormitory was pinpointed by one of the constables during the briefing. As it was a very small hostel – with just a single dormitory for each sex, plus an office, a bathroom, and the owner's living quarters upstairs – the view was that it should be quite simple to find the men. Each room was quite small, and the consensus was that the three men were likely to be the only male guests staying at the establishment that night. The big question mark, however, as first mentioned by Sergeant Hughes, was how the burglars would react upon the arrival of the police. "Remember, these men could be violent," he warned them.

Hartnell knew he was taking a risk, but he was feeling impulsive. He wanted the men now, so he could get his questions answered. He didn't want to wait for a more specialist squad to arrive or to wait until morning. He wanted to act now, and as the senior officer on duty that evening, it was the decision he was taking. He was by now governed by his belief that the men would come quietly. After all, they wanted to be found, right? And he needed to know why these three men wanted to be found. The experienced inspector backed his decision to act now.

The six police officers – Hartnell, Johnson, and the four uniformed police constables – left the station by the front door and hurried around to the yard at the back of the station. Hartnell and Johnson got back into the car they had arrived in twenty minutes earlier, and the others got into a large white police van with a light-blue roof and the words Three Shires Constabulary written down the side.

The two vehicles headed out of the compound and turned down the road towards the high street. The journey to the hostel would take under two minutes.

Hartnell parked the car outside of the estate agent's next to the hostel rather than directly outside it, and the white mini bus pulled up silently behind him. The six men stood on the pavement, speaking in whispers and using a lot of hand gestures so as to not waken anyone. It was, after all, just 3.35 a.m. on a chilly Thursday morning.

One of the constables hurried up to the door of the hostel, with his three uniformed colleagues plus Inspector Hartnell and Sergeant Johnson just behind. He bent down at the lock, and without the use of a tool or any kind of force, he released the door from the latch that usually required a large key to open. There were, of course, no other security features to the door, as it was the communal door to the hostel and guests were allowed to come and go as they pleased.

The six men slowly crept into the bright passageway, passing the small glass-partitioned window to the office on their left. One of the constables held up a drawing of the building and pointed to the door at the end of the corridor on the right – the male dormitory.

Hartnell's heart started to beat faster now. For the first time he was doubting his decision. Had he been too rash? He had convinced himself that this would be a simple arrest. Three petty criminals specialised in breaking and entering, fast asleep in a hostel, would be no match for six well-trained police officers. They would burst in and seize the three men, who would then be taken back to the station for questioning, with minimal fuss. That was the only scenario Hartnell had planned for. Now, however, all kinds of thoughts about the men being armed, dangerous, and lying in wait had entered his mind. What if they had been lured into a trap of some sort? What if something were to go horribly wrong, and he found himself dismissed for not following procedures? Had he now put himself, his men, and his career in danger? The policemen moved to the dormitory door and in unison looked at Hartnell for instructions. It was clear for Inspector Roger Hartnell that there was no going back now. This was it. He had done this kind of thing many times before, but usually he had the full backing of police protocols and a specialised squad behind him. He had never attempted this sort of early dawn raid simply because he was confused and wanted answers immediately and was too impatient to wait. However, the time had come.

One of the uniformed police constables put his hand on the door handle and looked up. Hartnell then gestured with his index finger pointing through the door, which signalled for the man to open it.

The six men burst into the male dormitory. The dormitory light was turned on by the first officer to pass the switch as he rushed in. Instantly, there were disgruntled male voices as they were woken from their slumber by the officers racing over to subdue them. There were no real scuffles, as the police acted very quickly, and the men could offer little resistance given the speed of the operation. Within about seven seconds of the door being opened, all of the men were standing there by the sides of their beds in their chosen night attire of boxer shorts and T-shirts.

Hartnell smiled as he realised his last-minute fears were for nothing, but as he started to properly survey the room, something hit him, and his smile changed to a look of confusion. Instead of seeing three men detained in armlocks, he saw four men standing there groaning and struggling, barely awake, having presumably been fast asleep just a few seconds previously.

Normally, at this point Inspector Hartnell would reveal to the detainees why they were being held and remind them of their rights, but he was stopped in his tracks by this question of number.

"What the hell is going on?" shouted one of the apprehended men, a very skinny, rough-looking person, but he was soon quiet again, as he was more asleep than awake. He had a real grimace on his face, though, with his shaved hair, a small scar on his chin, and a generally very unwelcoming look.

All four of the detainees had very puzzled looks on their faces, something that didn't escape Sergeant Johnson. He knew that you could often tell the guilt or innocence from the first reaction of a potential criminal upon arrest. People who made great crooks didn't often make particularly good actors, but these four had a genuinely confused look about them.

Hartnell was onto this also, but he couldn't decide among three questions he had: One, were the men still half asleep, and so their reactions couldn't be judged properly? Two, was he right that the men wanted to be found and were just standing there hoping to be taken into custody, and so their facial expressions were meaningless? Or three, were these the wrong men?

Had the strange behaviour of the guys in masks captured by the CCTV cameras been a double bluff by the culprits, and had he here before him innocent men? Why were there four people before him in the room rather than three? Was the fourth man part of the gang or just an innocent lodger, trying to get a good night's sleep, caught up simply because he picked the wrong hostel on the wrong night? And if this was so, which of the four men was it?

However, Hartnell's thoughts were abruptly stopped. He had been scanning the room whilst the other nine people were all seemingly waiting for him to say something, but then he saw it. There, tucked just under one of the iron-framed beds in the room, was a folder, carelessly left in view – a folder exactly like the one Frederick Leston had described to him as having been stolen earlier that morning.

Hartnell motioned at the folder and at Johnson, who smirked when he saw it.

The relieved inspector was at last able to speak. "You are under arrest for the unlawful entry and burglary of Linfield House, Sandy Lane, Arleswood, this morning at one thirty.

"You do not have to say anything; however, it may harm your defence if you do not mention when questioned something which you later rely on in court. Anything you do say may be given in evidence."

There was a moment's pause. The skinny, rough man simply shook his head. This procedure did seem all too familiar to him. The other three men were still shuffling and grumbling but didn't make too much of a scene either. What would be the point?

Hartnell spoke again. "Do you understand the charges put against you?" he asked the four men.

There were a couple of small head nods but no words. Silence and nods were always good enough for Hartnell in these situations.

"Then you will be taken from here now, remanded in custody at Arleswood Police Station, and questioned. Officers, please put these men in handcuffs and take them back to the station."

Hartnell then swiftly turned for the door, with Johnson in pursuit. The inspector wasn't smiling. "Something is still wrong here, Sergeant," he said to his colleague as they hurried back along the hostel corridor towards the front door.

"I'm sure they led us to themselves quite deliberately. They then left the stolen item in full view. They disturbed their own burglary. Our experts confirmed that these guys were professionals from the evidence, or lack of evidence, I should say, that was left at the scene. So what the hell is going on?"

"Well, sir," responded Johnson as the men left the hostel's inner door and paced across the porch area. "It should make for an interesting session of questioning over the next few hours."

"Yes. And it's always good to see another local celebrity in the line-up." said Hartnell. "Our old friend Marcus Stone. He's been out of trouble for a while now, but I'm not at all surprised to see him linked with a burglary of this kind."

"I didn't recognise the other three, though," said Johnson, getting back into the car.

"Me neither," said Hartnell. "So I can't wait to have a little chat with them all back at the station and try to find out what their little game is. Stone has way too much to lose, which makes this behaviour even more bizarre."

The senior officers sat in their car for a few seconds as they watched the four now-clothed arrestees being ushered into the van by the four police constables.

Hartnell turned to his colleague. "Oh, we'd better send someone down here at first light and let them know why their guests have vanished."

He still wasn't smiling, though, despite the obvious humour in his comment and the fact that the last few minutes had been a success. His sense of unease with the situation was evident in his shaking hand as he turned the key to start the car. They started the short drive back to the police station.

The arrested burglars were led into the main reception area of the Police Station by the numerous uniformed officers involved in the operation. Everything seemed abnormally low-key for a situation such as this. There was no shouting or struggling, and the lack of a hostile atmosphere seemed surreal. This pleased Inspector Hartnell, as the last thing he wanted was for this to get out of hand and aggression to raise its ugly head. He knew he would have to explain his actions to his superiors anyway; however, such a conversation was always much easier when things had been successful. He would feel even happier once he could start talking to the men. The arrests and transfer back to the station had gone as smoothly as possible, and the gamble he had taken in his decisive decision to apprehend the suspects could no longer backfire. The handcuffs had even been released early, such was the seemingly docile nature of the suspects. However, there was so much about this case that confused the experienced inspector; he knew he needed answers, and he needed them fast.

Hartnell's thoughts were broken into by Sergeant Hughes, who had approached him. "Sir, where do you wish to hold the men whilst we set up Interview Room 1?" he asked. "We only have two cells."

Arleswood Police Station was not large; it didn't need to be. As a small town of approximately 25,000 residents, with little in the way of serious crime given the predominantly upper-class stature of the residents, Arleswood was lucky to even have such a facility, let alone one manned twenty-four hours a day. Many slightly larger, rougher towns couldn't boast the facilities at Arleswood's disposal, yet this morning, even this station wasn't large enough.

"Put two in each cell temporarily," responded the inspector. "Normally we wouldn't put people together, as it would enable collusion in their stories, but in this instance it would mean we could end up with two different versions – and for sure they would all end up incriminating each other!" he added with a small grin.

"And also, please facilitate the contacting of lawyers and the usual other mundane procedures, and then get the boys to put the chaps in their cells," he said.

Duty Sergeant Hughes walked off to attend to his orders just as Sergeant Johnson walked over and replaced him at Hartnell's side. "It's funny," said Johnson, "but although Marcus Stone has been a good boy recently, he knows he's literally one burglary away from prison for the second time, and yet here he is caught red handed in his home town, leaving a trail so simple to track that we feel it was deliberate."

"Yes, I've been mulling it over ever since we turned the lights on in that dormitory and I saw him there," replied Hartnell. "So what could that tell us? Let's assume he's guilty here, especially as he doesn't even seem to be trying to hide it. What does that tell us?" he asked again.

"Well," replied Johnson, "perhaps there is a reason why he has done this. He has many enemies out there, and most of them would be only too happy to put a knife in his back, both literally and metaphorically. Remember, he dodged prison last year only because he revealed the names of a few of the wider area's drug dealers to us. He has been threatened and even beaten a few times since then. So perhaps the only place he feels safe now is, ironically, in prison. So he commits a minor offence, but serious enough to be sent down, given his record."

"So he makes sure he can be found," interjected Hartnell. "That explains why he had to disturb his own burglary. Let's face it, Sergeant, it could have taken months to find the culprits in a burglary like this."

"And also," continued Johnson, "Frederick Leston would have taught Stone at school, and he would certainly have looked on with sadness at his descent into the world of crime. Remember Mrs Leston said she thought that her husband's reaction suggested he knew the intruder? Could it be that he recognised Stone? I shall ask him when I return the folder to the old man."

The men smiled at each other. Although far from convinced they were at the bottom of this episode, they had finally found a simple scenario which *could* explain such a puzzling chain of events.

"Of course, there are many other questions here, Inspector," added Johnson, to ensure they didn't get too carried away. "So as soon as the solicitors arrive, we'll get going with our questioning."

"Yes," said Hartnell and smiled. "And we're starting with Stone!"

At that point, a flustered-looking Sergeant Hughes rejoined them. "Sir, none of our four suspects wish to have a solicitor," he said.

"What! Why?" exclaimed Hartnell, causing a few faces from the other side of the entrance hall to look over at their senior officers.

Johnson jumped in. "It's clear to me, sir, and I thought this might happen. It is so Stone can simply confess now and try cut a deal with us, without the complications of having a lawyer trying to save him from prison, which we now suspect is not what he wants. The other three are mates of Stone and don't wish for a lawyer to throw a spanner in the works either. They will offer confessions and then hope to walk out with cautions."

"Their reasoning is actually even simpler than that, Sergeant Johnson," responded Hughes. "They are all saying that they don't need to waste time with a solicitor simply to tell you that they were fast asleep."

There was a few seconds' silence, until it was broken by Sergeant Johnson. "What *exactly* did Stone say? What were his exact words?" he asked. He realised that Hughes' words implied that Stone and the others were actually denying their involvement and not confessing at all. This would then mean the scenario he and Inspector Hartnell had just discussed was considerably wide of the mark.

"Just as I told you, Sergeant," replied Hughes. "He says that as he was fast asleep when the burglary you have arrested him for took place, he doesn't need legal aid to tell you this over and over again when you question him.

"I reminded him, and all of the others, for a second time that it is not only their right but also advisable to have legal support – but they were all insistent," added Hughes.

"OK," said Hartnell. "I did not foresee this at all, and it really doesn't tie up with where Sergeant Johnson and I thought this was heading, so we'd better get on with the interviews. It all sounds like pre-planned collusion to me, anyhow. We clearly had enough evidence to arrest the men, so I'm not worried about any criticism I may receive from above. In fact, I'm quite looking forward to this."

The inspector smiled as he looked around the room. "All four men are now in the cells, right?" he asked Sergeant Hughes, who nodded.

"OK, give me a few minutes to get organised, get someone to make coffee for Sergeant Johnson and me, and let's go!" finished Hartnell enthusiastically. He walked out of the room and down the corridor towards the control room.

Meanwhile, in one of the cells, a dejected-looking Marcus Stone, his usual rough, troubled outlook intensified by his disturbed sleep, was joined by his dormitory mate, a man he had yet to have a conversation with.

It was this man who broke the silence. "Hello, I'm Billy," he said with his broad Yorkshire accent, holding out a hand for Stone to shake. There was no response.

Billy tried again. "Do you have any idea what is going on?"

Stone, looking thin and unwelcoming in the corner of the cell, again didn't speak, but he did muster the energy to shake his head before dropping his eyes to the floor again.

"Well, let me tell you, buddy!" said Billy again in a jovial tone.

This apparent knowledge of tonight's weird events finally ensured that Marcus Stone showed interest in his cellmate. His head lifted, his back straightened, and his eyes opened wide as he moved to speak. "Well, I know I didn't do that flippin' burglary tonight," said Stone in an uneducated Southern English accent. "So I assume you are about to tell me you did."

Billy grinned his trademark evil smile, this time flashing it across one of Arleswood's two Police Station cells at Marcus Stone. It was a facial expression which expressed cunning, self-appreciation, and deceit all with one minor movement of his mouth.

Cell B at Arleswood Police station was the smaller of the two cells. The walls were painted white but had plenty of scuff marks all over, presumably from the soles of shoes of the various unruly occupants over the years. There was a black hardwood bench running around three sides of the square room, which was just two meters by two meters. The one wall where there was no bench was, of course, the side with the door on it, which had a small window quite high up. Apart from that, there was no other window, the light solely coming from a two-foot strip bulb attached to the ceiling.

"Yeah, the three of us did it," answered Billy. "Me plus t'other two you were picked up with at the hostel. 'Bout two hours before they nicked us. Sorry to drag you in, pal, but we needed the cops to find four people, not three, or they would know it was us. Now we're going to confuse the hell out of 'em!"

Billy was sounding genuine. There was no aggression in his tone, meaning Stone wasn't sure whether this was real empathy or arrogance. History told him there was no honour amongst thieves and to trust no one, so he sat bolt upright and an uncompromising, angry look came over his face. "Are you framing me?" he said with a fierce, menacing look.

"No, pal, don't worry. We are de-framing *us*, if you know what I mean," responded Billy.

Stone didn't look impressed. "Look, *pal*," said Stone, mimicking the nickname his northern cellmate had given him. "Do you know who I am? I am not a nice guy. I fight, I steal, I deal. These cops hate me for all of the misery and overtime I've given them over the years. They can't wait to send me down again, and now you have put this on a plate for them. I'm trying to build a new life and haven't done nuffin for months. And now this. A burglary takes place in this town, and they follow a lead and find me at the end of it. Even though I've done nuffin wrong, as far as they are concerned, I did this. I'm an exception to the rule here. In this town, I'm guilty until proven innocent."

Billy was emotionless and stone-faced as Stone continued. "Of all of the people you could have ended up with in your attempt to 'de-frame' yourself, you ended up with me. And you'll never guess what. I only stayed at that hostel tonight as my pipes at home broke and flooded my flat. And that happened on the very day that I was handed a voucher for a free night at Burgin's. Talk about bad flippin' luck!"

By now Billy was smiling as he saw his cellmate starting to lose control and get agitated. He took a deep breath, however, as he knew that what he was about to say might tip the notoriously violent Marcus Stone over the edge.

"Yes. Yes I do know who you are, and it is not by accident that it was you in t'room with us when the cops arrived."

"What!" shouted an enraged Stone as he lunged forward at Billy across the small cell. Despite being a known local hardman, Stone was no match for Billy. His punches were simply blocked with ease by the big Yorkshireman, who then almost apologetically pushed his attacker back to the other side of the room.

"Look, man," said Billy with a sympathetic expression. "What I said earlier, I meant it. Sorry to drag you in. We needed a known criminal like you with us. Our plan wouldn't have worked if they had found us with a chuffin' chess champion, would it?"

Stone knew from his initial lunge that there was no point going after his new enemy with physical force again. He would easily be out-muscled, and after all, he was in a police cell and was already just one false move away from another jail term. He tried to relax and gather his thoughts. After everything he'd done in his life and got away with, was he really about to go down for something he didn't do? As time went on, though, his thoughts were becoming clearer and actually less dark. Yes, he was a bad egg. Yes, he was a known burglar. But most importantly, he genuinely had been fast asleep when the burglary took place. It could not be proved he was there at Sandy Lane this morning, simply because he wasn't there!

He lifted his head again to speak to his cellmate. "One thing baffles me, mate," he said. "Why did you tell me all of this? Why have you just confessed to me parts of your plan and the reason you dragged me into this? I don't want to go to prison. As soon as I go out there and they interview me, you must know that I'm going to tell them exactly what you told me!"

"Yes," said Billy with a smile, "which means that all four of us will have exactly the same story!"

8

I nspector Hartnell and Sergeant Johnson were already seated behind the desk in the small interview room when Duty Sergeant Hughes bought Marcus Stone into the room. Hartnell checked his watch. It was now 4.20 a.m. on this very eventful Thursday morning. Usually the interviewee would be accompanied by a solicitor at this point, but as Stone had refused the services of one, there was an empty chair on his left after he had sat down. Hughes moved over to the door and stood with his back to the wall.

The interview room was a lot more pleasant than Cell B. For a start, the room was bigger. It had a rectangular table in the centre, with four chairs around it, two facing each on each long side, with enough room to still fully circumnavigate behind the chairs. There was also a reasonably sized window behind the suspect's seat, but at this time of the morning the blind was drawn, and there was no light emanating from outside.

Inspector Hartnell cleared his throat and leant forward to press the recording device on the table in front of him.

"Interview with suspect Marcus Stone at Arleswood Police Station in relation to a burglary at Linfield House, Sandy Lane, this morning at approximately 1.30 a.m., Thursday, 7th April, 2016. The time is now 4.25 a.m. the same day. Present in the room are myself, Inspector Hartnell, accompanied by Sergeants Johnson and Hughes. Please confirm for the tape, Mr Stone, that you have refused, under no duress or external influence, to have the services of a solicitor at this time."

"That is correct," said Stone in a clear, confident voice. He no longer looked like a troubled man; he seemed very relaxed. He was still looking dishevelled and rough but no longer like a man with the weight of the world on his shoulders. He knew he was innocent and felt that after what he had just been told by his cellmate he would soon be able to clear this up and get out of there, despite the rather arrogant and physically intimidating Billy suggesting it might not be quite that straightforward.

"Look, Inspector Hartnell. I was—" he began but was immediately cut off by Johnson.

"We'll do the talking, Marcus, OK? Please remain quiet. I'm surprised you don't know the drill by now!"

Hartnell gave a half-smile and spoke next. "I may as well cut to the chase here, Marcus," he said sternly. "You were captured by the CCTV cameras leaving the scene of the burglary. You were tracked all the way back to Burgin's Hostel in real time by our surveillance team, where you were seen entering the building. Within just a few minutes of this, we entered the room where you and three other men all fitting the profiles from the CCTV images and the descriptions given by the victims just happened to be hiding. The victim also recognised you. You also have a well-documented history of similar burglaries in this town. And to cap it all off, the stolen item was there on the floor right in front of you."

Johnson spoke next, as if this speech had been rehearsed. "So please don't insult us by telling us that you are innocent."

There was a pause whilst the four men in the room all looked at each other.

"Would you like a lawyer now?" asked Johnson with a whiff of sarcasm.

There was a small murmur of laughter in the room, which added to the sense of ease that the policemen and the suspect all found themselves experiencing. It was a strange situation for Hartnell and Johnson, as they knew the accused so well from all of his various misdemeanours. The situation was made even more informal by the lack of legal representation for the accused. However, the inspector knew he needed to stay professional.

"So, Mr Stone, I am now interested in your story," he said. "Would you care to shed any light on things? Why that house? Why didn't you take anything of any real value? Why did you smash the vase? Come on, Marcus, what's really going on here?"

Marcus Stone was leaning back in his chair, supported by just the two back legs, with his arms behind his head. He was very relaxed now, and this was puzzling the policemen greatly. Based on the evidence, he effectively already had one foot back inside jail, and whether he wanted to go there or not, as the officers had pondered, this was not the pose of a worried or anxious man.

"I don't know what you are talking about," said Stone. "As I told PC Plod over there," motioning to Sergeant Hughes, "I was fast asleep at Burgin's at the time you are claiming I robbed that house. I got there at about 10.30 last night and didn't leave again until you lot dragged me out about an hour ago. Can I go now?" asked Stone flippantly.

Hartnell was now getting angry. "As I just summarised, Marcus, the evidence against you is quite overwhelming, and saying that you were asleep will not stand up in court, as you well know. Now I strongly suggest you get a solicitor."

"Do you want to go back to jail, Marcus?" added Johnson. "Is that your little plan? We are all well aware that your first stint inside was not much fun for you. Now, remind us, what was it? I think a broken arm, a broken jaw, several other little scuffles, and many run-ins with the prison authorities. So why do you want to go there again? Is it because there are people on the outside who would like to give you the beating of all beatings? I could name three people right now who would probably want to kill you. I think that is the plan, isn't it, Marcus? So come on. Level with us. Is that why you are choosing prison?"

A cold shiver came over Stone, as if had had been given a jolt of painful memories by Sergeant Johnson, but he was not to be broken.

"It wasn't me. I was asleep. I am very sorry to disappoint you, Officer. That was quite a moving memory you played out there. I don't want to go back to prison, which is why I don't do bad stuff anymore. It's why I became a super grass last year. You are off the mark here, Sergeant."

Hartnell shook his head and clenched his fist as if to smash it on the desk but stopped an inch short. He wasn't angry, just frustrated, and he needed to think. It wasn't that he felt he was being outfoxed. It was simply that Stone's sleep story wasn't helping to solve any of the puzzles or mysteries created by the events of the last few hours. He knew Stone must be guilty. In his experience, evidence like this was too strong for it to be coincidence, even if he had stretched a few of the facts when summarising it to the accused man moments earlier. Should he get the Lestons down to the station to identify the shapes they had seen and, in particular, get Dr Leston to identify the intruder who had lifted his mask? Stone surely was the man he'd recognised. Hartnell would rather he didn't have to do this, as the elderly couple were clearly in no state to come down to the station. But equally, if Leston had recognised his attacker, a claim at this point unchecked, then could it be done by phone? Simple: "Did you recognise the intruder, Dr Leston?" And if so, "Who was it?" He can't believe he didn't ask the old man that question back at the house, when Sergeant Johnson had informed him that Mrs Leston believed her husband knew the intruder.

Inspector Hartnell needed a way of getting Stone to talk. He needed to put him under pressure, somehow. He needn't have worried, however. His suspect was more than willing to talk. After a short break, whilst Hartnell and Johnson were conferring in each other's ears, Stone spoke, and this brought them back to face their interviewee.

"I do have a story for you, officers," Stone said calmly. "It may involve you doing a bit of police work," he said smugly. "But you'll get paid for it, so why not, eh?"

Inspector Hartnell and Sergeant Johnson were not amused. However, over by the door, the overworked duty sergeant, Sergeant Hughes, gave a little smile in response to Stone's comment, despite having just being referred to by him as PC Plod.

"The guy you put me with in the cell just told me everything, actually."

"I'm all ears," said Johnson, leaning forward and for the first time in the session trying to be intimidating.

"Answer me this first, though," added a smiling Stone. "How many people were you looking for in connection with this burglary?"

No one spoke. The question caught the officers off guard. Experience told them both that the best thing to do when that happened was to stop and think, to say nothing until their thoughts became clear. They should not start to blabber and show the suspect any lack of thought control.

The policemen knew they hadn't revealed to their suspects that it was clear only three people had committed the burglary. They knew that there was a chance that one of them was actually an innocent party in all of this. The likelihood was that all four were involved somehow, but the chance of one of them being an unwitting roommate was still there, albeit a low one. But surely, if there was an innocent party, that person was not Stone. In all probability, he was the gang leader.

"Shall I go on?" asked Stone. His question was met with the same blank faces.

"The other three guys you have here did the break-in. They came back to Burgin's and into the room where I was staying, so when you turned up there were four of us. Billy, the guy in the cell with me, said that they framed me so that when you all turned up, you wouldn't know which three you were looking for out of the four of us. I needed to be a known burglar and not someone with a clean record, or you would soon discount me and focus purely on them."

The police officers looked at each other. "So you were set up, Marcus? Is that what you are saying?" asked Hartnell in a bemused tone.

"It was quite clever actually, officers," continued an increasingly polite-sounding Stone. "Yesterday lunchtime, when I was at home, my water pipes burst and completely flooded my bedsit. Then, an hour later, after speaking to the plumbers, I was in town getting a few bits, and a man gave me a Burgin's Hostel voucher for a free night's stay. I thought it was odd in a town like Arleswood for that hostel to be trying to tempt local shoppers to become regular clients. But I had a flooded apartment and needed a place to stay. Looking back now, I'm thinking old man Burgin only set that place up for a refuge for people struggling to keep up with the cost of living. Not many of those are shopping in Arleswood high street on Wednesday afternoons. So, here comes your police work, chaps. You can check out my pipes at home and see that they have burst. And I bet the voucher offered by Burgin's was not real. Someone, presumably one of those three, just happened to stick one in my hand as I walked by. You can go down to Burgin's and ask them that. There was no one at reception when I arrived, so I just let myself in. The door was ajar. I had my voucher, so I didn't feel guilty."

Hartnell was intrigued. His eyes were wide open as he listened to Marcus Stone, a known burglar and fairly violent criminal, speaking like Sherlock Holmes. He was a constant thorn in the side of the local authorities with all of his various misdemeanours, yet he had never been considered a criminal mastermind. Quite the contrary: quite often he was implicated by his own silly mistakes. So was this a new Stone – or had this mysterious Billy fed Stone a brilliant story? Hartnell let him continue.

"And also, you can check my mobile phone. You will find no record of me ever having any contact with any of those guys. I have never met them before. I don't know who they are. That will become very clear to you when you do your homework. And of course, I'm sure when you dive into their lives, you will see that they are all connected to each other. Phone records, previous convictions together, even things like Facebook. I'm sure you will agree that you can't pull something like this off by plucking a couple of strangers off the street. So, plenty for you to be getting on with there, officers!"

He sat back in his chair and felt a well-earned sense of achievement after his monologue. He knew he was no angel, but he was not going to go to prison for something he hadn't done. His smugness was not to get back at the police for arresting him, however. He'd actually always quite liked them, Johnson in particular. No, he was actually thinking of his temporary cellmate, Billy, and the smart look on his face when he'd informed him of what had happened that morning, and why his gang had dragged Stone in – and how he'd smiled when he'd told him that getting off the charge might not be that straightforward. He was still puzzled, though. Why would Billy tell him what the gang had been up to? This would now be so easy for Hartnell and Johnson. It would be easy for the police to uncover that he was an innocent man and to implicate the others now. "Not as smart as you thought, *pal*," he muttered to himself.

The police officers were a little lost for words, as this clearly wasn't the direction they'd expected their interview with Stone to head off in.

"Thank you for that little episode, Marcus; we will indeed check out your story," said Inspector Hartnell. "Considering how close you are to another jail term, I hope for your sake you haven't just told us a little pack of lies and are wasting our time. That would probably seal the deal. And of course, we will also be speaking to the others."

"And checking their phones and Facebook pages," said Johnson in an unimpressed tone, annoyed at some of Stone's comments. "I would never have thought of that," he added sarcastically, even though he knew Stone was right. That would actually be quite clever.

Hartnell put his hand on his colleague's shoulder to calm him down. It was the inspector who spoke next. "You are free to leave the station now, but may I remind you that you are still under arrest and that you must report back to this station at 10.00 a.m. That is in just over five hours from now."

Stone nodded.

Hartnell turned to Sergeant Hughes. "Please escort Mr Stone out and do the necessary paperwork." He turned the tape off.

Hughes and Stone went out of the interview room and left the door open behind them. Sergeant Johnson spoke. "I'm good at reading people, sir," he said to Hartnell. "And he actually seems genuine."

"Yes, my past experiences with the man are of an angry, disturbed thug who barely tries to hide his guilt. Yet here he is laid back, calm, and logical. I know he's been quiet for a while. Maybe he's been to acting school these last few months!" quipped Hartnell.

"But he's guilty, right? He must be," responded Johnson. But then he doubted himself. "But what if he's not? What if that bullshit he just churned out is actually true? I'll get one of the chaps to check out his pipes at home and also the fake vouchers story, at first light, when they go down to Burgin's to explain what happened there. They probably don't even know we were down there earlier this morning, such was the ease of the operation, and they are still fast asleep."

At that moment, a very flustered Sergeant Hughes ran back into the interview room and caught the tail end of Johnson's sentence. "Fast asleep at Burgin's? You must be joking!" he panted as he gathered himself. "You are not going to believe what is happening there now!"

9

Three police constables ran out of the front door of the police station en route to the hostel they had attended earlier that morning. Inspector Hartnell and Sergeant Johnson briskly followed Sergeant Hughes down the short corridor back to the control room. Marcus Stone was still sitting in the reception area, a little bewildered at all the activity happening around him and more than a little frustrated that he wasn't yet allowed to leave the building.

Stephen Mortimer was still behind the desk of his computer when the senior officers entered the dark control room, and he immediately motioned to the officers to look at the big screen. The CCTV feed was still showing the front of Burgin's Hostel, just as Mortimer had promised it would just over an hour earlier.

Hartnell and Johnson stood open-mouthed as they looked at the large monitor on the wall of the control room. They could see a disturbance taking place on the pavement just outside the front of the hostel. Three men appeared to be kicking and punching a fourth man at the foot of the small steps of the building and were dragging him along the pavement towards the charity shop. Lights were being switched on all around, and then what appeared to be two females appeared at the hostel entrance door at the top of the stairs.

"What the hell is going on?" exclaimed Johnson. "The three other men we detained earlier, they are all still here, right?"

"Safely locked up in the two cells down the corridor still, sir," replied Hughes.

"So who the hell ...?" added Johnson, turning back towards the screen.

They all carried on watching the live feed on the screen as the two women ran down the steps and appeared to aid the lone man. The help worked, too, as two of the men broke away from the fighting group. However, they then ran straight up the steps and into the now unguarded hostel. One of the female figures turned and chased them into the building, leaving two men and the other woman fighting. Just moments later, however, the two men ran back down the stairs again, but they didn't join the fight. They merely ran past the scuffle and were joined by their accomplice, who finished his fighting duties and also fled the scene.

"Where are our boys?" said Hughes anxiously.

The three figures immediately left the scan and range of the CCTV camera that Mortimer was observing. All of the police officers were perplexed and fidgety, pacing around and waiting for the three officers to appear on the scene.

"Can we trace them?" asked a flustered Hartnell.

"Not really," replied Mortimer apologetically. "They have headed across the road and onto Arleswood Common. This is a fixed camera, so I can't turn it and follow the men. And even if I could manipulate the direction and zoom in, it's too dark. I'd be guessing."

The three police officers didn't speak, so Mortimer continued. "Although it's close to the town centre, the common is more than two miles long and is half a mile across at its widest point, and of course there are no cameras there. I think we are looking at a foot-pursuit officers."

More pacing from Inspector Hartnell and Sergeant Hughes ensued. Sergeant Johnson was looking at the watch on his left wrist, anxiously moving it from side to side with his right-hand fingers, presumably anticipating the arrival of the police car on the screen.

"Well, we know exactly where they are right now," said Johnson. "But they could exit the common at any one of about twenty points."

"Yes, I'm loading up a few of the cameras from the streets around the common boundary now," said Mortimer.

Just at that moment, the police squad car appeared on the road outside Burgin's Hostel, and the three officers jumped out. They ran straight over to the man and two women standing on the pavement outside the building.

Hughes grabbed a small handheld device from the table in front of him. "Constable McAllister, are you there?" he said. "Suspects have run onto Arleswood Common. Over."

"McAllister here, sir," came the reply. "OK, understood. No ambulance required here. Man down in need of medical attention only. Please send reinforcements for chase. How much of a head start do they have? Over."

"Ninety seconds, McAllister. We'll send cars to the perimeter also," added Hughes. "Leave one of your boys with the three from Burgin's, and you and the other get going. We will need regular updates. Over."

Hughes placed the device in his pocket and instinctively turned to his inspector. As he was his senior officer, Hughes was looking at Hartnell for a nod of approval for his swift actions and instructions to Constable McAllister and also to receive his next orders and instructions. These instructions duly came, but they weren't exactly what he was expecting from Hartnell.

"Call your men off the chase, Sergeant Hughes," he said after a large sigh.

"I'm sorry, sir?" replied Hughes with a puzzled expression and exasperated tone. "You don't want us to give chase?"

Johnson was also confused. "Sir. We know where they are. We can soon surround the common. We have a bit of a chance here. I know they may get away but—"

Hartnell held out his hand, shook his head, and said no. "Guys, it's OK," he said, trying to calm things down and hoping to reassure his two colleagues that he hadn't lost his mind. "I'm pretty certain I know what has just happened, and if I'm right, then we have no need to give chase. I think I know how to find these men, and it won't involve loud sirens, waking the whole town, and early morning chases across dark parks. But more of that later. If the people outside Burgin's don't need an ambulance, then we are not dealing with anything serious here, although I admit it could easily have turned out that way. Call McAllister back to the hostel after he's taken statements from the people at Burgin's. It is a better use of his time and energy than running around the common on a wild goose chase."

Both Sergeants Johnson and Hughes were still looking a little confused, but they followed their orders. Hughes radioed McAllister immediately. It was difficult for Constable McAllister to not sound too grateful on the radio when he found out he didn't have to run into the dark chasing who-knows-who for who-knows-how long.

After asking Mortimer to continue to monitor and record the CCTV cameras, especially those near the exits from the common, Hartnell asked his two sergeants to join him in one of the interview rooms. After all, he knew that the three men he had just seen fighting on the surveillance cameras were already long gone. He was relieved that the slightly injured man at the scene, presumably Mr Burgin himself, was not in a serious state. He was sure McAllister would look after him and also inform him that this was actually the second time the police had been there that morning. Burgin was probably still unaware of the first visit.

Hartnell gathered himself. "Sergeant Hughes, I need you to do me a favour. Marcus Stone is still in our reception area, right?"

Hughes nodded.

"I need you to go and sign his release papers and tell him to go straight back to Burgin's Hostel and collect his things before going home. Give him back his master key for the front door. Don't tell him that the police are there. And then please come straight back in here and tell me his reaction, OK?"

"OK, Inspector," he responded and left the room.

Johnson looked curious, but he suspected his partner was onto something here. "OK, that will take at least ten minutes," he said. "So, can you fill me in on your thought process here? What are you sensing? Why did we really not chase those men?"

Sergeant Johnson was a fine policeman, but when it came to hunches and unravelling unusual cases, it was his more senior colleague who seemed to have a sixth sense. After already getting so badly wrong the possible scenario of Marcus Stone wanting to return to jail, Johnson was only too happy to listen to his friend right now.

Hartnell motioned to Johnson to close the door, and then he spoke. "There are so many things about this burglary that are odd, and I'm not going to run through them all now. But after what we have just seen, actually, a few things have fallen into place."

"Go on," said an enthusiastic-looking Johnson.

"Well, it is a bit of a long shot, I must admit. But I think that the three men we just watched on the CCTV feed also went to the hostel to find the stolen folder."

Johnson's brow turned in on itself in confusion. Hartnell continued. "And apart from the police, who else even knows that a burglary has taken place?"

"The paramedics? The neighbour?" asked Johnson.

Hartnell smiled. "And even fewer people know anything was stolen," he added.

"Mortimer?" responded Johnson.

"And?" said Hartnell.

Johnson shrugged his shoulders and shook his head.

"The Lestons, of course," announced the inspector.

Johnson now looked even more puzzled.

"The paramedic told us that Leston was on the phone when he arrived, which delayed him receiving attention. He was also fiddling with his phone when I was talking to him in his living room. I told him very clearly that we were not going after the intruders and the folder tonight. It was only because of what Mortimer and Hughes found using CCTV that we did anything. Remember, Leston doesn't know this. He thinks we are sitting here twiddling our thumbs, drinking coffee and waiting until the morning. He desperately wanted us to go after the burglars. When I said no, he was hysterical, but then, after I reeled off some top-quality bullshit, he calmed down. I thought he'd bought it, but thinking back now, I remember he was again distracted by his phone. Maybe he was texting someone? Maybe he was saying, 'The police won't chase them, so you can do it, please?' I think whoever Freddie Leston sent a message to are the people we just saw running away from Burgin's."

"Interesting, Rodge," responded Johnson. "But there are many, many holes in that theory. Look, Leston is a rich man, but not that rich. He certainly doesn't have the wealth and power to control a rogue police force or hit squad able to track down suspects almost as quickly as the real police. We traced them using Arleswood's secure multimillion-pound neighbourhood security network – a few mates of Leston's couldn't do this. Who would Frederick Leston know that could possibly do this? He is a retired old schoolteacher who it just so happens can add up better than most. I don't think he's got any kids that could be Internet geniuses or anything, either. That kind of person would not have the ability to pull strings to do what you are suggesting. Do you agree with me?"

"I do agree," responded Hartnell. "But those men were clearly looking for something, presumably the folder. They did not know that it is currently in the room next door to us being analysed for prints by our forensics team. And here's the killer point, Dave. *Only Leston* knew anything was stolen."

Both policemen took a long intake of breath.

"I will head back to his house myself in a few hours to return his folder," continued Hartnell. "In the meantime, can we get someone to check his mobile phone? He called someone and texted someone, and we need to know who. I'm sure we have the ability to access his records. I see this line of evidence-checking on those American police TV shows all the time."

Hartnell was disturbed by a knock at the door, and Hughes put his head around the door without waiting for an invitation. "No reaction from Stone, sir," he said. "He just signed, smiled, and left as if he didn't have a care in the world."

"OK, many thanks, Sergeant. Will be with you in a minute," said Hartnell and waved him back out.

Hartnell spoke again. "And that brings me to my next hunch, Dave. Stone reacted as I expected him to. He is happy out there on the street, heading back to the hostel, blissfully unaware that if he hadn't been arrested by us earlier this morning he would have probably just have been beaten to a pulp by those three men we saw running onto the common. He doesn't know anything about that folder or the burglary at Leston's house."

"Go on," encouraged Johnson.

"Now I will try the same on the other three. Something tells me their reactions will be quite different. So, unless Mortimer has anything conclusive or McAllister has anything that he urgently needs us to assist him with, we'll start talking to them now."

"I'm not following, Rodge," admitted Johnson.

"My belief is that they knew someone else would be tracking them," continued Hartnell. "Someone who would perhaps not be as gentle with them as we were. And so they left a nice, simple trail so that we would find them first. They would rather be captured by us than be found by the three men we just saw fighting outside Burgin's. Now here is the crucial point, Dave. The guys we are holding here also don't know what has just happened down the road. I believe that when we tell them to go straight back to Burgin's, they may not react as calmly as Stone just did."

"Err, Roger, my friend?" responded Johnson. "It explains only part of the situation, as you know, and is ingenious except for one crucial and obvious point."

Hartnell knew exactly where Johnson was heading and was already nodding.

"Whoever broke into the Lestons' house disturbed their own burglary. If they hadn't done that, they could have been in France by now, and neither us nor these other men would have possibly been able to trace them. They wouldn't have needed to leave a trail so that we could save them from the mob if they had just left that bloody vase alone! Explain that one to me, mate!"

Hartnell was smiling helplessly. "Yep. I'm still working on that one! Now let's go and meet this Billy chap. I want to talk to him first!"

10

artnell and Johnson pushed for about twenty minutes on Billy in an attempt to get something sensible from him, but they got few details: Billy Morgan, 31 years old, originally from Leeds, West Yorkshire, Northern England, but now of no fixed abode. They knew they couldn't take too long if they wanted to test the suspect with the threat of being asked to go to Burgin's Hostel.

The uniformed PCs on duty had taken his fingerprints and ran a few checks on the computer but found no record on the system of any previous convictions or interactions. Hartnell had warned them not to expect to find anything anyway, as they were certain he was using a false name. This wasn't a concern, as the inspector was sure that in time the fingerprints would soon pull up his real details.

"So, let me run through this again, Mr Morgan," said Johnson. "You were asleep at Burgin's Hostel from about eleven o'clock last night until we woke you this morning. When you went to bed, there were three other men in the room, and when you awoke, there were three other men in the room."

"And a few cops!" chirped Billy.

Johnson wasn't impressed but continued unfazed. "You say you have never met any of those three men before, which of course we can easily check. You say you were staying in that hostel because 'that is what you do'. You regularly stay in hostels, as you have no address. We can easily check that, too. And you did not speak to your cellmate and talk him through an elaborate story about setting him up because he was a known criminal. You have no idea how a group of burglars could have gone to that hostel, left the stolen item at the foot of your bed, and then left again, but this time without being seen by the cameras. The same cameras that led us to that hostel in the first place."

"Have we left anything out?" asked Inspector Hartnell with a smirk.

"That is pretty much it, officers, yes," responded Billy. "Of course, as mentioned, the other three guys in the room could have been involved. I'm a heavy sleeper. But yes, that is it. That summary covers my answers to your questions."

"What do you take us for?" snapped Johnson. "Look at the evidence against you, Mr Morgan. You are totally guilty, and you know it, and more importantly, *we* know it. Now come on, mate, level with us. Was it Marcus Stone? Did he get you into this? Is that why you didn't want a lawyer? This was actually his grand plan, and he promised you a cut? This burglary was a trial, right? To see if Stone's plan works? Look, we can help you. We can cut a deal. Just give us Stone."

There was a short pause as the two policemen stared at Billy Morgan, neither of them aggressively – possibly they were intimidated by his physical presence.

"I assume, then, that Marcus Stone is one of the other three men?" responded Billy. "As I told you many times now, I don't know any of the others."

"Well, he didn't fall for that simple trap," thought Johnson to himself.

"OK," interjected Hartnell, ready to launch what he thought was his trump card. "You are free to leave, Mr Morgan. But remember, you are still under arrest. Please return straight to the hostel now, and report back here at 10.00 a.m. You will be given your key to the hostel by the duty sergeant."

Hartnell and Johnson then waited, ready to monitor the reaction of the suspect. Would he react as Hartnell predicted and flinch at the prospect of heading straight back to Burgin's? If he suspected another gang were after him, and he didn't know that the attack on Burgin's had already taken place, then he would surely give off a sign of being scared, and therefore aware of this baffling situation. Anything that suggested he knew unsavoury characters may be after him would go a long way towards proving Hartnell's theory.

"OK," said Billy calmly. "I'm going back t'bed."

This was not the reaction the policemen had hoped for, and they simultaneously let out an audible disappointed sigh.

Billy spoke again, forcing the officers to lift their gaze. "However," he said, "if you think I'm guilty, you would keep me here, or at least accompany me to the hostel in case I run. But if you now think I'm innocent, then you would have to drop all of the charges against me, surely?"

No one spoke for a few moments.

"So, which is it, officers?"

"Well, I think you are as guilty as hell, if that answers your question," said Johnson. "But with it being the early hours of the morning, and us therefore being pretty understaffed at the moment, we can't be bothered with you right now. The offence is minor, so if you did run off, I really couldn't give a shit. We now have your prints, and so I'm sure we'd catch up with you again sooner or later."

Johnson was quite dismissive in his style, which impressed Hartnell. "But just so that you are aware, Mr Morgan," he continued, "we used our surveillance team to track you to that hostel, and we will use the same team to ensure you head straight back there. If you deviate from the route, then we'll simply send a squad car down to pick you up. And then, I assure you, the charges will go from being minor to serious. And you don't want that. Do you understand?"

"Fair enough, Officer," responded Billy. "Think I've got it. Although you didn't track me anywhere earlier. I was asleep, remember?"

Johnson shook his head as Sergeant Hughes was summoned yet again to escort Billy away ready for release, leaving him with Inspector Hartnell to muse over the reaction of the accused man.

"Not convinced – sorry, Rodge," said Johnson. "Although he did start asking questions rather than just grasping at the chance of freedom, but that could just be down to him being smart. The questions he asked were valid. He didn't go for it. He seemed to have an answer for everything."

"I agree. Not what I was hoping for," replied Hartnell. "Still, the real test will take place now, I think. Will he start to walk there or run off? Once he's left here, let's go and see our young friend on the cameras and follow him live."

"I've never watched so much TV whilst on duty, mate!" said Johnson jokingly.

Hartnell smiled. "In the meantime, I want very quick statements from the remaining two suspects. I'm not in the mood to hear more stories about how they were fast asleep and have no idea how this could have happened. We get prints and names and then judge how they react when we send them back to Burgin's. They can't all be as cool as Stone or this Billy Morgan guy."

"I suspect we won't ever find any prints at the scene or on the folder; it's clear they were careful. And I'm not going to bother sending all their belongings off for DNA testing, either. Those guys are busy enough as it is looking at forensics for far more serious crimes than this one. This is simply a burglary where nothing of value has been taken, and even that object has been found. No one was injured, and I'm sure with 'a little police work', as Stone put it, we'll soon uncover the culprits, probably all four of them, and close this one."

"But it won't close it, will it?" said Johnson knowingly. "Someone, possibly Leston, sent a vigilante gang after his intruders and the stolen folder. That must be investigated, as we have an assault captured on camera. And I know, Rodge, that you won't close your mind on this one until you know what really went on. Why did the intruders disturb their own burglary, and why might the victim have sent a hit squad to find the culprits instead of leaving it for us? And how did he have the means to do it?"

"I know, Dave. There is far more to this one than we know at the moment. In a few hours, at the end of the shift, let's head back over to see Dr Leston and break to him the good news about finding his folder. I'm sure he'll be thrilled to see us!"

The men smiled at each other and left the small interview room. Sergeant Hughes was just doing the formalities with Morgan at the reception desk as they walked through, the large Yorkshireman towering over the diminutive Hughes.

At that moment, PC McAllister came back in through the front door of Arleswood Police Station alone, his two colleagues presumably still down at the hostel.

"All quiet down at Burgin's, Inspector Hartnell, Sergeant Johnson," he called loudly across the room at his senior officers, and before either of them could motion to him not to say anything else, he said, "I've left two PCs down there to make sure those thugs don't come back."

Morgan pretended not to have heard the comment, but a smile came across his face. He knew he would be able to go and have lie-down for a few hours after all. He knew that the hit men had already paid him a visit and been too late. But he was shocked that they'd found him and Burgin's so quickly. Were they better than he'd thought? Would he have to rethink his further plan? He also wondered where Stone was now. Had he also been sent back to the hostel? In any case, with the building safely under police guard, all he needed now was for his two friends to stick to the plan and not crack under the pressure of questioning. Then phase one of the operation could go down as nothing but a complete success.

11

The interviews with the final two suspects were meant to be quick and fruitful but inevitably proved equally as frustrating for Inspector Hartnell and his two sergeants.

"Incredible!" he cried, slamming his fist on the desk at just under full force. "All four of them, all the same damn story! Clearly it's a pre-planned set of responses, each one claiming he may have been set up by the others. All of them claiming they have never met any of the other three before."

"Ingenious, really, in terms of a short-term strategy," replied Johnson. "Mortimer has told us, from running back through the security video, that the four of them arrived separately at Burgin's throughout a two-hour period yesterday evening. But it won't delay us for long from finding out which are the three of them who left the hostel together in masks at around 1.00 a.m. and committed that robbery."

Johnson continued. "Three carry out the burglary, which means one definitely stayed behind and didn't take part. Because it was dark, the cameras aren't that sophisticated, and the men were wearing masks, we simply can't tell by studying the footage which ones they are. This means each one can claim he was the person left behind and is, in fact, an innocent party in this. The likelihood is, of course, that they were all involved and this is an extremely clever plan for them all to get off. Getting proof beyond all reasonable doubt here might prove tricky – unless we can prove that some of them, if not all of them, knew each other."

"Are the guys already going through phone records to find links between them?" asked Hartnell, referring to Sergeant Hughes and his team. Sergeant Johnson nodded.

"Good. That won't take long at all," continued Hartnell. "But right now, based on the fact that we know only three men were involved in the break-in, we have no choice but to let them all go. Stone and Morgan have already left. Please get Hughes to release the other two now."

"As I've just said," replied Johnson. "The question remains, was the fourth member there purely to hand us this complicated situation, or is one of them completely innocent? And we can't even start questions about why they broke the vase, and why they stole that folder, until we know we are actually talking to the right burglars."

"Well, Stone seemed genuinely confused and innocent, but I'd still bet my wife's brand-new car that he's involved," vowed Johnson.

"And she loves that car!" quipped Hartnell.

"And we have this Billy Morgan, who seemed so sure of himself," added Johnson. "Almost too sure. According to Stone, it was all this guy's idea. Maybe he is the brains here? He claimed it was *Marcus* who confessed to *him* that he was stitching him up – basically reversing the words Stone said to us. But I'm not convinced Marcus Stone has the mental capacity to create this clever situation, so my money would be on Morgan, and he's coached Stone into exactly what to say. We know he headed back towards Burgin's, so if HQ come back with anything on this guy, we can soon pick him up – the same if he skips his ten o'clock meeting with us."

"And what did you make of the Frenchman?" asked Hartnell. "He seemed very genuine."

"Yes. Philippe Le Sac," replied Johnson. "Or 'Phil the Bag', as we'll call him from now on! Well, his reason for being at Burgin's was the most feasible, but his English wasn't brilliant, and so it was hard to be sure he really followed our questions, but that could easily have been a clever ruse. We've sent his prints and details off to HQ for them to forward to France and see if he has a history over there. I have to admit he didn't strike me as a burglar, but I have to admit I'm not too familiar with what makes a bad Frenchman these days!"

Hartnell spoke again. "And finally, we met Peter Kerrigan," he said. "Who to me looked like the kind of cheeky chappy who had been in and out of trouble all of his life."

"Yes, funny one that one," replied Johnson. "His answers did seem a little rehearsed, but that could be simply because it was the fourth time he'd told the same story. He was furious that he had been set up by '*that Frenchman*'. He went bright red with anger when we told him that Le Sac had pinned it on him."

"And apart from Stone, we have no idea if any of the men gave their correct names," added Hartnell. "It's funny, but we've become so used to dealing with people we know. Not much happens in this town anyway, and when something does come up, then one of the usual suspects is invariably behind it."

"Like Stone," said Johnson.

"Exactly!" exclaimed Hartnell. "Anyway, talking of prints, I know the SOCOs were back from Linfield House. Do we have anything on that folder yet? You never know, Dave. Despite the obviously professional nature of this burglary, someone may have let his guard slip and handled that folder."

"Well, the records and mapping facilities are down at HQ," said Johnson. "So we won't get any results and matches for a few hours yet. But the folder is on Hughes's desk now and finished with."

"When I go down and see Freddy Leston, I can also return his precious stolen item," said Hartnell.

"I know I shouldn't have done so, Rodge, but I had a quick glance inside," said Johnson in a jovial tone, his voice becoming sarcastic as he continued. "It didn't look much like the finished article will be much of a riveting read to me! It was just a load of mathematical formulas and equations. Perhaps the aim of his book is to cure insomnia as well as tell the world about his past!"

"Anyway," said Hartnell, after he'd finished gently laughing at his colleague's comment, "can you come with me? I will need you to get hold of the old man's mobile phone when I'm talking to him and find out who he contacted. We're looking for a number he dialled at about 1.40 a.m. and a text he sent about an hour after that. They will probably be to the same number. That's what I'll need you to get."

"Are we allowed to do that?" asked Johnson.

"Probably not, David, my dear friend," replied Hartnell. "But no one will know, will they! Now, please ask Sergeant Hughes to send Phil the Bag and Mr Kerrigan back to Burgin's."

12

Billy Morgan gingerly walked up the stairs of the hostel, his key ready in his hand. Although he wasn't too scared as he knew about the police presence, he really wanted to avoid meeting Marcus Stone again. Morgan knew the police must have let Stone go too and probably also sent him to the hostel. He was tired and didn't want another argument.

The sun, although still not up, was starting to light the leafy town of Arleswood as Billy opened the door. He could see two police officers standing in the hallway. They nodded to him as he came in.

"Billy Morgan, I believe?" said one, clearly having been told by station officers that the burglar was on his way. Billy nodded.

"I'd get a few hours' sleep, if I were you," said the other. "Back up to the station for some more questions later."

Billy gave a small tilt of his head to acknowledge the words and headed straight for the dormitory door. His heart pounded a little bit as he wondered whether Marcus Stone would be waiting for him on the other side. He opened the door and looked around. He didn't flick the switch in case Stone was in there. He certainly didn't want to antagonise him any more by waking him up.

But the room was deserted. Even in the half-light Billy could see that the bed Stone had occupied was empty. He made the assumption that, as humans are creatures of habit, Stone would have automatically selected the same bed he had been in before. He would have done the same, he thought to himself. But all of the beds were empty. Letting out a small sigh of relief, he lay down on the same bed he'd occupied the previous night and soon fell asleep.

Within the hour, his two accomplices, Peter and Philippe, arrived back fifteen minutes apart, and both turned the lights on. Billy immediately motioned to each of his friends to remain quiet by holding his finger up to his lips and also by cupping his hand around his ear and pointing out to the corridor. He felt sure that the officers would be listening in, trying to very quickly and easily prove that the men knew each other, even hoping the men were so naive they might talk about the burglary itself. Who knows, they might have even very quickly bugged the room. Billy's actions made sure they didn't give themselves away.

Philippe Le Sac was a tall man, at around six foot about the same height as Billy. He was not as well built, though; indeed, he looked thin in comparison. He had short, tightly curled hair and had a healthy, cared-for look to his face. At around 35 years old, he was older than his friends, but Billy's toughened and troubled facial features in particular narrowed any visible age gap. He spoke English with a slight French accent, and contrary to the bewildered look he gave the policemen during questioning, his English was perfect.

The final man in the group, Peter Kerrigan, was the shortest of the burglars, at around five foot ten inches. He was around 30 years old and had thinning brown hair and a small stud earring in his left ear. He had a kind, boyish face, but there was sadness present in his eyes, perhaps a pleasant facade hiding deeper troubles.

The three men gathered at the side of Billy's bed, where he pulled out some paper and a pen.

"All OK?" he wrote.

Peter took the pen.

"Yes. Stuck to the story. They let me go after five minutes."

Philippe took the pen.

"Same."

Billy took over the pen again.

"Havelock's men have already been here," he wrote. Peter and Philippe both inhaled sharply and looked frightened.

"Clearly looking for us. Beat up the owner. But proved our plan was required."

Peter and Philippe looked worriedly at each other and then down at Billy. What had they got themselves into? Billy started a new line.

"Based on what I know has happened, and my knowledge of police procedures, I predict that in a few hours when we go to the station they will have to formally let us go. They simply can't prove it was us. Then we disappear again. Havelock tracked us here, so he is active and mobile. So go far away. Travel only using cash, and lay low until you get a message from me on the pay-as-you-go phones I gave you.

Never contact me, as it could incriminate you. Never use your normal phones. The police will give you those back today too, but they will be monitoring them from now on, for sure."

Peter took the pen. "What will you do?"

Billy responded. "I'll also be hiding. But will stay here in this town. I can disappear. I know how to blend in. I have money. The total amount of cash I stole from that warehouse last week came to several thousand pounds. There is plenty of it for each of you in the lockers at the railway stations I told you about. You have the keys secure somewhere, I hope? Lay low, and only use that money. No cards. You could be tracked. And I mean by Havelock, not the police. They won't bother with us."

Philippe took the pen.

"How long approx do you reckon? Can I go home to France?"

Billy smiled at his French friend as he took hold of the pen once more.

"Two weeks maximum. Please, no France. UK is not part of Schengen. You would need to show your passport and could easily be tracked if you use it. I'm not sure who Havelock is using, but they are good. They traced us here. Sorry, *mon ami*."

Philippe nodded; he was comforted by the use of French to be called "friend". He understood why he couldn't do what he wanted. Billy continued writing on the paper, switching over to the other side.

"So, this afternoon go far away and disappear. The two of you can stay together, but be careful. You could be found in time, but you won't be watched from here. Havelock's men won't risk being around with all the police presence here. The offence they committed is far more serious than what we did. Violent assault. So they will not be close to the police station either when we walk out of there again in a few hours. But they will quite probably still be around town and possibly the train station. Keep your eyes open.

"This is the last time we'll be together for a while. You did great. Well done, and thanks. Watch for instructions on the phone. Be careful with money. Stay in hostels. And get a couple of hours sleep now."

The men all shook hands. Billy took the paper and started ripping it into tiny pieces, making sure it was indecipherable. He handed out small parts to each of his accomplices to dispose of. He walked over to the light switch, gave a thumbs-up and a wink to Peter and Philippe, and turned the light off.

13

It was just after eight o'clock on Thursday morning when Inspector Hartnell and Sergeant Johnson felt they could leave the station to go and reunite the stolen folder with Dr Frederick Leston. Inspector Gerald Middleton, who was the other senior officer alongside Hartnell to operate out of Arleswood Police Station, arrived at around seven o'clock, and after about an hour of briefing, it was felt he was now up to date with all the events of the previous evening.

Middleton was a short, stern-looking man in his early 60s, with a full but undeniably thinning crop of grey hair. Although he didn't need to wear a uniform whilst on duty, being old school in his approach he always chose to do so. He felt uncomfortable in civilian clothes whilst at work. He had been policing for forty years, thirty-five of them in Arleswood. He was very much a by-the-book policeman, and he disagreed with many of Hartnell's decisions of the last few hours. Most notably, he thought Hartnell had been wrong to make the arrests at Burgin's without having the proper clearance and teams in place, and he also questioned the order given to not chase the attackers at Burgin's Hostel across the expanse of Arleswood Common. Although they were the same rank, Hartnell had been granted overall leadership of Arleswood Police Station however, and therefore, he could issue orders to Middleton if he ever needed to.

"Sometimes you just have to go with your instinct, Gerry," said Hartnell during the discussions, much to the older man's annoyance.

The two inspectors did agree, however, that holding the men for any longer was pointless, given the nature of the crime and the effort it might take to identify the guilty trio from among the four suspects. No violence had occurred, the stolen item had been returned intact, and the men had all given fingerprints which were now on file. It was deemed by both that resources would now be better used elsewhere. Quite often something is found or something happens later which can help solve a case retrospectively, and that was how it was agreed that this particular file would be closed for now.

"So, you didn't at all discuss the fact that you will be doing a few checks on Leston's phone, then?" asked Johnson as he and Hartnell got into their car in the police station yard.

"Of course not," replied Hartnell with a smile. "Firstly he would disapprove. It isn't in the coaching manual, and it is slightly underhanded, so he would give me that disappointed, you-should-know-better look he is so good at. And secondly I think he and Leston get on well. I don't think they are close, but Gerald always seems to put the well-being and the opinions of the very wealthy in this town above that of most of the people. He would accuse me of trying to drive away his star residents."

"Well, let's see where this takes us then, Rodge," said Johnson as Hartnell handed him the folder so he could put the keys in the ignition and start the car. "Assuming that there isn't any screen-lock code on Leston's handset, then I'll quickly find the numbers he called and texted. If these numbers and whoever they belong to reveal something, then I expect I'll need to tell my wife that I'll be working overtime!"

"Well, I was going to take the kids to school today, so I'm already in trouble, Dave!" said Hartnell with a wry smile. "Not the easiest of conversations I've just had with Mrs H, but it doesn't happen very often."

The short journey to Linfield House was uneventful, with the only topic of conversation whether Mr and Mrs Leston were going to be up and about to greet them. When they arrived at the house, the gates were open, and so Hartnell drove the car onto the stony drive. As the policemen were getting out of their vehicle, the front door opened, and Frederick Leston came out to greet them.

"I win! Told you he'd be up!" said Hartnell quietly to Johnson.

"Good morning," said Johnson loudly across the driveway to Leston, holding the folder up as he did so. "We've got it, sir."

Leston looked very tired as he stood at the front door, understandably so, given the events of the last few hours. He had changed his clothes, but the policemen wondered whether he'd had any sleep at all.

"You'd better come in, officers," said Leston with a beckoning wave of the arm. He continued as Hartnell and Johnson walked past him and into the house, "I'm so glad to see my folder again. But it does seem strange that you have it, given that you told me you wouldn't chase the men. I'd like to know how it came to be in your possession. I hope it wasn't simply thrown aside and abandoned."

Leston led the men straight into the kitchen and offered them a coffee. Though they had sat there just a few hours before, it now seemed like days ago.

"Your forensics guys said they had finished and that we could tidy the place up a little bit," he said whilst filling the kettle at the sink. He could see that the policemen's gazes were drawn to the broken window and the fact that the shattered vase had been cleaned up.

"And we found the chair by the wall in the driveway, Inspector!" he continued, this time addressing Hartnell directly with a dry tone.

"Where is Mrs Leston, sir?" Hartnell asked.

"Upstairs in bed, Inspector," responded Leston. "As you can imagine, this morning was pretty tough for her, and so she is catching up a little bit of rest."

"And what about you, sir?" asked Hartnell. "Were you able to get some sleep?"

"A little," came the response. "But I was very anxious, as I'm sure you can imagine. And so, apart from falling asleep on the sofa, I've not had much sleep since you left."

Leston poured out three cups of coffee. Both policemen were scanning the work surfaces in the kitchen for a glimpse of Leston's mobile phone, but as of yet they couldn't see it.

"Shall we take these drinks through to the sitting room?" asked Hartnell in an attempt to see more of the house. "It will be much more comfortable in there for you, sir."

Hartnell wasn't quite sure how Leston would feel about being given instructions in his own home, but the polite tone and reassuring voice he used should have been enough to ensure the old man didn't feel he was being dictated to. Sure enough, Leston smiled and asked the police officers to follow him out of the kitchen.

Hartnell felt that Leston's large lounge looked very different in the daylight. At the far end, a huge set of double curtains were wide open, and the morning sun was now streaming into the room, making it very light and forcing the men to squint slightly as they entered. The trio sat down on the large sofa once again.

"Here you go then, Mr Leston," said Johnson, and he handed the folder over to the mathematician. "One stolen folder. Does everything seem in order?"

Leston didn't answer or look up. The folder was undeniably his, but he started to look through the contents suspiciously, giving no eye contact to his guests. He glanced at page after page of equations and symbols before looking up.

"Well, everything seems in order, officers," he said. "But please, I need to know the details and timelines of how you got it. Was it abandoned? Did you catch the intruders? These may sound like strange questions, but I need to know every last detail."

"These questions are not strange at all," Hartnell thought to himself, given how he suspected that, however unlikely, Leston might have done some chasing of his own.

"It was quite simple, Dr Leston," said Johnson. "After we left you early this morning, we got a call from the station, telling us that they had tracked your intruders from here to a location in the town using CCTV. We immediately went to that location and recovered your folder."

"And arrested and removed the culprits?" asked Leston.

"Indeed," said Johnson.

"So, let me be sure I fully understand," said Leston again. "The folder was found soon after it was taken from here. And it was recovered by the police?"

"By me personally, Dr Leston," said Johnson. "And apart from allowing our team to dust it down for prints, it hasn't left my sight."

"Well, that is a relief, officers," said Leston. "So there is no way that my work could have been tampered with or even looked at?"

"Well, in my opinion absolutely no way," interjected Hartnell. "We can see the folder clearly on the CCTV feed from near here at the precise time just after the burglary and when your wife first called the police. Then it is in view of the cameras and visible the entire time from then on right up until the raid we made and recovered your work."

"I'm not sure what those intruders were up to, sir," interjected Johnson. "But I suspect they never even opened your folder."

Leston took a sip from his coffee. Although he said he was relieved inside, he wasn't yet showing it externally. Perhaps the whole ordeal had really taken its toll on him.

"So, these men you arrested," he said. "Did they say why they did it? Why did they only steal my memoirs?"

"Actually, sir, there were complications," responded Hartnell nervously, as he would now have to break it to the old man that his intruders weren't in fact being hung, drawn, and quartered at this very instant. "When we tracked the suspects, who were all wearing balaclavas and masks, of course, we found more people than we were expecting."

Leston frowned.

"And so, whilst we carry out our investigations, the men are released on bail," said Johnson.

The policemen stared at Leston, trying to read his reactions.

"You look perplexed, sir," said Hartnell, starting to fish. "The men won't come back here, if that is what you are worried about."

"Yes, yes, I know," said Leston. "It's not that, it's just … well, I don't know. It's that they are still out there."

"I understand, Dr Leston," said Hartnell in a reassuring tone. "Maybe you can help, though. Your wife seemed to think you knew one of the intruders. She said he lifted his mask and looked at you from the top of your wall, and that is when you collapsed."

"Did you know the man?" asked Johnson. "And if you don't know him by name, do you think you could you identify him?"

Frederick Leston seemed to shudder, and he looked a little ill again.

"I'm sorry, sir; I know this has been a nasty experience," said a sympathetic Hartnell. "But with your help, we can charge the right people. Right now we know that three people did this to you, but we have a longer suspect list. If we could just get the identity of one of the men, sir, we are certain to identify the other two."

Leston shook his head and looked at the floor. "No, sorry. I'm sorry, but I didn't know the intruder," he said in a melancholy tone. "But when you see people on your land in balaclavas, who have clearly just burgled your property, and they are smiling at you, I assure you it is a horrible sight. And that, I suspect, is why I collapsed. I assumed it was a former pupil."

"I understand, sir," said Hartnell again. "But did you get a good look at this man? Could you identify him in a list of suspects? Was he big, small? Fat, thin?"

Again Leston shook his head. "It was very dark, Officer, and although I could see the man had lifted up his mask, I couldn't see any features at all, even his size. I'm sorry."

"It's OK, Dr Leston," said Hartnell. "We will soon be able to identify the three men who broke into this house from the eleven men that were present at the scene when we picked up the folder."

"Eleven!" said a shocked Leston, as if understanding now the difficulty the police were having in identifying the guilty men. "I thought that Burgin's was a small place!"

Leston sprang to his feet in a move which defied his age and frail, tired state. "More coffee, gentlemen?" he asked enthusiastically as he gathered all of the cups and headed for the door. "I have many more questions for you about this whole episode."

"So have we," thought the policemen and gave each other a wink. Leston had fallen into a simple trap. Both men had been careful not to have named or described in any detail where the intruders had been picked up. But Leston had just mentioned Burgin's. Neither Hartnell nor Johnson had done so. Leston knew something.

"Yes, please, Dr Leston!" replied both police officers in unison as Leston walked out of the room and away to the kitchen.

"We've got to get that phone," whispered Johnson as soon as the sound of the footsteps faded. Hartnell nodded. "We won't get the resources to do a full trace on his phone records, given he is classed as a victim right now, so I need the physical object in my hand."

"Time for a little bit of a search," responded the inspector excitedly. "This is now very urgent, and it just got a whole lot more interesting. I'll invite him down to the study and keep him there for a while, and you have a good look in the other rooms. Mrs Leston is asleep. I'll tell him you are making calls if he asks where you are and why you haven't joined us."

Just then, Leston walked back into the room, saying, "Right, the kettle is on," forcing the policemen to quickly break from their conversation and look up.

"Can we have another look at your study, sir?" asked Hartnell. "It's possible we may have missed something in there."

"Of course; follow me," said the homeowner. Hartnell jumped to his feet, but Johnson didn't, staying put on the large sofa. "Are you not coming, Officer?" asked Leston.

"No, sir," he responded. "If it is OK with you, I'd like to check the back door and the kitchen again. The behaviour of the intruders in that room bothers me greatly. I need another look around."

"Of course, Officer. You can make another coffee too whilst you are there!" said Leston jokingly. The pain from the events of the previous seven hours or so now seemed to have vanished. The three men left the lounge but headed in different directions once in the hallway.

Hartnell knew that Leston's mobile telephone was unlikely to be in the small, untidy study. It had been clear to him earlier that morning that the room was hardly ever used by the elderly couple. The inspector's plan was to spend as much time in there with Frederick Leston as he could whilst Johnson searched for the handset. The best-case scenario was that it was lying around on a table somewhere with no code required to access the various menus. The worst-case scenario was that the phone was in Leston's pocket, or upstairs, perhaps in the bedroom where Mrs Leston was sleeping.

Johnson headed in the direction of the kitchen but didn't go in. He knew that what he was looking for was not in there, having had a chance to survey the room just twenty minutes or so earlier. Instead, he headed through another door off the main hallway, which led into a kind of informal dining room. In a house of this size there were many reception rooms, and it was difficult to know exactly which was used for what. This room had a modern-looking wooden table in the middle, with four chairs surrounding it. There were a few pictures on the wall; one was unmistakably a replica of John Constable's *Hay Wain*, but this was not a grand room. Johnson suspected that, as it was next to the kitchen, the room was used as a breakfast room, although the kitchen itself was large enough to fulfil that role and there was a main dining room somewhere else in the property.

Halfway along the left-hand wall was what looked like a closed hatch about a meter square in size. Based on where he was, he knew it would open out into the kitchen on the other side. On the wooden table near to this hatch was a daily broadsheet newspaper, open at the sports pages, and a plate with a few crumbs on it.

"Leston was obviously having his breakfast when we arrived," thought Johnson, and he made his way over to that side of the room. Then, as if Johnson knew the kind of scene he needed to look for, he calmly closed the newspaper to reveal a mobile phone. The phone was not even meant to be hidden from view. It would have simply been placed on the table as breakfast began and been covered up unnoticed as Leston began to read his morning paper and turn the pages over.

Even so, the experienced sergeant was both pleased and shocked to have found the phone this quickly.

Glancing back towards the dining room door and listening intently for any sound of approaching footsteps, Johnson picked the phone up. His enthusiasm was immediately dented, as there was inevitably a code lock on the handset. He was unable to progress beyond the first screen. He had been hoping that with Frederick Leston being so old, he might not have been aware his phone had a screen lock, and it might not have been activated, or at the very least it would have had an inactivity delay of about twenty minutes before kicking in. Unbowed, Johnson turned the phone towards the light. Over time, the buttons that are regularly used to enter a pin code tend to have smudges on them, especially if used whilst someone is having a greasy breakfast, for example. It soon became clear to the policeman which four digits formed the code. He just didn't know the order and knew he would have to employ a simple process of elimination.

He then froze. Sergeant Johnson could hear footsteps coming back down the hallway, presumably Leston on his way to the kitchen after dropping Hartnell off at the study. He put the phone into his pocket and the paper back onto the table.

"I don't think the intruders went in there, Officer," said Leston into the doorway of the informal dining room as he walked past. Johnson hurried out of the room and followed him.

"Please don't pour the coffee, Dr Leston," said Johnson as he joined his host in the kitchen. "I've just been paged by the station. We need to head back."

"Very well, Officer," replied Leston. "But you must come back. I have many questions for you."

Johnson scurried down to the study to tell the inspector the lie about being paged.

"Get some rest, Doctor," said Hartnell as they hurried back out of the front door.

"We'll be back," said Johnson as they ran across to their car.

Hartnell drove the Three Shires Constabulary squad car rapidly out of the gates of Linfield House, leaving tyre tracks in the neat stones of the property's driveway area and onto Sandy Lane. At the end of the street, he turned into Lacey Drive, where he brought the car to an abrupt stop.

"So I assume you have got it, then?" Hartnell asked Johnson.

"Yes, but it's locked," responded Johnson. "I can soon unlock it, but I couldn't very well do it with Leston around."

Sergeant Johnson then proceeded to press a few buttons, holding some carefully selected ones down simultaneously.

"Bingo!" he exclaimed after just thirty seconds or so. "There are not many smartphone handsets I don't know how to override the security locks on, especially when I know which numbers the code is made up of."

"Genius!" exclaimed Hartnell, beaming with pride at his friend and colleague.

"OK, let's see. Menu. Phone Log. Dialled numbers." Johnson was thinking out loud.

"OK, Rodge, write this down. 04994 661001. Dialled at 01.43 this morning. The name given for the entry is Smith. Great! Smith! Only a few Smiths in this country! He texted that number too, at 02.29 this morning. That must have been whilst you were sat with him. Interesting, the text is blank. And he received a call back from that same number at 04.48. That call lasted twenty-five minutes."

"Good work!" said Hartnell. "Are there any other interesting messages?"

"Nope," said Johnson. "This is the only text message in the log. Strange."

"OK," said Hartnell. "Let's speed back round to Leston's house now, and you give him his phone back. Say it is the same as yours, and that you must have picked it up accidentally whilst you were walking around."

"Yes, that was my plan when I took the phone in the first place," said Johnson. "Then what do we do? I'm shattered."

"Then we both go home," responded Hartnell. "And we get a few hours' sleep. I think we've got some work to do, David, my old friend!"

14

As ordered to by Sergeant Hughes earlier that day, the four suspects all headed back to Arleswood Police Station. Marcus Stone made his way in from the house of a friend, having chosen not to sleep at Burgin's as instructed, whilst Billy Morgan, Philippe Le Sac, and Peter Kerrigan made their way up from the hostel, albeit separately, in an attempt to continue the premise that they were strangers to each other.

The police staff in the station were all new faces to the men now. Sergeant Hughes had been replaced by a day-duty sergeant, and the various uniformed constables who had worked the early hours had also gone home. It seemed strange, as there were many fewer people around now in the reception area than there had been in the middle of the night. Inspector Hartnell and Sergeant Johnson were nowhere to be seen. The accused men all sat in the waiting room, consciously making sure they didn't make eye contact with each other. The innocent Stone, despite not being part of this façade, also had his head down, avoiding all contact.

Inspector Middleton decided to look after the formalities at the front desk, having been briefed thoroughly by his colleagues an hour or so previously. That left the day-duty sergeant to see to an old lady who had wandered in asking to speak to an officer. Calling up the dishevelled and rough-looking Marcus Stone first, Middleton handled the process with clinical efficiency, issuing individually various instructions to the men whilst returning their personal belongings, including their mobile phones. Stone was simply asked to report again the following day, and he left the building, but the three suspects new to the Arleswood Police were instructed again to give their personal details in the hope that something would differ from the answers given last night. No one at the police station believed the men had given any correct information, but unfortunately, the required information of whether the prints had showed up on the master file was yet to be confirmed by the force's head office in the city, five miles to the south. After a frustrating half-hour of questioning each, Inspector Middleton discharged all of the suspects, requesting that they return again – not the following day, as there would be nothing new to discuss – but in one month's time.

The last one of the four suspects to leave the station was Billy Morgan, who was still keen not to have a confrontation with Marcus Stone. He gingerly looked up and down the street from the front door of the building for a sign of the local man, but he wasn't there, so Billy casually descended the steps. Once on the path, he then thrust his head down straight at the floor, effectively hiding all of his features. There were, of course, potentially other, even more violent men than Stone waiting to greet him. If he could shuffle away and then blend in to the world as quickly as possible then he knew he'd be OK. He was very good at disappearing.

The time was now 10.30 in the morning, and despite the events of the last nine or so hours, Billy was still running on adrenalin and not remotely tired. Despite his caution in not looking up to reveal his features, he was confident that he was one step ahead of everyone else in this bizarre set of circumstances as he orchestrated the whole thing. It was time for him to lay low for a while. He had no intention whatsoever of returning to the police station the following month and had instructed Phillipe and Peter also not to do so, should that be the instruction they ended up receiving. This whole situation would be resolved long before then, and if things went as planned, he knew perfectly well that the police would not have the time, the resources or, frankly, the will to find them.

A mere five minutes after Billy left the building, Sergeant Johnson came back in.

"Sergeant Johnson," the WPC behind the desk greeted him. "Everything OK? Your shift has finished. I wasn't expecting you until seven o'clock this evening."

"Everything is fine, Officer," replied Johnson jovially. "I can't sleep, but everything is fine!"

He headed down to the duty sergeants' office, which was currently empty, and let himself in. There was no sign of the day-duty sergeant or Inspector Middleton as he made his way down the short corridor past the interview room and the holding cells. He logged onto a PC and pulled out a series of notes he and Hartnell had made so far on the case. He felt he had to do the investigation into that phone number and the mysterious "Smith" by himself. He couldn't pass the work on. The method he'd used to acquire the phone in the first place was against many written and unwritten rules. Inspector Middleton would never approve, and so he couldn't very well ask one of Middleton's team on duty that day to do some police work for him on this.

Johnson heard a female voice outside saying, "Hello, Inspector." Johnson knew she must mean Inspector Middleton and that he was outside nearby, and so he thought that, out of courtesy, he should inform the senior officer that he was in the building. Before he could stand, however, the door to the office he was occupying was pushed open, and there indeed stood the inspector – Inspector Hartnell!

"What are you doing here?" Johnson asked him, finally rising to his feet.

"Probably the same as you, old chap!" responded Hartnell. "Too many things going round in my mind. Too many unanswered questions. Kids at school, wife at work, so what the hell, eh? I had a shower, a bite to eat, and I've headed back."

"I'm pretty much the same," responded Johnson. "I need to get answers!"

"You are turning into me, David, my friend!" replied Hartnell. "I couldn't simply leave this case hanging after we got our proof that Leston seems to be informed here, and clearly neither could you. The question is, is he getting information from someone in the police? After all, he has many friends here."

"Including Middleton," interjected Johnson quietly.

"Yes," said Hartnell with a smile. "Or maybe he runs his own detective agency and private hit squad! Either he or someone else has access to our surveillance network, and to that end, we must find out if we have a leak, or at best, a computer network breach."

"I was just going to let Inspector Middleton know we were here," said Johnson. "Was he out there when you came in?"

"No. He's out somewhere, according to PC Watton on the front desk," replied Hartnell. "We'll catch up with him when he's back."

When Sergeant Johnson ran back up to Leston's house to return the phone handset, he and Hartnell had already decided not to push the old man further on how he knew the men had gone to Burgin's Hostel. That line of questioning would come later. They had returned to Linfield house just three minutes after they'd left it, and so the two officers were convinced Leston wouldn't have suspected a thing. Surely he would assume that picking up the wrong phone had just been an honest mistake. What they most wanted to get on with was investigating that phone number, the one dialled and texted by Leston in the early hours.

"So, will you dial it, or shall I?" asked Johnson.

"We'll do it together – here, now," replied Hartnell. "You do the talking though, Sergeant. Just try and keep them talking for a while, and see what we can find out. Say that you have been asked to dial this number by a friend. Play dumb and ask open questions from the outset. And let's make sure we dial out using the number-withheld facility. This can't be traced back to the police."

"It is an interesting number," added Johnson. "Most, if not all, UK mobile numbers begin with 07. It is not a landline either, as then it would be 01 or 02 something. The premium rate numbers for banks and companies tend to be 08 or 03 numbers. This one is 04. I'd be interested just to run 04 numbers into Google and see what we get. Then maybe we can put the whole phone number into Google. Sometimes things pop up."

"Seems like your department, this, Sergeant," said Hartnell. "All things to do with phones, it seems. I'm impressed."

"OK, let's see, then," said Johnson. "This number, 04994, brings up some place on the south-west Indian coast. That can't be dialled from the UK in that format; you would need an international code for India prefixed before it. But keep that in mind."

"And the whole number?" asked Hartnell.

Johnson typed it in. "Nothing. No entries appear. So now I want to see what 04 numbers in the UK are."

Hartnell stared at the screen as his colleague typed the number. The search directed them to a British Telecom overview page. They quickly scanned the information on the screen.

"04 – Not used" appeared.

"So, secret police, secret phone numbers, Sergeant!" quipped Hartnell.

Johnson laughed. "Well, whatever it is, it isn't supported by BT, that's for sure," he said.

"Well, I suppose we should dial it and see what happens," said Hartnell.

Sergeant Johnson leant over the telephone and began to dial. He pushed a series of buttons to ensure the call couldn't be tracked back to the outgoing phone set, and then he punched in 04994 661001, and the two men waited as it started to ring, their hearts pumping a little.

After three rings, it sounded as if someone were answering, yet just an automatic message was played. There was a recording of a man's voice with a very strong London accent. "Hello. This is Smith. Please enter your personal reference number after the tone by using your keypad, and someone will call you back. Bye."

The phone then produced a continual beep for two seconds, and Johnson reached forward and cut the call off by pushing down the grey button where the phone handset usually docked.

"Well, he sounds like a nice, decent sort of chap," said Inspector Hartnell sarcastically. "What do you make of those few words?"

"Well, this is way beyond my basic knowledge, Inspector," replied Johnson. "We will need to ask HQ to get someone at the telephone company to help us. It's a number automatically set up to go straight to a message-capturing service. We would need to know who owns that number and who dials in to access the messages."

"Can we not ring back and wait to see what happens?" asked Hartnell.

"I wouldn't recommend it, sir," responded Johnson. "I suspect that there are not many people who know this phone number, and any suspicious activity on the line would point to the security and integrity being compromised, and it would be immediately shut down. We can't risk that. We could be onto something here, and we can't risk letting it slip away."

"OK. Very good, Sergeant," said Hartnell. "And so we need to pass this on to more specialist help, you say? Like BT, or whichever operator deals with this kind of thing now?"

"Yes," replied Johnson. "I think you and I could jeopardise this if we tried anything now."

At that moment, Hartnell's own phone rang, and he answered it. Sergeant Johnson headed out of the room to see if he could find Inspector Middleton to let him know he and Hartnell were in the building. When he came back, Hartnell had finished his call.

"Close the door, Sergeant," he said as he beckoned his colleague back into the room. "We've got the results from forensics of all of their work this morning at Linfield house."

"OK, Inspector," replied Johnson. "Middleton is back. Shall we fill him in now to save doing it all again later?"

Hartnell shook his head. "No, Sergeant, let's keep him out for now. We may need to bend a few more rules, and I don't want him reminding us how irresponsible we are all of the time. And besides, we may need to bring Leston in for questioning if we can prove he is behind a little vigilante stunt, too, and I know Middleton would not like that at all."

"OK," said Johnson. "So what did the SOCOs find?"

"Well, nothing at all at the house, as you can imagine," said Hartnell. "If intruders like these are anything worth their salt, then they simply don't leave prints anymore. SOCO have also had a look at the clothing, to see if any fragments from the clothes found at Burgin's match anything found at Leston's place."

"And even if it did," said Johnson, jumping in. "Then it would hardly be a surprise, would it, as we are 99.9 per cent certain that three out of the four men we found were the intruders."

"Indeed," agreed Hartnell. "But there was one funny thing they found."

Johnson could tell by the inspector's tone of voice that he thought he was about to tell him something that would add considerable mystery to the case.

"They obviously also dusted down that folder," continued Hartnell.

"Go on," said Johnson.

"They obviously didn't have the time and resources to analyse every single page in there, so they did the front and back cover and a few of the pages. On the cover they found three sets of prints, and all three can be matched in our system."

Johnson leant forward in anticipation.

"The first set has been confirmed as Dr Frederick Leston's, unsurprisingly. The second and third sets, however, are very old prints. Apparently fingerprints can last for up to twenty years if the surface they are on is well protected. And that folder lay behind a glass cabinet at Leston's, didn't it?"

Johnson nodded and spoke. "Yes, it did. But that also means he has been writing those bloody memoirs for at least ten years then?"

"Mmm. Anyway," mused Hartnell. "Here is where it gets really interesting. The second set belong to a former policeman. His name was Chief Inspector Ian Riley, from the North Midlands Constabulary, which covers many of the large cities up there. He retired from the force about six years ago. We will definitely need to track him down and ask him if he remembers the circumstances in which he held that bit of card. It will help us."

"It could be an innocent way of starting to delve a little deeper on Leston," said Johnson. "I mean, we can give him this information and ask him, without making it known we are probing him, how this former policeman had his grubby hands all over his prized possession."

"Yes, but it could lead nowhere," responded Hartnell. "The prints are so old it is almost certain that they have nothing to do with this case."

"Indeed, they probably don't," said Johnson. "But what it will do is get Leston talking and hopefully revealing a little more about this folder than he has done so far. He might inadvertently offer up some information that helps us further. After all, we are now certain on your theory that he knows something about those other men who went to Burgin's."

"OK, I like the idea," said Hartnell.

"And the third set of prints?" asked Johnson.

Hartnell cleared his throat. "Well, the third set, which are also very old, as I mentioned, belong to a Mr William Hastings, who died some time ago, aged just 20. He was in and out of youth detention centres for most of his adolescent life. He had convictions for drug dealing, assault, burglary, and car theft, including carjacking. He was an all-round wrong'un, it seems. Anyway, he drowned off the coast of Devon. He fell overboard from a fishing boat. When the body was found, his system was full of drugs, and he had a large knife wound in his back, but the post mortem revealed he had, in fact, drowned."

"So I guess we will never know how he ended up coming into contact with that folder," said Johnson.

"Well, actually, we might," said Hartnell. "Here the plot thickens even further. According to the official police records, it was PC Riley who identified Hastings' body."

15

Peter suddenly stopped and dragged Philippe to one side in the busy shopping street.

"I'm pretty certain we are being followed," he said to his French companion. "Every time I look around, he is there."

"Who?" asked Philippe.

"A short, muscular man in jeans, white trainers, and a dark baseball cap."

Both men glanced back down the street. There he was, peering into a shoe shop window.

"I first saw him in the previous street, the high street," continued Kerrigan anxiously. "I thought nothing of it until I looked over my shoulder a few minutes ago and saw him again, about the same distance behind. And there he is again now, for a third time."

"Do we turn ze next corner and run?" asked the Frenchman.

"I reckon we do," responded Kerrigan. "It could only be the police or one of the gang sent to beat us to a pulp. And as the police just let us go, it is unlikely to be them wasting resources following us around. So my money is on it being one of Havelock's men."

Phillipe nodded so that he could inform his English compatriot he understood and agreed. Both men now were scared, and they starting walking briskly down the street away from the man.

"Do we need to warn Bill?" asked Philippe. "Zey could be tracking him, too."

"No," responded Peter forcefully. "He said not to contact him, and as we both know, he can look after himself. Besides, it might be my paranoid imagination. And I don't want him to worry about us."

"*Oui*. I mean yes," said Philippe. "*J'agree*. Let's just get out of 'ere."

They turned the next corner by a small greengrocer's and burst into a fast sprint down the residential road they found themselves in. They knew they would have to quickly find a place to hide so that when the man following them turned the corner he would not be able to see them anywhere. The road was too long to get to far the end and turn the next corner in time. After just three buildings, the first possible opportunity, Peter and Philippe ran off the path and entered a small archway splitting the ground floor of two large, terraced Georgian houses; this was used for access to the rear gardens, and they hoped to find a place out of sight.

At the end of the archway, on either side, were two small gates leading to the gardens of the two properties served. There were numerous wheelie bins parked here too, presumably pushed down the alley under the archway for emptying by the bin men.

Peter and Philippe were lucky in that on both sides of the street there were similar passages and alleyways between many of the properties. If indeed they were being followed, when their pursuer turned the corner, he wouldn't be able to spot them. His targets could have chosen any one of about twenty passageways to hide in. The advantage the man in the baseball cap would have, however, was that he could simply wait for his targets to reveal themselves again. He knew the men would have no idea when he had passed by or given up. To be fully hidden, Peter and Philippe had had to hide behind a garden fence, out of the line of sight down the archway that they had run up. They would no longer be able to see the road or, therefore, any foot traffic on the adjacent pavement.

"We 'ave made a 'uge error," whispered Philippe to Peter. "We are stuck 'ere!"

Meanwhile, back out on the street, the man in the cap, who had also quickened his pace in the previous road, was now standing looking down an avenue with large, grand terraced houses on both sides and steps up from the pavement to their respective front doors. There were quite a few parked cars on both sides of the road, and a few small trees lined the street for aesthetic decoration. The two men he had been asked to follow were no longer in sight, but he knew they had to be here somewhere, either hidden behind a car or maybe in one of the gaps between the ground floors of the terraced properties. "Not even Usain Bolt could have got to the end of the street and out of sight in that short time," he thought. But he would have to act fast. He didn't know which side of the road the men were hiding on, or if there were accesses out of the back of the gardens, if that was where they had indeed headed.

Finding himself lying horizontal behind a garden fence, Peter was starting to panic. He wasn't a criminal. He worked in a shop. Although no angel, he had never been in trouble with the police at all, in fact. And he certainly wasn't the kind of person used to situations where he feared for his personal well-being whilst hiding behind a garden fence and hyperventilating. However, in the space of the last ten hours or so, he had been arrested by the police, narrowly escaped a brutal attack at the hostel, and he was now being potentially tracked by a gang member for a second time.

Philippe tapped him on the shoulder and pointed to the back of the garden.

"Can we climb zat fence?" he asked. "Do you zink we can zen get out on the parallel street?"

Peter jumped up and ran the instant Philippe had finished talking, knocking over an empty plant pot next to him, which smashed. It was clear his answer was yes. The adrenalin was already pumping in his veins, and as soon as the Frenchman put the idea of another way out into his mind, he was up and off. Adrenalin and sitting still do not go hand in hand.

The two men ran across the back garden of one of the houses. The grass was well kept and the fringes of the garden neat and tidy, with shrubs and flowers in the border. A small swing was sitting proudly in the centre of the lawn, which both men used as a small pivot as they ran around it. It was around lunchtime now, in the middle of a working day, so there was a high probability the house was not occupied at that moment, but they couldn't be sure. Peter wondered if it would even be a good thing if someone did spot them and come out. It could scare off the pursuer. They reached the large fence at the far end of the garden and immediately jumped up and started to scale it. Looking around, they could see the man in the baseball cap. He must have heard the noise of breaking porcelain, for he was drawn off the street and into the garden they were hiding in.

Peter and Philippe were quickly over the fence. The man started to run across the garden in pursuit of the duo, who were now running across the garden on the other side in the hope that there would be an exit onto that street somewhere.

"Stop! Police!" shouted the man twice.

"Don't fall for it, mate," said Peter, gasping for breath. "He is not the police – keep going!"

They reached the house at the end of the garden and were lucky enough to find an alleyway leading down to the road. They turned around to see how much of a lead they had, but there was no sign of the man. Perhaps the fence was too high for him to climb. They'd had to jump to reach the top to lever themselves over, and the man chasing them was considerably shorter than they were. They were free for now.

"We need to get to the railway station – and fast," said Philippe. "I'm done with zis town now."

"I agree," responded Peter, still panting after all the physical exercise. "But we stay sharp and alert. There could be more of them, and I bet they are expecting us to go to the railway station."

Arleswood Railway Station was only a short walk away from the town centre, so the men knew they must be close. "Ten minutes maximum," thought Peter uncertainly – he wasn't too familiar with the town – as he and his French accomplice briskly walked in the correct direction.

"Keep your eyes open," said Philippe. "Zis time we both know what he looks like. He'll be running around trying to find us, for sure. He's only one street away. It won't take 'im long to figure out where we went."

"Should we lay low for a couple of hours then, and get a train away from here when the coast is clear?" suggested Peter.

"No way, my friend," replied Philippe. "I'm getting out of 'ere now."

There was a clear determination in the Frenchman's voice. Peter didn't really want to wait either. He also wanted to be away, and Philippe had told him exactly what he wanted to hear.

As the men approached the station, they could see in the distance a train approaching from the direction of London, heading north. They would have to run to catch it, but it was clear from their body language that they both wanted that train. Arleswood was a popular, affluent commuter town about half an hours' train ride from Central London, and it was these fantastic transport links to the city which made this area attractive to the rich who wanted a more sedate alternative to London whilst staying close enough for daily travel there.

Peter Kerrigan glanced back over his shoulder as they broke into a run. The short man in the baseball cap was about fifty yards behind them. He had found them all too quickly, but deep down they'd suspected he would. They knew that the railway station was too obvious a destination. Their desire to get out of the town by the quickest means possible had clouded their thoughts. Ahead of them on the station approach were quite a few people. Some were standing around talking, plenty were going in and out of the ticket office, and most were coming and going from the stairs, which gave access to the platforms and led over the four train lines to the other side. This railway station was an open station in that you didn't need a ticket to go through any barrier to access the platforms, something Peter and Phillipe were very grateful about right now.

The train was pulling into the station as Peter and Philippe arrived, forcing them to break into a sprint. They knocked into a couple of people as they went running up the stairs to get across to the correct platform in time. People running for trains was not an unusual sight, and so most people in the vicinity didn't pay any attention. Peter and Philippe looked back to see the man in the baseball cap also running. He was seriously gaining on them. It looked as if he, too, might make the train, which would be a disaster. Maybe they could double-bluff him? Peter thought cleverly – although he knew that was risky and that he was probably safer on the train even if the man did make it too.

Just then, a large man in a brown overcoat, probably a businessman just going about his business, stepped right into the way of the chasing man in the baseball cap, knocking him to the floor. A few other people then gathered around and helped the man up. He dusted himself down frantically whilst moving away, seemingly ungratefully from those who had tried to help him. His baseball cap had been knocked off in the collision to reveal a completely bald head; it also showed off his rippling neck muscles. He was a bright shade of red from all of the running he had been doing, and there was an angry look upon his mean features. The damage had been done. He had missed the train. Hands on hips, he looked across from the other side of the bridge he had failed to make it to, as Peter and Philippe boarded the train. The doors shut, and the train moved out of the station. He had failed.

Peter could see out of the window that the man had not boarded the train and was in fact over at the other side of the bridge rather than right behind them as he'd feared. He refrained from giving the man a sarcastic wave that could come back to haunt him. He turned his head back and breathed a huge sigh of relief. Gasping for breath, he patted Philippe on the shoulder.

"Well done," he said. "Now we disappear too."

"It was a bit of luck for us zat those men bumped into each other," said Philippe. "It was the difference between that man also being on this train or not."

Peter shook his head and smiled. "That wasn't luck," he said warmly. "The man who knocked over the guy in the baseball cap was Bill."

16

There was a knock at the door of the small office currently occupied by Inspector Hartnell and Sergeant Johnson.

"Come in," said Hartnell in a clear, confident voice.

It was Inspector Middleton. "Good morning, boys," he said. "I understood you were hiding away in here."

"Yes," replied Hartnell. "We had been looking for you, actually. I wanted you to know that we were still here on your watch. Didn't want you to think anything was amiss."

"I had popped out to see an old friend," answered Middleton. "But anyway, I thought I'd warn you, Inspector Hartnell. Chief Inspector Gault is on his way over here now. He didn't seem very happy."

"Our boss is coming here now?" asked Hartnell, as if to clarify the situation.

"That is correct," responded Middleton. "Details about all of the various bits of fun this morning at Leston's and Burgin's have made their way onto his desk down at HQ, and he wants to come here and ask a few questions about it. I'm sure he'd be delighted that you've extended your shift somewhat." He sounded quite condescending and sarcastic, unsurprising given his disdain for many of Hartnell's policing methods.

"Then why didn't he ask me to go down to him?" asked Hartnell. "It's not like him to come over here. I'd be surprised if he even finds the way!"

"I wouldn't joke, Inspector," said Middleton. "The main reason he is coming to Arleswood at all is to personally visit Frederick Leston, to sympathise with him on the burglary and apologise for, and I quote, his 'officers' bungling of the investigation'."

"What!" shouted Johnson, clearly insulted by the remark. "What bungling?"

"Look, gentlemen," said Middleton in a calming voice. "Please don't shoot the messenger."

"Well, OK, Inspector," said Hartnell cuttingly. "I just wonder in which direction you have been playing the role of messenger. I know you don't like my style and that you disagreed with my actions. I'd like to think that you didn't go running to Gault about all of this. I'd hope that nothing underhanded is going on here. I have nothing to hide, and I can justify why I made all of the decisions I did."

"Well, good luck, Inspector," said Middleton in an equally unfriendly tone. "You know what I think about most of your decisions, and not just on this case. But I assure you it isn't me who has been in the chief inspector's ear."

Although Hartnell and Johnson were suspicious of Inspector Middleton right now, there was a clear ring of honesty in what he was saying. Although the policing methods between the inspectors differed somewhat, Middleton was a good man and certainly not a back-stabber, and neither was he in any way out to score points off other officers. His career was coming to an end, and he had nothing to gain by any black marks Hartnell or Johnson might receive.

"OK," said a clearly apologetic Hartnell. "I'm sorry; I didn't mean to accuse you."

"It's all right, Inspector Hartnell," said Middleton again. "But pull yourself together; he'll be here soon."

Inspector Middleton turned and headed down the corridor, shutting the door firmly but not slamming it behind him, whilst Sergeant Johnson thumped his fist on the desk.

"Bungling police officers!" he muttered out loud.

"Calm down, David," said Hartnell. "It will be fine. As you know, my friend Chief Inspector Gault is just an even more highly strung version of Gerry Middleton when it comes to the wealthy in these parts, especially if they happen to be famous as well. As soon as he got to work this morning he would have found out that Leston had been burgled and he would have immediately demanded to know all of the details. If one of his precious wealthy residents has been a victim of any crime, then that case will receive all of his attention. He's paranoid of any negative press against this force, you see."

"And that means him coming here personally?" asked a confused Johnson.

"Well, normally, no," replied Hartnell, "and that is now why I'm starting to worry. In usual circumstances, I would receive a call whereby

I'm summoned to HQ to debrief the chief inspector with the full details and am told to double my efforts and increase my visibility with the victim until the case is closed."

"So, someone from here, or maybe one of the people we contacted overnight at HQ, has fed him some details which he feels are important enough for him to go and see the victim personally, you reckon?" suggested Johnson.

"It would appear that way, yes," replied Hartnell. "Maybe one of the SOCOs?"

The inspector then turned a little pale and continued, "Or the scary version is that Leston himself contacted Gault – or at least somehow ensured he would get the details."

"Good grief! What on earth are we dealing with here?" pondered Johnson.

"Probably not a lot," said Hartnell. "And our imaginations are running away with us now. But I think something much bigger than a simple burglary is in motion here."

"Well, this is better than being bored, I suppose," quipped Johnson.

"Indeed," responded Hartnell. "And just in case you *are* bored, here's what I need you to do whilst I'm getting my wrists slapped by Gault. I need you to follow up with British Telecom on that strange telephone number that you retrieved off Leston's mobile. Secondly, see if you can track down Chief Inspector Riley. He's probably on a beach somewhere in Spain, spending his enormous pension, but someone down at HQ will know how and where to find him. And finally, see what you can find out about that youth who drowned. You know, the one whose prints are also on the folder. William Hastings. He seemed like a really nasty piece of work by all accounts, so it seems very strange that he'd have been in contact with Leston's memoirs all those years ago. We need to know why and to check out the whole story, as Riley is involved there too."

"You forgot to allow me some sleep, sir!" said Johnson jokingly.

Hartnell smiled warmly. "No, but I did forget something else, too. I received an email reply from the operators down at HQ about the French guy we took in and questioned. He didn't use a false name, which was a surprise, and it seems he has a very interesting story too. Please start the digging on that one also; I've already forwarded you the message."

"Of course I'm happy to do all this, Rodge," said Johnson. "But it seems like an awful lot of investigating for a botched burglary."

"Yes," responded Hartnell. "But two things, my friend. Firstly, as we both just agreed, this could be way more than just a simple burglary. And secondly, knowing Chief Inspector Gault and his love of all rich residents, he will insist that we drop everything else and concentrate purely on finding out who broke into Leston's house and stole that folder. He probably doesn't even want to know why, and I suspect he cares even less about the fight outside Burgin's a couple of hours later. He's always hated places that attract the wrong sort of person to his beloved corner of England."

"Got it!" said Johnson. "I'm beginning to understand your governor. I just hope that he comes here before he goes to see Leston so that he at least hears our views first. The last thing we need is Leston telling him he pleaded with us to send resources straight away and we ignored his request. That will really piss him off."

Hartnell glanced at his watch. "Judging by the time, he went to Leston's first. He would have been here by now otherwise. Bugger! Oh well. Anyway, make some calls here or on your way home to set all those enquiries in motion, and then leave me a voicemail with all of your findings. Try to get some sleep, and let's meet back here later, before our shift begins."

"OK. Thanks, Rodge, and good luck," said Johnson as he got up to vacate the room. The two policemen looked at each other and warmly shook hands. With one handshake, Johnson was able to show empathy and support for his friend and colleague who was about to get a roasting from the chief inspector and Hartnell was able to thank Johnson for his unwavering support.

Hartnell sat alone behind the desk in the office. He, too, was now desperate for some sleep and was understandably a bit apprehensive about the imminent meeting with his commanding officer. It was his view that many senior officers in the force seemed to get overly twitchy when a victim just happened to be quite wealthy, something Hartnell really didn't like. And if Chief Inspector Gault learned that he'd arrested the suspects in the burglary and then subsequently released them without charge pending further investigations, he was going to have some difficult explanations to make. Even though he was confident he'd made his choices for the right reasons and could back them up with sound logic and reasoning, he knew his boss wasn't going to be very happy.

He logged off the computer in the small office and switched it off. As soon as his meeting was over, he planned to head home and bank a few hours' sleep; he felt like saving every second he possibly could. Then, from down the corridor, he heard formal greetings and pleasantries being shared in the reception area. He knew that the chief inspector had arrived, and he left the room to greet his superior.

Inspector Hartnell headed towards the front of the police station, but he didn't get far, as the man he was going to meet was already heading purposefully in his direction. Wearing a smart, creaseless uniform and shoes so shiny you could almost see your reflection in them, Chief Inspector Gault held out his hand for Inspector Hartnell to shake. Gault was a tall, thin man, well over six foot and about 55 years old, with a dark moustache. He removed his cap to reveal a healthy crop of hair that was whitening but still had plenty of black visible all around, particularly on the sides and back. He had piercing blue eyes that housed a look of determination and, in today's case, anger. These eyes were not smiling as he greeted Hartnell.

"Shall we go down to one of the small offices, Chief Inspector?" asked Hartnell as he firmly shook Gault's hand.

Gault nodded. It wasn't unusual for Hartnell to have taken the lead in this situation. After all, he was the joint most senior officer operating out of Arleswood, and Gault was effectively his guest, one who rarely visits the sleepy commuter town. Upon entering the small office, the same one which Hartnell and Johnson had just occupied, Gault immediately went around to the side of the desk where the computer faced. This, by default, is where the person to whom the office belongs would sit; thus Gault had instantly taken the position of psychological power in the room.

"Well, Inspector Hartnell," he said whilst frowning, "you've had a busy morning, haven't you?"

"You mean the burglary at Dr Frederick Leston's house and subsequent events thereafter, I assume," responded Hartnell.

"Of course, Inspector," said Gault in a patronising manner. "And I'm afraid your report card on this one looks particularly poor."

"Well, I had to make several quick decisions, sir," responded Hartnell. "But I assure you I can justify all of my actions."

"Can you?" continued the ever-more-condescending Gault. There was a stern look in his eye as he leant forward and stared at his inspector. "Well, we have a long list to go through, don't we?"

"I'm begging your pardon, sir," said Hartnell. "But I'm not entirely sure what you mean."

Gault chuckled slightly before changing the look on his face to one of anger. "Really, Inspector? Really? Well, let me help you figure out what I mean."

Hartnell swallowed and a lump came to his throat. Chief Inspector Gault looked furious, and during the three years Hartnell had worked for the man since he'd moved from the London force, he had never seen his boss look like this.

What was going on? There was nothing to make Gault so furious. Something was wrong here.

The very tall Chief Inspector Gault stood up and stared down at Hartnell as if to make himself even more intimidating.

"Firstly, you send a team down to that hostel to apprehend three suspects without the proper backup or appropriate team in place. You did not know if the men were armed or dangerous. In fact, you knew nothing, and yet you went against all known procedures and put yourself and five other officers in grave danger."

"But, sir—" interrupted Hartnell.

"Quiet, Inspector!" shouted Gault. "Let me finish."

"Yes, sir," said Hartnell sheepishly.

"Then I understand that there was a serious physical assault at the same hostel some time later. Yes? And that you ordered your men not to pursue the perpetrators despite them being more or less still in sight at the time."

Gault looked at Hartnell as if he wanted a response, but having been told to be quiet moments before, the inspector decided to say nothing.

"What were you thinking!" Gault screamed down at Hartnell from across the desk.

Hartnell now did move to speak, but Gault held up his hand as if to stop him from saying anything.

"If it gets out into the general public domain, or to my superiors, that we are not taking violent crime seriously, then we may as well all pack it in. We have three men at large who are capable of such a crime, who could easily have been detained, and what did you do? You said, 'No, don't bother, boys'!"

There was a silence.

"And you said no," repeated Gault, whilst shaking his head.

"Can I—?" asked Hartnell but was again instantly silenced.

"And, of course, they are not the only three men at large right now, are they Inspector Hartnell? You were able to detain four men, one of whom we know is a perennial pain in the backside, who were caught red-handed with the stolen item, and you let them go. *You let them go!*"

"I had no ch—" chipped in Hartnell.

"I'm not even close to finishing yet, Inspector," said the very angry Gault. "I'm just getting started, in fact. Because I also understand that you, along with sergeants Hughes and Johnson, conducted all of the interviews with the suspects without them having legal representation present. I have no doubt that you asked them for their lawyers, but upon their continued refusal you should not have continued with the interviews. You know the rules, Hartnell. You could have held them here until they saw sense on this matter. If the overpaid – and frankly, over-devious – selection of defence lawyers polluting this area became aware that we at Three Shires Constabulary were grilling suspects in this fashion, they would have a field day and take us to the bloody cleaners. They could cry foul, and literally hundreds of cases could be reopened citing procedural errors, and many of the worst scumbags we've got safely locked up could be acquitted and released. Your decision-making beggars belief here, Inspector."

Gault finally sat back down in his chair but never once took his eyes off the inspector. Hartnell didn't know if now would be the right time to speak. He didn't want to antagonise Gault any further; the senior man was sitting there red-faced with veins pumping.

Gault took a deep breath to compose himself and spoke again, once it became clear Hartnell had chosen not to say a word just yet.

"And to top it all off, you then went back to see the victim of the original burglary and decided to steal his mobile phone."

Hartnell swallowed the lump in his throat and slumped back down in his chair.

"I may have got this wrong, Inspector," said a sarcastic but at least calmer, quieter Gault, "but I thought that when a crime has been committed, it is usual policy for us in the police to investigate the potential criminals, not interrogate the victim and pinch his belongings. I'll check that one in the manual as soon as I'm back in my office."

"How did Leston know we took his phone deliberately?" thought Hartnell. "Mistakes happen. It's not too unknown for people pick up the wrong handsets. We were only gone three minutes. Leston should not have suspected anything."

Then the penny dropped for Hartnell. It must have been that number they'd dialled, he realised. That must have triggered something.

Gault continued. "Now listen very carefully, Inspector Hartnell, unless you want to be sat behind a desk filing reports in alphabetical order for the rest of your police career. I have promised Dr Leston that we will find the men who burgled his house. He has agreed to not issue a complaint against you and Sergeant Johnson for taking his phone, providing we find the men who entered his house. I don't know why, but he wants to meet them personally. I know it is a strange request of his, but right now I will do anything to protect the reputation of this force. Do you understand, Inspector?"

"Yes I do, sir," responded a relieved and enthusiastic-sounding Hartnell, who for a short moment there had felt he was facing a suspension. "But I feel that I have much to tell you about all of the things you just mentioned, sir. Not least why we felt we had to examine Leston's phone, sir."

"In good time, Inspector Hartnell, all in good time," said Gault calmly. "I have no doubt you will have good explanations for your stupid decisions, as always. Listening to your bullshit would take up more of my time and yours, and frankly, I'm bored with hearing why you continuously break tried-and-tested police protocols. Consider this a final warning, Inspector, as I haven't got the time to fire you either. The paperwork is horrendous. Right now, as I'd said, I'd like you to bring me the four people who you had in here earlier as suspects for the break-in."

"But that is the problem, sir," said Hartnell. "Only three people were involved in breaking into Leston's house, and yet we have four suspects. Unfortunately, we simply don't have enough evidence or details yet to know which three of the four it was, sir."

Gault scratched his chin.

"So you see, sir, I had to release the men pending further investigations, which Sergeant Johnson and I have continued to do for several hours after our shift finished."

"Harassing victims, Inspector," said Gault with a fierce look on his face. "Is not what I'd call investigating, would you? I'd call it a recipe for a PR disaster."

"Sir, I feel you must know something," said Hartnell gingerly, not sure whether he was about to incur the chief inspector's wrath again. "There is a chance that the three men responsible for the assault outside the hostel were sent there by Dr Leston, sir. That is why I needed to get hold of his phone."

"A chance, Inspector?" said Gault sarcastically. "Oh good, a chance. That is a brilliant way to prioritise, Inspector. We know for certain that three of the four men you held here were responsible for the burglary. We know for certain that three men just assaulted another man and two women outside Burgin's *and* that they are definitely on Arleswood Common. But no, you waste your time on 'a chance'."

"Sir, people other than the police were also looking for the men who burgled Dr Leston," said Hartnell. "It was too much of a coincidence that the same building was the location for two major incidents on the same night. I feel they must be connected."

"I'm listening," said Gault, as if encouraging Hartnell to carry on.

"So, I thought that if we could quickly find out who Leston had contacted whilst I was interviewing him the first time this morning, straight after the burglary, it would either confirm or eliminate Leston from the enquiries about who the second set of men at Burgin's were."

"Go on," encouraged an ever-more-interested-looking Gault.

"We managed to get a number, sir. Frederick Leston contacted the number both verbally and by text in the minutes after he was burgled and was contacted back by the same number a few hours later. Sergeant Johnson was working with the phone companies to work out who the phone was registered to and where this person is."

"So you have confirmed my fear, Hartnell," said Gault.

"Really, sir," responded Hartnell enthusiastically.

"Yes," retorted Gault, much less warmly than Hartnell had hoped. "My fear that you are spending more of your time on harassing a victim of a crime than solving the crime itself."

"With all due respect, sir," said Hartnell. "I feel that if we have some kind of vigilante police force roaming the south-east of England, enforcing their own form of justice, and with the ability to track and locate people as quickly as we in the real police did, then we must follow this up, sir, surely?"

Gault sat back and took a huge intake of breath.

"The reputation of this police force is on the line here, Inspector Hartnell," said Gault. "And you are responsible for most of the potential ways in which the reputation breach could occur, with your rather colourful morning's work. And so I would suggest you remember who you are talking to."

"Yes, sir," responded Hartnell in an apologetic tone.

"I'm positive you are way off the mark with Dr Leston," said Gault. "He is a frail old schoolteacher and a globally renowned mathematician. And after I met him this morning, I'd like to add 'a thoroughly decent all-round good guy' to his synopsis. Despite your little game earlier today, he harbours no hard feelings towards you and Sergeant Johnson and was very complimentary of your work. And you accuse him of being involved in these kinds of things?"

Hartnell sat back up in his chair and focused in on the Chief Inspector's face, trying to study Gault's expression. Had he lost this little battle with his superior?

"However," said Gault. "I do trust you, Hartnell. You are not normally as reckless as you have been today. You have earned my trust these last few years, despite your scant regard for policy. You get results, and the local people who matter like you, and that is good for me. So, tell me about this phone number and where you are going with this. However, do remember, Inspector, I'm not happy with this at all. I am now using my time to follow a line of enquiry I don't agree with. If it turns out you are wasting my time with this, I will not be impressed."

"Of course sir. Thank you," said a seemingly rejuvenated Hartnell. "Well, I and the paramedic who first attended to Dr Leston both noticed that Leston contacted someone in the middle of the night. Once when he was first being treated – literally minutes after the burglary – and secondly when I was interviewing him, much to my frustration, as I felt I didn't have his attention fully. He was preoccupied with something. Leston later let slip that he knew we'd tracked his intruders to Burgin's. We hadn't told him that, and so my hunch was born that he'd sent a hit squad to the hostel to recover his stolen item. I felt we therefore needed to find out who he had contacted. We checked the time in his phone records with the time he was seen using the phone, and there were appropriate matches with a mysterious number beginning 04. Sergeant Johnson is checking the number out with BT or someone, as I said, sir, because when we dialled it we just got a dead-end voice recording."

"And so, can we call Johnson now?" asked Gault.

"Better than that, sir," replied Hartnell. "We can go straight to the contact we use at the phone company for this kind of thing. They have been very helpful."

"Very well, Hartnell," said a stern-looking Gault.

Just then Hartnell's phone beeped. It was a text from Sergeant Johnson. "I'll read that in a second," thought Hartnell, and he proceeded to type into the desk speakerphone a phone number he had stored in his handset.

The phone started to ring and was picked up. "Dean Marshall," said the cheery voice at the other end.

"Hi, Dean," said Hartnell. "Inspector Hartnell from Three Shires Police again."

"Oh, hi again, Inspector" said Marshall. "I've just been speaking to your colleague, Sergeant Johnson, actually."

"About that funny 04 number, right?" asked Hartnell.

"Yes," replied Marshall. "Not much to tell, really, I'm afraid. I've checked the details. It is a premium line set up in the name of Smithfield's Healthcare. We ran a quick Google check on them, too, for you, sir. They offer private mobile specialist healthcare services for a small, select group of wealthy elderly people around the south-east."

Hartnell slumped. "OK, many thanks, Dean," he said.

"You are welcome, Inspector, but there is something else," said Marshall.

Leaning forward and speaking into the speakerphone, Chief Inspector Gault took over. "No, I've heard enough. Many thanks," he said. He hung up the phone and sat back in his chair with a face like thunder.

"So," Chief Inspector Gault said, clearing his throat for an extremely sarcastic rant. "Leston is old, frail, and wealthy and has just had a nasty fall and experienced an event which would make him feel unwell – and so he calls a company offering him a service to make him feel better!"

He let out a large breath as he got to his feet. He placed his cap on his head and turned to Hartnell as he left the office. "You complete prat!" he said as he stormed out and slammed the door.

Darkness was beginning to fall over Arleswood as Inspector Hartnell returned to work at the police station for his shift, passing a very tired-looking Inspector Middleton on his way out.

"Good night, Inspector," offered Hartnell cheerily to his colleague, but he received nothing more than a gentle nod and weary half-smile in return. "Been a busy one then, chap?" he asked sympathetically.

"Twelve hour shifts are not good for me at my age, Inspector," replied Middleton with a little more enthusiasm than he had given in his initial greeting. "And next week I'm back on nights, which are even harder. Might be time I jacked it all in."

"Oh, there's plenty of life left in you yet, sir," said Hartnell, and he patted his elder compatriot on the back as he left the building.

Looking around the reception for an initial indication of what the day shift might have been up against, or more importantly, what the next twelve or so hours might hold for him, Hartnell silently prayed that things would be quiet. He muttered the words "need to concentrate on solving the Leston burglary case" as he looked skywards for inspiration. He had got his fingers burnt earlier with his wrong assumptions about the reclusive mathematician ordering some kind of mob hit on Burgin's Hostel. He felt like a fool. How could he have got it so wrong? It would have been fairly easy for Leston to find out that Burgin's was the place his intruders had been found hiding out. After all, various members of the police had been coming and going from his house for several hours between the burglary and the second time he'd interviewed him. Any one of them could have passed on that information or inadvertently shared it. Even the forensic team, dusting away while looking for fingerprints and other evidence, had known that Burgin's was the target, and no doubt their radios would have been cackling away during the entire operation. Hartnell felt he had learnt a lesson.

He could still hear Chief Inspector Gault's angry voice clearly in his head, pounding away and giving him a severe headache. "Find the three actual burglars from the four suspects – and quickly, Hartnell," the voice kept telling him over and over again.

He wasn't used to making mistakes. He felt he had been too fixated with wondering why the burglars had disturbed their own burglary and then left a simple trail for the police follow, and also trying to pin an assault on Leston simply because it fitted a scenario.

He said good evening to Sergeant Hughes, who had also arrived already, and headed again straight to the sanctuary of the small office he had been using before he'd gone home to rest. Luckily, he had been so tired by the end that he had indeed gotten plenty of sleep, despite Gault's criticisms and humiliations being fresh in his mind.

"You complete prat, Hartnell!" echoed again in his mind. He knew that various things Gault had said to him earlier today were going to reverberate around his head for some time, until he solved this peculiar case. He felt unusually low but was looking forward to getting deep into some investigative work and, hopefully, vindicating himself.

His phone then rang.

"Ah, David, there you are," he said as he answered the call, having glanced at the name on the display. "On your way in?"

"Yes, Rodge," replied Johnson. "But I've got some things to update you on, so may as well do it from the car on the way."

"OK, my friend, what do you have?" asked Hartnell.

"Well, firstly," said Johnson, "the Frenchman. As mentioned before, he did indeed give his real name and address, which is unexpected and a breath of fresh air. His story seems a sad one though, Rodge. His family used to run a successful restaurant in a small town in the south of France, but that was shut down over a health scare some time ago. From then on it seems he spiralled out of control a little. He has been convicted in France on counts of burglary several times."

"OK," said Hartnell. "That's our second convicted burglar in our line-up after Stone, so it's all coming together nicely. Any links to the UK at all? Why this town? Why now?"

"Well, that is the strange thing," responded Johnson. "The boys have run a quick check on his passport, and this is actually his first-ever visit to Great Britain. He arrived at London Stansted just a few days ago, on a budget airlines flight from Montpellier."

"That explains his poor English," said Hartnell, "but not why he turned up in Arleswood and just so happened to come across a group of like-minded burglars and petty criminals and rob Frederick Leston!"

"Well, as you know," replied Johnson, "not one of the four guys we had in custody seemed to have ever had any contact with any of the other three before. No common, mutual links were found on any of their phones. So it is truly baffling how this particular Frenchman ended up committing a burglary here."

"A long way to come to steal an old man's memoirs, don't you think, Dave?" asked Hartnell. "Any details of a return ticket purchased?"

"Nope," replied Johnson. "Nothing is showing up. He only bought a ticket for one-way, although admittedly he could easily have booked something with another airline or mode of transport altogether, like a train or ferry. They haven't had time to check everything. He could be here on an open-ended crime spree!"

"I doubt that, my friend," replied Hartnell, "or he would have gone to more trouble to not get caught. I think we need to stop calling this event a burglary and give it another name. There is clearly something else going on here. It's almost as if the guys just wanted Leston's attention."

"But then, why get caught? Why not just get his attention and then bugger off back to France or wherever?" asked Johnson.

"I still don't know!" said an animated Hartnell. "Anyway, so we now know at least two of the four are known burglars. Stone we already knew about and now Philippe, this Frenchman. What else do we have, Dave?"

"Well, not a lot really," responded Johnson. "Peter Kerrigan also gave his real name and details, but he has nothing on file at all. No prints and no profile. He has no convictions and hasn't even been questioned by the police before. Anyway, he lives somewhere in the Midlands, near Nottingham. Considering what Gault wants you to do, I'd suggest we go and pull him back in. At least we know where to find him. And which force would we need to help us with that?"

"Err," said Johnson after a short pause, "that would be the North Midlands Constabulary. The same one as our retired policeman Ian Riley, but that must be incidental."

"And the fourth chap?" asked Hartnell. "Anything on our overconfident Mr Morgan?"

"Nothing at all," answered Johnson. "He certainly gave a false name, as he doesn't exist on any police database or electoral roll, and he has no credit history. His prints didn't match anything on any of the UK systems and records."

"So finding him again will be tough?" suggested Hartnell. "But he was the only one who lied to us about his details, though, correct? The other three all check out, right?"

"Yes," responded Johnson. "That appears to be correct. However, finding him might not be a lost cause. If we continue to assume that all four of them were in on this together, if we manage to find them and drag them back here, then I'm sure that with the appropriate pressure we can get at least one of them to give up Morgan."

"Yes, I like it, David, my friend," said Hartnell. "They can't all stick to their 'I was asleep' story if we start over-inflating the possible punishments for this crime. I'd bet on that Peter guy cracking if he has never been in trouble before."

"And the Frenchman too," said Johnson. "If we can scare him with stories of the British justice system and our tough, harsh prison conditions, he might panic."

"And Stone?" asked Hartnell. "I do genuinely think he is innocent in all this. I do think he was set up by the other three, just like he told us."

"Well, yes, that was going to be my next point, Rodge," said Johnson. "His story about his pipes bursting at home and this bogus offer of a free night at Burgin's both check out. His flat *is* flooded, and Peter Burgin has told us that neither he nor his daughters have never created 'free nights' vouchers."

"So everything now points to this Billy character," said Hartnell. "Who is he, and why did he set Stone up only to then reveal to him his entire plan?"

"No idea," responded Johnson, "which is why we need to find him. It's been about ten hours since anyone last saw him. He could be anywhere in Europe by now, as could they all."

"OK, Rodge, I'm nearly at the station," said Johnson. "I'll tell you what we've got on PC Riley and that Hastings lad whose prints are also on that folder once I'm there."

Hartnell hung up his phone and put it back on the desk. He pondered about what he had just been told for five minutes, making several notes on an A4 pad of lined paper. He started drawing lines and linking comments, people, and dates, until Sergeant Johnson walked into the office.

"OK," said Hartnell enthusiastically, "what do we have? Tell me more about the guys whose prints were on Leston's folder, then. This is starting to really come together."

"OK. Riley retired in 2008," said Johnson. "And then it seems he disappeared completely off the police grid. Our systems have no onward address and no next-of-kin details. Nothing. No one in either this force or the North Midlands seem to know how to contact him."

"His pension?" asked Hartnell.

"Well, I also drew a blank there," responded Johnson. "It seems that against all advice he took a lump-sum payment when he retired and is not receiving any kind of regular payment from the Police Pension scheme. We could try council tax records and the electoral role, for example, but as we don't know where he lives, we would be entering the realm of needles and haystacks."

"Well, that makes things a little harder," said a downbeat Hartnell. "I've just received a huge ticking off from Chief Inspector Gault about digging deeper into Freddie Leston instead of chasing the 'baddies', as he put it. I really don't want to get my fingers caught in the till again by trying to find a former policeman who in all probability is not connected to the case. I wouldn't have Gault's support on this. He already thinks I'm concentrating on everyone else and neglecting the four suspects from the burglary."

"I could get one of the men to do it discreetly," suggested Johnson.

"No," said Hartnell in a sterner-than-usual voice. "Somehow, I think all investigations we ask our guys to do now will be compromised and will find their way back to Gault. He's made Leston a promise that we'll present to him his intruders soon and is blinded by the thought of anything negative being said about his force. If he finds out that we are trying to find this Riley guy, albeit just so that he might be able to help us, Gault will fire me, make no bones about that. His prints may be on that folder, but they are over ten years old and therefore almost certainly not relevant to this morning's burglary."

"OK, I see," said Johnson dejectedly.

"And anything else on Hastings?" asked Hartnell. "Did you and the troops come up with anything?"

"Well, not a lot more than we already know, unfortunately, Rodge," said Johnson. "We know he was a proper nasty piece of work. I won't run through his list of convictions again, boss."

Johnson put a file onto the desk in front of Hartnell. "It's all here," he said.

Hartnell picked the file up and began to read out loud. "Was transferred from Leeds to Nottingham at the age of 13, for his own protection. Was then placed in a home for adolescents with behavioural problems. Several convictions. Drugs. Assault. Robbery. He was schooled at a special school for young offenders. Crime spree continued into adulthood. Six-month jail term for series of violent carjackings. Suspected he became involved in the notorious Nottingham gang scene. Inspector Riley investigated him on several occasions."

"And then the bit about the fire," added Johnson.

"Yes, I think that bit is coming next," said Hartnell, continuing to read the file. "Large warehouse fire. Hundreds of thousands of pounds of damage. Hastings among others suspected but never found. Was traced to south-west England. William Hastings found washed up on a beach in Devon. Inspector Riley identified body. Fell from a tourist fishing boat in front of eleven witnesses."

"Yet the body was found with a severe knife wound in it," said Johnson. "Although drowning was the cause of death given by the coroner."

"Was there any scuffle on board that fishing boat, then?" asked Hartnell. "Any of the eleven witnesses say anything about that?"

"I don't think so, Roger," said Johnson. "If you were to carry on reading, it says he just sort of 'fell in'."

"Are you saying suicide?" asked Hartnell in alarm.

"No way," said Johnson immediately, picking up the file and reading it himself. "Hastings was staying at small hotel. In his room they found a wallet with over a thousand pounds of cash in it and a laptop left on the desk; there were clothes, a mobile phone. No note was found. No evidence whatsoever of suicide. Clearly no evidence here for a faked suicide, either. The cash and phone would certainly be needed. Hastings clearly intended to return to his room, there is no doubt about that. When I first read this, Rodge, I immediately thought murder."

Hartnell's eyes widened considerably. Murder was not a word very often heard in and around Arleswood Police Station. Not since he'd left London's Metropolitan Police had he investigated such a crime. He drew a big breath.

"Well, I think you may be right," he said. "He either drowned, as per the file, or was murdered and it was cleverly disguised as a drowning. This discussion means we are still no closer to knowing how Chief Inspector Riley's or William Hastings' fingerprints ended up on Leston's folder."

"No, Rodge," said a despondent Johnson. "We are not. And I'm not even sure that if we were to investigate this any further we would find out who burgled the Leston house this morning."

"Correct. Only solving the Leston burglary case can save my reputation with Gault," said Hartnell. "But by now I'm convinced that everything is linked, and therefore I will indeed investigate further. I need you to get to France, my friend. Dig into Philippe Le Sac's story. I'm pretty certain it will help us understand why he came here to Southern England. There must be a reason. And my gut is telling me that he will return there soon too, so you never know, you may be waiting for him when he gets there."

"I assume we don't have the resources or clearance to put a check on the ports and airports to see if his passport is used," asked Johnson.

"No, David, we do not," said Hartnell. "And anyway, I think you can find a lot out about him and his whereabouts and travel plans whether he turns up or not. It's Thursday evening. Go there first thing in the morning. Depending on the flight times, you could be back tomorrow night, so get on the Net and get booking. I'll arrange for you to meet the gendarme who runs the shop in Philippe's hometown."

"France! OK, I'm in," said Johnson jovially. "I'll do a little more reading on him and his family in the meantime. It would look good if I turn up with more than basic knowledge of his background. I'll also brush up a little on my *français*. What will you do, Rodge?"

"Well," replied Hartnell, "I *should* go to the Midlands and try to find Peter Kerrigan. I'm sure he'll be easy to track down. Having never been in trouble before, I'm certain he'd have got scared and headed to the comfort and security of his home. This time I can be a little tougher with our questions on him. I'm certain he'll break."

"Nice plan," said Johnson.

But Hartnell held up his hand to inform his friend that he wished to continue to talk. "But actually – and for heaven's sake don't tell anyone – I think I'm going to go to Devon. If I leave early tomorrow morning towards the end of our shift, I'll be there before lunchtime. I'll ask Middleton to come in and start early. He'll be OK. He knows I'm up against it here after my cock-up with Leston's phone."

"But how will investigating a case closed over ten years ago help you solve this latest case?" asked Johnson. "Gault could have your head, remember. I know there is a link with the stolen item, but it is ten-year-old evidence. There is no proven link with the burglary that your career hangs on solving, Rodge."

"Maybe not," said Hartnell with a smile. "But I'm not so sure. There is something all too strange here, as usual. We have a drowned man with a fresh knife wound in his back but no mention of an attack by the eleven people who saw him go overboard. And we also have a policeman who seems to have gone to great lengths to not be found post retirement. I'm sure there is a connection, and I need our friends in the West Country to help me find it."

T he following morning, as instructed, a weary yet enthusiastic Sergeant Johnson arrived in the small town of Rocheville, about half an hour's drive north from the Mediterranean beaches, near the city of Montpellier, in southern France. It was still only eleven o'clock on a busy Friday morning, as he had caught the early flight from London, but already the temperature was approaching twenty degrees Celsius.

Rocheville was bathed in sunshine as the Englishman parked his hire car and treated himself to a quick look around *le centre ville* before heading to the police station. The buildings were typically French and very traditionally Mediterranean, mostly rendered or washed in different shades of white to reflect away the summer's intense heat. The houses were all terraced, with only a small maze of narrow, cobbled alleyways separating them, and the windows bounded by different shades of wooden shutters in various states of repair. This was an old town, full of rustic charm, with streets barely wide enough to walk down, let alone drive a car. It seemed each street ended in a small square with attractive plane trees reaching up to grab the light, the only splash of green in view. The largest square, in the heart of the centre, had a small fountain in it, invitingly spurting out water into a large stone catchment before inevitably being sucked up and pumped out again.

The town had a permanent population of around ten thousand people; however, in the summer months that number often swelled to triple that figure, thanks to the hordes of Northern European tourists heading for the golden Mediterranean climate. In early April the streets were still owned by the locals, coming and going about their daily business. The hordes of tourists wouldn't arrive to claim the town for themselves for another month. The police station was located in a small street just off the main square, in Rocheville's beautiful old town, next to the marvellous seventeenth-century town hall with its tricolour proudly flying in the light breeze.

"Ah, you must be ze policeman Johnson, from England," said the smallish, charming gendarme in a smart French police uniform behind the desk of the small police station. "We 'ave been looking forward to you arrive."

"Bonjour et merci, monsieur," replied Johnson in his best French. "I am pleased to be here. I have come to meet Lieutenant Floregge. Is he here?"

"Yes, Policeman Johnson, zis way, *mon ami*," said the gendarme as he led Johnson down a small corridor in the police station. Old plaster was flaking off the walls of the station, and the general feel was of an interior that required more than a little TLC, but it seemed nonetheless a friendly and welcoming work environment.

"'Ello, good morning," said Lieutenant Floregge with the most cheerful of greetings, leaping to his feet as his guest was shown into his office. "I am so pleased to meet you."

He was a charming, handsome man who reminded Sergeant Johnson quite a lot of Inspector Hartnell. He was maybe a little older, perhaps in his late forties, with a kind face and smile. He was around five foot nine inches tall, so not a short man, but by no means did he appear large or intimidating. His uniform, although smart and formal, wasn't immaculate, telling the story of a man who was probably happier in plain clothes, much like the British police officer standing in his office before him. He was a slim man with a tanned, weathered face typical of the area.

Johnson looked around. The lieutenant's office was quite large, with exposed sandy-coloured bricks on all four sides, designed years ago to keep the room cool. There was a small window above the only desk in the room, but that was enough to adequately light the square space.

Floregge waved away the front desk officer, who shut the door behind him, and he invited Johnson to sit down by pointing at a chair with wheels, strangely placed next to the one he himself had just risen from when his guest arrived.

"Can I get you a drink, Sergeant?" he asked. "I assume you are thirsty after your trip."

"Well, that would be nice," responded Johnson as he wheeled the chair around to the other side of the desk and sat down. "Just a glass of water would be perfect."

"Of course," said Floregge in an equally enthusiastic manner. "It will be 'ere in one minute," he said as he pressed a button on his desk.

"*L'eau pour Sergeant Johnson et aussi pour moi,*" he said into a hidden speaker, giving instructions in a very formal voice. This was refreshing to Johnson considering the jovial nature he had heard exclusively so far.

Lieutenant Floregge had lived in the town of Rocheville all of his life and had been a policeman there for twenty-five years. He was fluent in both English and Dutch as well as his native French. This was a result of the changes over the last fifteen years or so, since the town had become home to numerous ex-pats from the UK and the Low Countries, not to mention the annual influx of tourists.

"I learnt English so I could do my job properly, Sergeant Johnson," he said proudly when complimented by the Englishman on his language skills. "I believe my ability to speak these languages well 'as 'elped me to defuse many situations when things could 'ave got out of control."

Johnson smiled as he recognised the self-satisfaction his counterpart was getting from using his English. "*Mon français c'est pas bon,*" he said with a wide grin. "So I too am very pleased that your English is so good."

Both men had a small chuckle. "It's funny," said Floregge. "I meet thousands of British people every year, and they can all speak plenty of words of French. And yet, I'm afraid to say, so few ever go on to learn the language properly. It is a real shame. It is of great credit and respect that most of your countrymen will always try to speak the words they do know, but so poor that only a fraction could really say they 'speak French'."

"Well, guilty as charged," said Johnson putting his hand up. "*Désolé!*"

At that moment there was a knock at the door. Floregge pressed another button, and there was a whirling sound as if a lock were being released. Then the charming officer from the front desk entered the room with two glasses of water and placed them on the desk. Johnson muttered *merci* towards the man, but without so much as even looking up, Floregge waved his colleague out of the room again and moved forward to speak.

"So, you are 'ere to talk about Philippe Le Sac," he said, his face taking on a much more serious look. "You must be very curious, Sergeant Johnson, about this man to have come all the way down here to the sunny south. But I too am intrigued. It's quite lucky for you because I know Philippe quite well. Very strange he showed up in England."

"Yes, it is very strange, Lieutenant," replied Johnson. "And that is exactly why I'm here. I'm hoping to see if we can work out why he went to my town, which is called Arleswood. You probably haven't heard of it. It's about forty kilometres north of central London."

Floregge gave a small shrug of the shoulders which suggested he hadn't. "I don't know why 'e went there, *non*."

"Well," continued Johnson, "considering he has never even left France before, and now he turns up in Southern England and is placed at the scene of a burglary, it doesn't look great for him."

"I was led to believe, Sergeant," said Floregge looking slightly agitated, "that you don't know if 'e did commit a crime or not, and that you were 'ere to find this out. For several years 'e would 'ave made friends with people from Great Britain. There are many 'ere in Rocheville. There are many reasons why 'e would want to visit your country."

"You are correct, Lieutenant – forgive me," said an apologetic Johnson. "We don't know for certain, but based on the evidence from Arleswood and his record here in this region, we have to assume he may be involved at this stage, even though I do accept it is unlikely."

"Maybe," responded Floregge. "I'm not sure 'ow it works over the water, Sergeant, but in French policing we don't make assumptions, 'owever."

Johnson felt he was meeting a little resistance from Lieutenant Floregge simply because he had spoken as if Philippe were already guilty, which hadn't been his intention. He knew he'd have to choose his words carefully here, as he was a guest here in France, and he didn't want to offend. He also knew he needed local help, and so he let Floregge continue.

"Philippe is a good person, Sergeant Johnson," he said with less frustration than before. "'E may have been involved in a few things 'ere in the last few years, but at 'eart 'e is a good man. I 'ave known him for many years. I will never give up on 'im. I know the real Philippe."

"The real Philippe?" asked Johnson.

"Yes. The real Philippe," Floregge snapped back. "I am sorry to say that I don't believe there is any chance that 'e was involved in your crime in England, Sergeant. I simply cannot 'elp you. As there is no open crime 'ere in my jurisdictive region of Languedoc, I can't put any resources on this for you. It is the start now of the busy time, with all of the English coming 'ere, and I am not permitted to waste time investigating a small crime in another country."

Johnson was taken aback, but he understood. He suddenly felt ridiculous that he had come all that way. He also now could see that the lieutenant was quite fond of Philippe. Then he remembered what he had been told by his colleagues back in the UK about the collapse of Philippe's family restaurant, and he felt confident enough to ask Floregge.

"I was wondering about Philippe's past, actually, Lieutenant," he stated. "I understand from the records your team sent to my police force back home that he has a few convictions for petty crime in the last few years or so, but before that he was never in trouble."

Floregge nodded. "That is correct, Sergeant. I have known 'im for 'is whole life. 'E was never in trouble, but when his family became ruined, 'e started to turn to small crimes. But I mean petty, Sergeant. Just to get a few euros together to feed 'is family when they were desperate. A bit of theft from supermarkets, for example. 'E is a good boy from a good family. I do not believe that he would go to England to do this. There must be another reason why 'e was there."

Johnson could hear the passion in Floregge's voice. There were almost tears in his eyes as he spoke about Philippe.

"I understand, Lieutenant," said a calm Johnson. "I am hoping that he returns to his home here whilst I am around to talk to him and find out why. He was found with the stolen item, along with some other men. I can tell from your words that he is a good man, Lieutenant. I would love to remove him from our enquiries."

"If you are so keen to talk to 'im, Sergeant," said Floregge assertively, "then why did you release 'im in the first place? I am confused by your actions. Just one day later you are all the way down 'ere in the south of France wanting to speak to 'im again."

Johnson was starting to get a little agitated, having his decisions and actions picked at, but he remembered he had to stay calm. Reluctant help was better than no help, and now that he was here, he should try to gather as much information as he could.

"I am aware how this looks, Lieutenant," he said. "It is a long story, but I need to speak to him again. We may have made a mistake. Nothing makes any sense in this case."

"*Oui*, I 'ave read the report," said Floregge. "Very puzzling."

"My inspector and I do need your help, sir," Johnson continued. "I would like to review the files about Philippe. I'd like to know more about how he became a petty thief. I'd like to know more about how his family business was ruined and also to read up on the reports on the crimes he has committed here in France. I'm hoping that I find something, no matter how small, that gives us some indication as to why he flew to London this week."

"OK, Sergeant," said Floregge as he got to his feet. "I will give you everything you ask for. I 'ope you find something that can clear Philippe's name with you, as I'm no longer enjoying 'earing these accusations."

He walked over to a table at the far side of the room, away from the window and the desk. On it were a stack of papers, which the lieutenant picked up.

"'Ere you go, Sergeant," he said as he handed the files to Johnson. "I already 'ad them prepared as per the request we received from your office before you arrived. Everything is in French, I'm afraid, apart from a few statements taken from British or Dutch people. But feel free to use your computer and the online translation services. You can use my office. I am off out for a few hours. My colleagues will bring you some lunch. The wifi code is simple. It is on a yellow sticky note stuck to the corner of the desk."

"That is most kind, Lieutenant," said Johnson. He also stood up, and he shook Floregge's hand. "I hope I find what I need."

"Good luck, mon ami," said Floregge, reverting back to the friendly tone he had used at the start of the meeting. "Remember, Sergeant Johnson, Philippe Le Sac is a good man."

"I'm beginning to get that mental picture of him, Lieutenant," replied Johnson. "But, of course, I need to keep a fully open mind whilst I go through all of these files. If he is innocent, we'll find something in here that can clear him."

"Indeed, there are many files, Sergeant," said Floregge. "Can I recommend you start with the file I've placed on the top? It is about the episode when his family's restaurant was closed down. It effectively marks the beginning of Philippe's involvement with the police. Before this incident there was nothing. And also, many parts of the file are in English. There was an Englishman involved."

Lieutenant Floregge gave a small wink, turned on his heel, and then left his office in the capable hands of his guest. Sergeant Johnson deliberately left the office door wide open. Floregge had mentioned that food was on the way, and given that Johnson didn't know which button his host had pressed to release the door earlier, he wanted to make sure he didn't miss out on his lunch by being locked in the room!

He sat back down at the desk, this time in Lieutenant Floregge's chair, picked up the first file as instructed, and began to read.

19

The last of the day's sunshine was just visible above the rooftops of the old town of Rocheville. It was a truly idyllic scene with the old town square full of people sitting at tables having dinner or simply enjoying an early evening drink. Plenty of non-diners were around too, tourists mostly, walking through the pleasant streets. Some had pushchairs and others dogs; all were enjoying the gentle heat. They were soaking up the atmosphere and buying the odd souvenir. Several children were running around too, some splashing in the fountain outside the grand town hall, others enjoying rapidly melting ice creams. The square was full of life, as it so often was this time of year. The restaurant owners had placed as many tables and chairs as they possibly could onto the cobbled stone base of the square in an attempt to maximise revenue on this fine evening.

One restaurant was particularly busy this evening. La Vieux Lion was located directly opposite the town hall, on the south side of the square. This was the oldest restaurant still in operation in Rocheville, and the fact that it attracted locals in their masses was an indication of both the quality and affordability of the establishment. The tables had spilled over well into the open rectangle, and all appeared to be occupied. Inside the restaurant it was busy too, with the air conditioning working hard to keep the many diners cool.

At one table, an English lady in her early thirties, with long blonde hair, was enjoying a glass of white wine. She was tall, thin, and very elegant, wearing a lovely all-white dress and black shoes. She was with a short man who was probably around 50 years old. The couple had already finished their meal and were contemplating dessert.

"George, I really don't feel well," the lady said. "I don't want to sound dramatic, but I feel like I've been poisoned." The comment was meant to be flippant, but right then she started to perspire furiously, and her companion could see just by looking at her that something was seriously wrong.

"Oh Jesus! Sarah, my love," said George. "You look terrible. Shall I call over the waiter?"

"No, George," she responded. "Can we just go? I need some air. Can you get the bill and meet me outside?"

"Of course, my sweetie," he said, again in a slightly patronising fashion, as if he were talking to a schoolgirl.

He stood up, walked around the table, and helped his ill girlfriend to her feet. She was taller than he was by a good three inches, but due to her slight frame she was easy for George to support. Indeed, he was able to hold her in one arm whilst taking the time to finish off his own glass of wine and then hers with one large gulp each. Holding his lady close, George then manoeuvred the two of them between the other tables and headed towards the door at a rapid but safe pace.

One of the waiters, Luc, had seen George rapidly emptying the contents of the two wine glasses down his throat and watched as the couple headed swiftly for the exit. His immediate thought was that they were trying to leave without paying.

Across the noisy, crowded restaurant, Luc shouted, "Stop! Please stop! You must pay."

Desperate to get his girlfriend outside for some air, George simply turned around and waved away Luc with a gesture to indicate "one minute" by holding up a finger. However, in the fading light and with the large numbers of people around, Luc erroneously thought that George had made a very different signal with his solitary finger. The waiter was furious, and he called loudly across the restaurant for assistance from a colleague to apprehend the runaway diners.

By this time, all of the diners inside La Vieux Lion had been drawn to the situation that was occurring before them. The background sounds of idle chatter and cutlery and plates chinking that usually dominated the ambience of the restaurant quickly evaporated, and just as the room fell into a semi-hush, George lost his temper.

"Look, I'm coming back, you French idiot," he boomed across the restaurant in Luc's direction, a comment which was met by many gasps. Complete silence followed, with all eyes trained either on him and Sarah or at Luc and the other staff, waiting to see or hear a response. You could have heard a pin drop.

George glanced around the room and took stock of the embarrassing situation he had found himself in, noticing that most of the eyes in the room were on him. In a rush of adrenalin, as if to justify his description of Luc as a French idiot, he spoke the ill-fated words, "As you have just poisoned my friend, I need to take her outside for some air."

The sound of muttering amongst the other diners started up again. Everyone had heard the word *poisoned*, and the diners at each table were no doubt individually discussing it. The English couple headed for the door again and made their way through to the outside, where the people were unaware of the fracas inside. Luc and his companion, Florian, caught up with them before they could get beyond the closely grouped tables and out into the open square where the air might be easier to breathe.

"Sir, I must insist you come back inside at once and pay for your meal, or I will call the police," said Luc, tugging hard at George's free arm, not yet noticing that the lady on his other arm was genuinely ill.

George was furious at being manhandled in this fashion. "Big mistake, pal," he said with an angry look on his face. "How dare you touch me! Now let go of my arm."

All of the diners seated outside in the square were also now drawn to the altercation between the Englishman and the French waiter, and not just those at Le Vieux Lion. People sitting outside at other restaurants and many passers-by also stopped to focus on the argument dominating the square.

Luc did not let go, however, and moved around behind the couple towards Sarah, forcing George to yank his own arm down sharply to loosen the grip that was on him. Suddenly Sarah fainted, crashing onto a table she was standing next to and sending a plate of food and a glass of beer crashing to the floor.

The poor family at the disturbed table jumped to their feet, and the man there who had just lost his drink attended to Sarah. Luc finally let go of George's arm and placed his hand over his mouth in a kind of what-have-I-done gesture. George, seeing that the man at the table was helping his girlfriend, was able to focus his anger on Luc and his friend Florian.

"You have done it now, matey," said George with disdain and anger because of the physical state Sarah was in. "She's just eaten something dodgy in your restaurant. I was only taking her out for some air. I'm going to shut you down for this."

Luc looked genuinely shocked, but he couldn't hold George's gaze any longer, which infuriated the Englishman further. He had been distracted when he looked at Sarah, noticing she had come round but was sitting on the floor with blood pouring down her forehead.

"Please, someone call an ambulance!" the man at the table who had attended to her shouted in the general direction of George, Luc, and Florian.

Florian immediately ran back inside, and George at last went over to see his girlfriend, who had a large cut above her left eye and was losing colour. He knelt down to her side to be at her eye level.

"Don't worry, my sweet," he said calmly and quietly. "We'll get us some nice compensation for this."

Sarah was shocked at the apparent lack of sympathy from her man, and then she fainted for a second time. George stood up, thoughtlessly leaving Sarah lying on the floor, and he again turned his attention to Luc. The rest of the people in the square were still listening and watching every move.

"And you better tell your friend that the medics need to know that she is suffering from food poisoning. That is why we were getting some air, and that is why she fell to the floor so easily after you pushed her," he said, deliberately loudly, so that Luc and all the other people around could be in no doubt they hadn't misheard the comment.

As Luc turned to head back inside, an older, overweight man appeared in the doorway, wearing a tatty old apron. He was clearly one of the chefs. Upon seeing a sizeable group surrounding the young blonde lady with blood streaming out of her head, he put his hands on his head with an expression of anguish.

"*Monsieur Le Sac. C'est un catastrophe,*" said Luc as he passed the chef on the way to catch Florian.

The plump man, Jaques Le Sac, had a completely bald scalp but thick, dark hair all the way around the sides and back like a monk. He was the owner of the restaurant. He made his way over to Sarah but was intercepted by an incensed George, who had noticed the man was wearing a chef's uniform and by his age had judged him to be senior management.

"I suggest you get cleaning your kitchen, mate," said a still-angry George. "Your place is not fit to serve. I'm taking this one all the way."

Jaques shook his head, and there was a bewildered look on his face. Clearly he hadn't understood the English words, but George's body language could not be misinterpreted. A man then spoke to him in French from a nearby table, translating the words and cementing his worst fears.

"Non, non, non," Jaques proclaimed loudly. "C'est pas possible." He then gestured apologetically to George and held his hands together in a praying motion. George simply ignored him and knelt back down to Sarah's side, finally showing a degree of concern for the woman.

Within just a few minutes, the silence had ended. Groups were muttering to themselves about what they had seen and heard. The phrases "food poisoning", "the waiter assaulted the lady", "not coming here again", "I don't feel great, either", and similar exaggerated comments could easily be heard in the immediate vicinity.

A policeman also rushed over upon hearing the disturbance; he checked on Sarah's condition before asking various groups for an explanation of what had happened. The ambulance was struggling to make it to the scene through the crowded, narrow streets of the old town. By the time it did arrive, the injured lady had lost a lot of blood, but she was at least sitting up now. The paramedics knelt down and attended to her.

"No, forget my head," she said with a grimace. "It's my stomach. I feel as if my stomach is about to explode. I've eaten something bad."

Sarah was quickly loaded into the ambulance by the medical men, but not until they had placed a bandage around her head and had done a few quick tests on her. In the middle of the square, in full view and with everyone in earshot, one of the paramedics naively relayed the sentence that would rock the world of the concerned-looking Jaques Le Sac.

"*Monsieur. Peut-être qu'elle a été empoisonné à votre restaurant.*" Your restaurant may have poisoned her.

George, understanding the French well, felt vindicated and knew that the crowd staring at him would see him as the innocent party in these unsavoury events. He then spoke loudly and callously across the square, like a politician addressing a crowd at a small rally.

"The magnificent Vieux Lion. They give you food poisoning, then harass you, and finally assault you. *Au revoir.*" He then climbed into the ambulance, the door was closed behind him, and the vehicle slowly made its way out of the hustle and bustle of the old town.

Gradually things got back to normal in the area around the restaurant. People returned to their meals and drinks; the gathering of people more or less dispersed. But one man – Jaques Le Sac – sat alone at a table in his own now-deserted restaurant, crying. He had heard what people had been saying in French, and he could read the body language of the British all too well. Surely there wasn't a hygiene problem in his kitchen? And surely his longest-serving waiter, the dependable Luc Detroux, had not assaulted that wounded lady and her companion?

*   *   *

Despite its size, Rocheville, like most small French towns, still had the benefit of a well-equipped hospital with an emergency department. George was waiting anxiously in the corridor for an update on Sarah. He had been informed that she wasn't in any real danger, despite her heavy bleeding. They were concentrating solely on the stomach pains now.

The hospital building was old but charming. It had been built in the late nineteenth century and was in serious need of external renovation, but it was nonetheless clean and tidy inside. The ambulance had earlier bought Sarah and George to the side of the building, where there was a platform with a purpose-built concrete dock so that patients could be offloaded from the back of the vehicles quickly, without the need for the lowering of steps or carrying people. From there Sarah had been rushed into an older part of the hospital, where doctors had set to work on finding out what was wrong with her and what treatment they could administer.

Two hours had passed since George had last seen his younger girlfriend when a spectacled male doctor came out and spoke to him. The man was wearing an open long, white lab coat with a grey shirt underneath and black trousers. He looked more like a cricket umpire than a medical man.

"Hello, I'm Dr Williams," he said in perfect English with a Welsh accent. "I'm afraid the lady does indeed have food poisoning. Nothing too serious, don't worry, but we'll have to keep her in for a couple of days until the virus has passed through."

George nodded his head in understanding and looked relieved at the news. "And her head?" he enquired.

"Oh, that will be OK," replied Dr Williams. "She hit her head hard on the table, but apart from a bad headache, she'll be OK there too."

"Oh, good," said George. "Can I go and see her?"

"Of course," replied the doctor. "You know where she is, don't you?"

Just as George was about to walk away, Dr Williams put his arm on George's shoulder and stopped him.

"Sorry, sir," he said, "but I have to ask. What did your friend eat for dinner?"

"She had a fish soup followed by a prawn salad," replied George.

There was a pause, and Dr Williams nodded.

"I needed to check, sir, but yes, we believe it is from fish that she has picked up her bug," he said. "Quite a nasty one, I'm afraid. I'll have to go and give a short update to the administrators. I think we need to get that restaurant temporarily closed."

*   *   *

The following morning George wandered into le centre ville alone from his rented villa on the outskirts of town. He didn't feel like driving. His head was pounding, the after-effects of helping himself to three bottles of wine alone the previous evening. His girlfriend was still in the local hospital and in a lot of pain. The scene was quite different today as he stood in front of the town hall and looked at the deserted old town square and La Vieux Lion. A few children ran across the cobbles, their parents slowly heading for one of the side streets, beckoning their kids to follow them.

As he stood there looking at the restaurant, he noticed that many people walking past were looking and pointing at it. Had word got around already that last night an "incident" had taken place? He looked harder, taking a few paces towards the restaurant, and could see that there was a sign up in the window, and so he wandered over.

"Fermé. Closed. Gesloten" the sign read, handwritten in French, English, and Dutch in black marker pen on a sheet of white paper. Below it was a further notice all in French. This one was typed and official looking, and on the headed paper at the top it said "La Ville du Rocheville." George read the notice, his French proving very useful, and he learnt that the restaurant had been forced to shut down until further notice.

George smiled as he finished reading the notice. He was still angry from last night. His trophy girlfriend, a stunning lady twenty years his junior, had been hospitalised as a result of their incompetence. "And they were rude to me," he thought to himself as he walked off.

He had only taken a few steps when a middle-aged man in shorts came running up behind him.

"Sir! Stop!" said the man, panting a little. "I recognised you from last night. You were the one whose wife was taken away in an ambulance, right?"

The man was of medium height, and he had a neatly trimmed beard with a short crop of brown hair. His face was tanned rather than red, but straight away George could tell he was British, despite not being able to recognise his accent due to the heavy breathing.

"That is right," replied George. "And how can I help you?"

"Well," said the man. "My name is Steve Abbott, and I produce a newsletter for the British ex-pat community here in Rocheville and the surrounding villages. I was wondering if you could tell us what is happening at La Vieux Lion."

"Happening?" asked George.

"Well," said Steve. "We understand that a complaint has been filed against the Lion and they were forced to close their kitchen last night. We can only assume that it was to do with your incident."

"Mmm," pondered George. "Well, I can tell you this, Mr Abbott. It was confirmed last night by the hospital that Sarah – my girlfriend, not wife – had picked up food poisoning from this restaurant and that it would probably have to shut down temporarily."

"And you filed a complaint?" asked Steve. "And please call me Steve."

"Well no, Steve, I did not," responded George in a determined tone. "Someone else must have done it, but I quite readily will make another one, if required, to anyone who will listen. My girlfriend is in a bad way as a result of this place, and also, as you may have seen, she fell when the staff here were harassing us, and she hit her head hard."

"And the police were here too," stated Steve. "Maybe they are involved?"

"Could be," said George. "I gave a long statement to the police last night at the hospital, detailing what happened. I didn't make an official complaint, but I did make it very clear to them that I wanted the place investigated by the health authorities. As I told you, Steve, the hospital told me that my girlfriend's ill health was a result of eating something at La Vieux Lion."

"And did it seem to you they were taking you seriously?" asked Steve.

"Well, after the fuss I made in the square last night, and with the analysis from the hospital, I think they had to, don't you?" replied George. "And the fact that it is indeed now shut probably tells its own story."

Steve nodded in agreement and was about to ask another question, but an increasingly impatient George cut him off. "Anyway, I have a girlfriend to go and see, so can I help you with anything else?" he asked.

"No," said Steve. "But just so you know, I'd like this incident to go into my newsletter because this place is a favourite among the Brits who live here. They will be aware the place is closed, and they will need to know why. Can I use your story?"

"Be my guest, Steve," said George. "My name is George. George Havelock."

*   *   *

Word had soon spread around the town of Rocheville about the incident and the temporary closure of La Vieux Lion. Cuisine is a very big business in France, and the reputation of any chef and restaurant is of huge significance. Rumours and hearsay about anything untoward in the food industry would travel very quickly around a community like this.

Two days later, George Havelock arrived back at the hospital for what he hoped would be the final time, to collect his girlfriend and then catch the flight back home to England. It was not the ending to a holiday they had hoped for. Sarah still felt very weak as she was helped into the passenger side of the large SUV-style hire car the couple had rented, but at least she was well enough to travel.

Dr Williams appeared at the doorway of a side entrance to the old building and ushered George back in to speak with him.

"Sir, we have just had the preliminary results of some tests we have been running on Sarah," he said. "We will send the full details when we get them to the forwarding address in the UK you have given us. This may come as a shock, but there is a chance that the virus had been in Sarah's system for some time. It's just such a shame it came to the surface whilst you were on your summer holiday, sir. The full details will show us for certain, and we'll inform your GP back home, too."

George smiled and shook the hand of the Welsh doctor warmly. "Many thanks, Doctor. You have been most kind and helpful," he said as he walked away to return to the car.

"What did he want?" asked Sarah as George sat down beside her and started the engine.

"Nothing really, dear," responded George, smiling. "He just told me to ensure you take things easy for a while."

The following day, the local French newspaper ran a front-page story that told how Le Sac and his restaurant were under investigation for suspected poor kitchen hygiene. They printed full details of the food poisoning and a less-than-complimentary account of how Luc and Florian had behaved in their altercation with that "poor English couple". Steve Abbott's English language newsletter was published later that week and also led with an article warning people to be very careful if they wished to attend La Vieux Lion upon reopening. Word had indeed got around.

Jaques Le Sac, his restaurant, and his family's good name were now ruined.

20

Sergeant Johnson had been so engrossed in reading the police file about the incidents in July 2003 which had led to the closure of the restaurant owned by Philippe's father that he didn't even notice that a ham and cheese baguette had been placed on the table in front of him. He looked at his watch. It was just before two o'clock local time. He decided he would eat the roll and then head out of the gendarmerie and wander around the corner to the former site of the restaurant, to visualise for himself the events he had just read about. Then he would call Inspector Hartnell, who should be in Devon by now.

"Did you find anything, Sergeant?" asked Lieutenant Floregge, walking back into his office as Johnson was taking his second bite. "I see you forgot to 'ave lunch. This would never 'appen in France! We look forward to lunch from the moment we 'ave finished breakfast and count down the minutes!"

Johnson giggled slightly childishly but soon regained composure upon finishing his mouthful. It was comforting that Floregge had returned from his appointment, probably a grand lunch somewhere, in a very good mood.

"Maybe I have, Lieutenant," he replied. "I read a statement from the doctor at the hospital who claims he told the man, George, that the sudden illness the lady experienced had nothing to do with the restaurant. Did anything come of that?"

"Indeed, Sergeant," replied Floregge. "It did. It was concluded by the hospital that there was a high chance that the food bug would have been already in the lady's body from much earlier. They believe that the symptoms the lady had could never 'ave materialised that quickly from anything she ate that evening."

"But did they tell the public?" asked Johnson. "Did they tell Monsieur Le Sac?"

"They tried, mon ami," said Floregge. "But it was too late. And also the hospital could not be 100 per cent sure. But the damage had already been done to old Jaques. His reputation was ruined. He tried to reopen the place under a different name, but no one wanted to go there. The other restaurateurs in the town turned on him rather than 'elping 'im. Always warning people of the dangers of Le Sac."

"What a shame," said Johnson. "Could the papers not help? The same ones who printed the story in the days after the incident? Could they not now reveal that there had been a terrible mistake?

"Non," said Floregge shaking his head. "The hospital couldn't be sure, and 99 per cent wasn't good enough. No newspaper would want to be associated with trying to help a restaurant with a bad reputation. It would be too risky here in France, Sergeant."

"OK, I understand," replied Johnson. "And what about the lady? Did she make a full recovery?"

"What another good question, Sergeant Johnson," said Floregge. "The answer was yes, she did. And it was then felt that if the Englishman came and made a public statement to clear the name and reputation of Le Sac, it would really 'elp."

"And so?" asked Johnson.

"So the hospital had his address. They tried to pass on their findings to him. They tried a few times, actually, but never got a response. It seemed he did not want to 'elp. The hospital did finally get a response from England which read, *"Merci. Fin de cas. Fermé. Au revoir.* Which means—"

"Thank you. Case closed. Goodbye," the men said in unison.

"Oui, monsieur, very good," said Floregge. "So it seemed Monsieur Havelock did not want to 'elp poor Le Sac. Perhaps he was still angry about how he was treated that night in the restaurant? Or perhaps it was just too much bother for 'im?"

"This is a very interesting story," said Johnson. "And so after that, Philippe, his son, became a bit of a problem for your team here?"

"Only a little," replied Floregge. "He was there that night at La Vieux Lion. He was working as a chef with his father in the kitchen. He blamed himself initially, but there was nothing he could have done. He was 23 at the time, and suddenly he had no job, no family business to inherit, and two parents and a younger sister to support. So he became a *petit* thief. Nothing more."

"And this was thirteen years ago," added Johnson. "So probably no link to what happened in England early yesterday morning. As you say, he's met many British people over the course of his life, so his finally coming over this week is almost certainly not linked to these events. But I'd like to read more about him in your other files. Can I scan these other files across to my office and get them translated into English? I can then work on them from there. I'd love to stay, but I have a flight to catch."

"Maybe," said Floregge suspiciously. "But again, I must remind you of my view that Philippe is not responsible, even if he was there in your town. So what are you exactly 'oping to find?"

"Well, don't worry, Lieutenant," replied Johnson. "I no longer believe that Philippe is really who we are after. I feel sorry for him, and I am moved by the file I've just read. But something bought him to England and placed him at the scene of a crime yesterday morning, and I need to know what that was. I actually believe he is in a great deal of danger. You may have read in the report that a vicious gang of men came looking for him."

"Well, I read that a gang came looking for someone," responded the Frenchman abruptly.

"Exactly," said Johnson. "I think I can help him, but I need to figure out how on earth he became mixed up in all of this. And that is why I need these files."

"OK, Sergeant," said Floregge. "You can scan the files with my blessing. I believe you are indeed trying to help him. I'm sure that the British police do have better things to do than fly around Europe tracking a small-time *petit* burglar. So if you think he's got mixed up in something bigger, then you have my 'elp. Philippe is a good man, as I've told you several times now." The two men smiled at each other.

Over the course of the next twenty minutes, Floregge instructed one of his junior officers to scan all of the pages from the files of misdemeanours committed by Philippe Le Sac over to Sergeant Hughes, who had been called into action to help. Johnson, in the meantime, went for a walk, as planned, to the Old Town Square and made a phone call to Inspector Hartnell, who had indeed just reached Devon and was about twenty minutes from his final destination.

Johnson told his inspector that he had "charmed" the French police into giving him all of the files on "Phil the bag", and he ran him through the story of how Phil's family had lost everything, causing the boy's descent into petty crime. Hartnell updated Johnson on a few things, most notably the fact that Chief Inspector Riley had been tracked down; he was now living on a secluded farm in the Peak District of northern England in his retirement.

"How did you find that out?" asked Johnson.

"My wife did a little bit of digging," responded Hartnell. "I couldn't trust any of the boys at the station or down at HQ, in case Gault was on their backs, spying on us. So I asked her! It's amazing what you can find out with just a few clicks on the Internet, Davey boy!"

Johnson hung up the phone and stared at the deserted building that La Vieux Lion had once proudly occupied. The site hadn't been reoccupied in the years that had passed since its closure. No new business wanted the stigma of being located in the spot where a failed and disgraced restaurant had once traded. The windows were boarded up, and various plants had encroached on the fabric of the building itself, causing it to crack and crumble. The rest of the square was still pretty and beloved, but this small section across from the town hall was derelict. A small tear ran down the cheek of the usually steely Sergeant Johnson.

"Pull yourself together, David," he said to himself as he turned his gaze away from the building and returned to the police station to say goodbye to Lieutenant Floregge.

"I will contact you if I see Philippe," said the lieutenant warmly. "Good luck."

"*Merci beaucoup pour votre … err … help!*" said Johnson, trying out his French again and bringing smiles to the officers in the small police station's entrance area.

"*Avec plaisir, mon ami,*" replied a smiling Lieutenant Floregge.

Johnson returned to his hire car and headed to the airport to catch his flight home.

"Incredibly, I might be home earlier than I sometimes am when I work the day shift back home!" he thought to himself as he drove through the pleasant vineyard-lined roads back to Montpellier Airport, the sun just starting to set on the beautiful April day.

21

By the time Inspector Hartnell pulled into the car park of a small hotel in the seaside town of Listingbourne, in the south-west English county of Devon, it was approaching two o'clock in the afternoon in Great Britain. He had been fully briefed on the details of the original case over the phone on the four-hour drive from Arleswood, via a call with a local Devonshire policeman.

"This is it," he thought, looking out of the car windscreen. "The Rose and Crown hotel. Where William Hastings was staying but one day never returned."

Hartnell looked around him at the beauty of the place he found himself in. "What a very strange place for a rotten guy like Hastings to end up in," he thought, and indeed it was. He said to himself, "I suspect the only crimes that happen around here are when someone does thirty-two miles per hour in a thirty zone."

Listingbourne was an old fishing port, with a beautiful stone harbour along the seafront. It seemed to be quite isolated at the foot of some fairly impressive cliffs. On one side the town was cut off by the sea and on the other side by these sharply rising hills.

There was a beautiful array of old stone buildings aligned along the harbour edge, overlooking the numerous boats of different shapes and sizes bobbing around in the water. The town also had a lovely old square-towered Norman church located on slightly higher ground as if governing over the buildings below it. However, the crowning glory of Listingbourne's beauty had to be the vast array of wonderfully coloured cottages that flanked the hillsides overlooking the town.

"What a wonderful place to live," thought Hartnell to himself as he got out of his grey saloon car and looked around. "Even on a mediocre day like today, it is wonderful."

The Rose and Crown hotel was just one street back from the road that ran along the side of the harbour. Hartnell suspected that some of the rooms around the hotel's front might boast "sea views", although even the most optimistic marketeer would be really stretching it to call them so. The hotel was a simple structure in two connected parts, built in the early 1900s out of the local grey stone. It was just two stories tall, with some of the sloping roof covered in grey tiles. The slightly older front part of the establishment doubled as a pub. It had a thatched roof and was accessed from the main door straight off the road. The hotel part of the building was slightly newer, and the guests' entrance was around the back off the car park. It was through this door he headed, hoping that his wife had managed to successfully make him the reservation.

The inside of the building was quaint and full of character. Just along the corridor from the outside door was a little alcove which operated as the hotel's reception. Hartnell could see down this corridor and across a small beamed room the main bar of the Rose and Crown. There were a few people in there enjoying a drink in the midafternoon. To his left was another small corridor, flanked by a sign saying "All rooms this way". There was an open area next to the bar, effectively separated by a feature fireplace, which looked as if it was the restaurant and breakfast area. This section was deserted at this time. Hartnell pressed the little call bell on the desk of the reception area, and within a few seconds a youngish-looking girl came around the corner with a huge smile on her face.

"Good afternoon, sir," she said with a heavy Eastern European accent. "Can I help you?"

Hartnell took a moment to respond. He was immediately struck by the girl's age and features. She was fairly short, perhaps just over five feet tall, with long, dark hair, very protruding cheekbones, and a beautifully cheery smile. She was wearing blue jeans and a black turtleneck jumper with long sleeves. She could not have been any more than 20 years old.

"Hungarian?" Hartnell asked. There was a short silence. "Are you Hungarian?" he asked again.

"Oh, I see!" answered the smiling girl. "No, I'm from Serbia. I've not been here that long, and my English isn't great. I had turned my head so my ear to you to hear the response to my question and misunderstood you. I'm sorry for the delay in answering you, sir."

"Please, you must not apologise," said Hartnell in a kind voice. "I was very rude. I answered a question with a question. We are taught not to do this, and I did it. I'm the one who should be sorry. And besides, your English is perfect!"

The girl smiled again; she was clearly embarrassed by the compliment. Hartnell could see she had gone red in the face, so he tried to save the situation.

"You should have a reservation for me, my dear. The name is Hartnell."

The girl scurried around to the book on the desk surface and ran her finger down the page. "Ah, Inspector Hartnell!" she said with a wink. "So, you are in the army?"

Hartnell chuckled. "Err, no – I'm actually a policeman! My wife made the reservation for me. She was obviously being a little bit official. My name is Roger Hartnell."

"Well, welcome to the Rose and Crown, Roger Hartnell, sir," responded the girl. "My name is Ana Flavic. I've just finished my first year at the University of Exeter and am here working at the hotel for the summer."

"Good for you," said Hartnell in an equally cheery fashion. "It's nice to see someone so friendly. I'm normally surrounded by people who are upset because we have just arrested them, or they are upset because they have just had a crime committed against them. I'd forgotten what it is like to see a happy person during daylight hours!"

"Let's see if I'm still so friendly by the end of the summer," replied Ana. "I might hate it by then and be praying for Serbia!"

They both laughed as she handed Hartnell his room key and pointed him along the corridor to a set of stairs. The interior of the hotel was clean and light, with a fresh smell of disinfectant. The place did seem quiet to Hartnell, but presumably the summer months were when a place like this would really be full. In spring even a beautiful place like Listingbourne would struggle to attract the masses.

Once in his room, Hartnell placed his small suitcase onto the bed and headed over to the window to see what kind of view he had. He pulled aside the white net curtains to reveal the car park. "Well, no one has pinched the car yet," he thought to himself as he looked down at his vehicle. Beyond the grey tarmac of the car park area, however, the hills and cliffs overlooking Listingbourne rose up before him. The tops of the hills were covered in trees, and the steep slope down to the town was a mixture of exposed chalk, shrubs and, of course, the coloured cottages. "Magnificent," he thought.

The room itself was exactly what it needed to be. There was a double bed with a cabinet on either side, a built-in wardrobe with a sliding glass door doubling as a large full-length mirror, a small desk area with a phone, a kettle, some tea and coffee, and a chair to sit on. Just past the desk was the door through into the bathroom. The bedroom walls were painted in a fairly standard magnolia colour, and this continuous shade was only broken by a large painting hanging on the wall of what Hartnell assumed to be the Devon wilderness of Dartmoor.

"This will do, Roger," he said out loud. He took out a spare shirt from his case and hung it up in the wardrobe, followed by placing his toiletries in the bathroom. He then made a quick phone call to his wife to tell her of his safe arrival and that she hadn't messed up the booking. Then he got to work.

The inspector was already in possession of all of the case notes from the Hastings drowning incident of September 2004, having stopped off at the headquarters of the Western Counties Police Force some thirty minutes north of Listingbourne and collected them. He wasn't even sure what he was looking for and had several times during the drive down questioned his decision to come. However, he had to solve both a crime and a riddle, and he felt that this hotel was somehow a key link in the story. He remembered what he did know for certain: the stolen folder had only ever been handled by two men apart from its owner. One of those men had spent his last-ever night's sleep in this very hotel, and the other had definitely been in this town the day after. "There must be a connection," he again spoke out loud to himself.

After about twenty minutes of staring out of the window at the beautiful cliffs overlooking the town instead of concentrating on the case, Hartnell decided that he would probably be more comfortable in the bar downstairs. He had already been fully briefed on the main parts of the case, so it wasn't as if he had to spread anything out all over his room and piece things together. He wasn't starting from scratch. He picked up some of the papers he had and headed downstairs, picking up his phone as he left his room and letting the room door swing shut behind him as he headed down the corridor.

The bar now only had one man in it when Hartnell arrived there. Instead of walking up to the counter to order a drink, he took himself over to a table away from the other man and left his notes there before heading back over to find someone to serve him.

"Hello, Roger!" came a familiar cheery greeting. The other man in the bar let out a short laugh.

"So, you are the barmaid as well, Ana!" said Hartnell. "Multitasking – I like it! I'd like an orange juice for now, please. I've got some work to do, so no beer for me yet."

"OK. Go and sit back over there," said Ana, motioning to the table Hartnell had just deposited his papers at. "And I'll bring it over to you."

Hartnell said thanks and did as he was told, sitting down at the table with his back to the wall and looking out across the bar area. He picked up the first few pages of the notes he had with him. They were the statements from the people who had been at the hotel that day. He summarised the chronological order of events from that day twelve years ago.

Hastings left the Rose and Crown. He went down to the seafront. He boarded a tourist fishing boat. He fell in and was seen splashing around in the water, and heard calling for help. The boat crew tried to find him and hopefully rescue him. The body was found washed up on the beach eight miles from there the following morning, identified as William Hastings by Chief Inspector Riley.

He was just about to start reading the first statement when he felt a presence in front of him. He lifted his gaze, and there was Ana, sitting at his table and holding out his orange juice with a mischievous smile on her face.

"Here you are, Roger," she said, handing the drink over.

"Thank you," came the reply from the policeman. He smiled at her and didn't say anything else, expecting her to get back up again and walk away, but she just sat there smiling back at him.

"I really need to get on with this work, Ana," he continued, with a dismissive voice, and it had the desired effect. The smile instantly disappeared from Ana's face, the look in her eyes sank, and she stood up to walk away. Hartnell was suddenly full of guilt.

"I'm sorry, Ana," he said. "I didn't mean it to sound like that. That sounded terrible. I really am sorry."

Ana stopped and turned round to Hartnell. The smile was back. "It is OK, Roger. I should know when to not disturb important policemen like you."

"Not just me, but anyone," Hartnell thought to himself as he contemplated what to say next. Should he just let her walk away? No, he thought. He would still feel a little guilty. He felt he needed to say a few more lines to make sure that that there were no hard feelings.

"I bet you have lots of work to do anyway, Ana?" he asked her.

"Actually, no," came the unexpected response. "There are only two people in the bar, and usually the people staying in the hotel don't turn up until six or seven at night. I'm bored, Roger." The mischievous look was still on her face.

"Oh my God!" Hartnell thought to himself. "Is she coming onto me?"

"Is the manager not around?" Hartnell asked, almost dreading the response. "Can he not give you some work to do?"

"I suppose so," replied a disappointed-looking Ana. "I'll go and ask." Again her face had dropped, and with drooped shoulders she walked off. Again Hartnell found himself feeling guilty, but it didn't bother him this time as he knew he had to focus. There were very few women in Hartnell's life who called him Roger, and it was making him recall the security of a more innocent age. Although the girl was very attractive, he wasn't having feelings for her, as she was under half his age. He could actually sense that he was becoming quite fond of her, however. He then had a brainwave.

"Oh Ana, dear," he called out before she reached the other side of the bar. "I do have some things you could do for me!"

Ana rushed back over with a hugely enthusiastic expression on her face again. Hartnell wondered what could be going through her mind, and so he spoke again quickly. "I assume you are familiar with the Internet?" he asked her.

"Of course I am," said Ana. "Unlike you, Roger, I grew up with it!" she added cheekily.

"Then, as you are so bored," added Hartnell. "I have some investigation work for you to do for me."

"Oh yes, please," said Ana. "I would love to do something like that for you. I'd love to be a policeman-woman."

"Genius," thought Hartnell to himself. "I can get her digging through newspaper archives from this area and in the Midlands for everything she can find out. She can do keyword searches of September 13 and 14, 2004, Inspector Ian Riley, William Hastings, and so on. She might uncover something that connects a few of the dots here."

Hartnell then spent a few minutes explaining to Ana as much of the Hastings story as he felt was necessary and exactly what he needed her to do. She could work on her laptop from the bar and break each time she needed to serve someone a drink.

"Please, can you also find out for me which room William Hastings stayed in?" he requested as he put a jacket on. "I'd need to get in there."

"And where are you going now?" Ana asked disappointedly, her infectious smile fading and her large brown eyes dilating as he headed for the front door.

"I'm going for a walk around the harbour, my dear," he replied. "I've got all the statements from the fishing boat company and the other passengers that were on that boat. I'm going to have a good look around."

22

It was a fairly cloudy and breezy afternoon down on the South Devon coast. Every ten minutes or so the sun managed to break through the clouds but just for a few moments each time, it seemed. However, at least it wasn't raining. Hartnell made his way along the road from the hotel's pub exit, and after just a couple of minutes' walk he found himself at the water's edge. He immediately made his way over to a bench by the stone wall of the small harbour, looking outwards at the water rather than back at the town, and he sat down. There were plenty of craft inside the small enclosed haven. Most of them were commercial fishing boats, already back from their daily outing to sea, and some were small private yachts. This wasn't exactly Monaco, thought Hartnell, but the scene was tranquil and idyllic.

He took out the old notes containing the various statements from the boat's crew and its passengers the day Hastings drowned. The vessel Hastings had been on was a fishing boat that tourists could pay to go out to sea on. Usually they would be taken a few miles offshore, given a rod, cast their lines, and fish for mackerel for about an hour. However, that day back in September 2004, the fishing boat the *Artful Dodger* hadn't gotten that far. Hartnell began to read the account given by the deck steward:

I remember that the afternoon was sunny but breezy. This trip was our last scheduled outing of the day, as there was approximately forty-five minutes' daylight left when we left the quayside at Listingbourne. We in the crew knew that we would be returning in near darkness, and I'm sure many of the passengers knew this, but nevertheless there were more than enough people wanting to go out to make the trip viable. There were eleven paying guests on the boat plus us four crew members: myself, the captain, his trainee co-pilot, and another deck hand. The man who fell overboard was sitting alone until the incident. He had been joking with another couple, however, for much of the journey. He wasn't acting strange in any way, but there were a few things that struck me as being odd, though. Firstly he was alone. We rarely get lone passengers anyway, but he must have been about 20 years old, and he didn't look like the kind of person who would be on holiday alone in Listingbourne. To be honest, he looked quite unruly, and he was also quite a large man. He made me feel a little uneasy. And another thing I thought was odd was that he didn't have anything with him, either. No coat, no bag, nothing. Pretty much everyone brings a small rucksack or something with them. Perhaps to put a bottle of water in it or a sandwich, or maybe a jumper in case it turned cold. At the very least, somewhere to keep their wallets and phones. But not that man. He came aboard completely empty-handed, with just the clothes he was wearing, which was a pair of medium-length versatile swimming shorts and a thin, long sleeved, dark-blue top.

At approximately 18.30, about fifteen minutes after we left the harbour, several of the passengers started making a lot of noise, drawing everyone on board's attention, shouting, "He's fallen in!" and "Man overboard!" I rushed over to where they were seated and could see the man in the water, struggling and shouting for help. I remember vividly him shouting back at the boat, "Help me – I'm drowning! Help!" It was only then I noticed his accent was a northern one, Leeds or Manchester, maybe. Given the speed the boat was travelling, we were already quite some considerable distance from the man. I would estimate fifty meters at least. I immediately threw a lifebuoy into the water, to at the very least mark the spot from where I saw him. I ran to the bridge and informed the captain, who had already began to turn the vessel, having heard the commotion. By the time we had done this, I would estimate we were well over 150 meters from the point where the man fell. The water was quite choppy for a September, given the strong breeze. I couldn't see the man. None of us could. Our captain called the coastguard immediately, and we continued to circle the approximate spot where the man fell. Looking back at Listingbourne, I could tell we were about two miles offshore, in choppy waters, and given what few clothes he was wearing and gauging on how much he was struggling when I saw him, I feared that we were facing the worst-case scenario. We did not find him, and neither did the coastguard.

"So there was clearly nothing about a fight or anything remotely resembling an altercation," mused Hartnell. "Hastings was found with a deep stab wound in his back, yet this account makes no reference to such an event. He could already have been on board with the wound, but surely that would have been visible, or at the least the blood pouring out of the wound, so that is unlikely. I don't think any of the accounts from the passengers mention either a struggle or the fact that the man was injured. A wound like the one documented would have been debilitating and impossible to conceal. I'll read the accounts again, but I don't think I'm going to find anything on this," he decided.

We were sat next to the man on the boat. He and my husband chatted and joked about the weather. I remember he had a northern accent and that he had a kind smile, but he did look a bit rough. Dare I say it, but he looked like the kind of person that if you met them on the street you would give them a wide berth. I wasn't really paying much attention to them until I heard him fall in. I know he had been sat on the edge of the boat, but he wasn't the only one; in fact, most of us had been. He made a "whoa" noise, presumably as he was falling backwards. I looked around in time to see the splash as he hit the water. My husband and I stood up and shouted for a member of the crew, as did many of the others, and the man rushed over and threw a red ring into the water. Even though we had already travelled some distance since he fell, I could see the man in the water calling for help. It was horrible. We started to turn around, and I hoped to see him there calling out still, but we never saw him.

"So, according to the lady sitting next to him, he just fell in," thought Hartnell. "No tussle, no disagreement, no nothing. Something doesn't add up here."

The puzzled inspector then spent a little time reading a few of the other accounts; they all portrayed a very similar story. No incident, nothing violent. He just fell in.

Hartnell continued to sift through his thoughts. "Is there any way in which the stab wound was already there before he fell? Could it have been a slightly older cut, already sufficiently healed to allow him mobility? Hopefully Ana will have found something that might explain that. Or did he somehow make it back to shore alive and was then attacked, knifed, taken back out to sea, and thrown into the water again? Now, that would simply be too far-fetched, Roger – concentrate!"

A frustrated Hartnell berated himself as he put the statements back inside a see-through plastic sleeve and selected a new section of papers. These were actually some photographs taken by the police of the body they'd found on the beach the following morning. The first one wasn't particularly gruesome. It showed Hastings' face, the long-sleeved blue top, and a pair of shorts. Judging by the background, this was still dawn, so he must have been found early. The light was low, but the quality of the camera used had been good enough to capture the time of day. There were long shadows created by the cliffs above the shoreline, and the beach was fully shaded, meaning there wasn't any light falling directly onto the body.

Picture two, however, was not a pleasant sight. The first officials on the scene had rolled the body onto its side. Just below the left shoulder blade was a clear incision, which had pierced through the blue top and had spewed blood all across the area. There was sand already in the wound, and it had combined with the saltwater; the skin had turned a frightening shade of deep purple.

"Well, that puts to bed the debate about whether the stabbing took place before the boat trip," thought Hartnell upon seeing the image and studying the extent of the pierced clothing, the skin damage, and the blood. He thought that it must have happened afterwards. And yet the pathologist had said the cause of death was drowning but that it was inconclusive as to which event had come first, the drowning or the knife wound. Apart from being able to tell the wound was at least three hours old, he hadn't really been able to tell at what time in the previous twenty-four hours the skin had been punctured. Perhaps the seawater made the wound look worse than it was? Or maybe the salt somehow preserved the skin temporarily, thus making it hard even for an expert to be really accurate?

He paused momentarily in his thoughts. "Surely not?" he said out loud before looking up at the sky for inspiration.

"Don't be silly, Roger. No way. There is no way that someone would put a knife into the back of dead man they found lying on a beach. Would they? And if so, why would they?"

He looked at a few more of the photographs of Hastings' dead body lying on the deserted Devon beach. He found confirmation of the time the police had arrived on the beach after a dog-walker alerted them that he had found a corpse. It was noted as 7.19 a.m.

Just then, after a parting of the clouds, Listingbourne Harbour became bathed in April sunshine, and Inspector Hartnell's first thought was that it was divine intervention. Unfortunately, nothing new entered his thoughts, and he slumped dejectedly on his bench on the quayside. But he did spot something that he hadn't previously seen. Moored up over on the left-hand side of the harbour as he looked out was the *Artful Dodger*, bobbing away quietly on the ripples of the water. He scratched his head.

"In the last thirty-five hours or so, I've received nothing but questions I can't answer," he reflected. "I don't even know what I'm doing here, but I'm so engrossed in this now that I have to find out more. Something is wrong here. I think the answer must lie with events before Hastings took that boat trip."

He stood up and gathered all of the pieces of the file together. "Let's see what Ana has turned up back at the hotel."

* * *

"Roger!" Ana called out joyfully to him as he re-entered the bar area of the Rose and Crown hotel. "I have found out some really important, brilliant things for you."

The young Serbian was still standing behind the bar, laptop on but now plugged in for a well-deserved battery boost. Hartnell had been gone around an hour, and during that time the number of people enjoying a drink in the bar had gone up from one person to three. She still wasn't exactly busy with bar work, noted the inspector, and so his hopes for something – no matter how small – were quite high.

"OK!" replied Hartnell happily in response, pointing at a table over at the far side of the room. "I'll settle down over there again, and you can come and tell me your important, brilliant discoveries."

Ana was so excited that she made it to the table where they had sat an hour earlier before Hartnell did. She placed the computer down and sat staring at the policeman with her wonderfully enthusiastic smile firmly printed on her face – like a small puppy waiting for some affection or a treat, Hartnell felt.

"So, what do you have, my dear?" he asked. "Just why are you so excited?"

"Well," said Ana. "On the Internet I have found all of the press cuttings from the local and regional papers from around that time. The story of the drowning wasn't covered as much as such events usually are because there was a big fight in the next town along the coast on the same evening. That seemed to get more attention, despite the dead man. I also dug around a little bit, as you asked, on William Hastings and Mr Policeman Riley. It seemed Riley was already in Listingbourne town, looking for Hastings."

"I already knew that, but thanks for looking," thought Hartnell; he had found that out in his own research to date.

"I even managed to get the full report from the hospital on their examinations of the body found on the beach," she added, a comment which caused the policeman's eyes to widen.

"How the hell did you get that?" asked a startled Hartnell.

"I hacked into the hospital's computer!" answered Ana with a mischievous smile.

"You did what!" exclaimed Hartnell. "You could get into serious trouble! More importantly, you could get me sacked. That is highly illegal, Ana."

"Relax, granddad!" said Ana jokingly, mocking the inspector. "There is no way anyone can ever trace me and find out. No one will know I even looked! And most of the information was published publicly anyway. It is hardly a secret, Roger."

"So you can hack in without being noticed?" he asked. "I thought you always left a trail."

"No!" said Ana dismissively. "I'm just looking at their files and records as if I worked at the hospital. I'm not going to change anything. I'm only looking. Stop fussing!"

Hartnell smiled a little as he shook his head. "Different world," he thought.

"Anything else?" he asked.

"Yes!" answered the young girl. "I have much more for my Roger. That was all I found on the web, but I also found many interesting things here in the hotel. You know that Mr William stayed here. Well, the police must have spent many hours here searching for things. They left behind lots of items, too. Notes, photographs of his room, statements. Loads of things. They were all in our store cupboard."

"Really?" asked Hartnell. "And you found out which room he stayed in?"

The girl nodded, with that same mischievous look on her face.

"The room he was given is vacant," she said. "We can go up there now together, Roger. Room 9. No one will know."

Still uncertain whether she was making a pass at him or not, Hartnell quickly replied, "Or you can just give me the key. You are busy down here with the bar."

Ana smiled. She was well aware that her comments were suggestive, and she was teasing Hartnell. She sensed he probably enjoyed the attention, but the reference to his wife early on in their meeting had told her that he was a happily married man.

"Of course," she said, looking at the three customers with their drinks. "I need to stay down here."

"Brilliant work though, sweetheart," said Hartnell. "In a few minutes we can go through what you found in the newspaper cuttings and the hospital reports. But now I'd like you to give me the photographs you found and the key to room number 9."

She handed everything over with a smile.

"I also have the statements given by the hotel staff who worked here that day twelve years ago. I will go through everything up there in the room," Hartnell informed her.

"OK, darling Roger," Ana said provocatively. "Take your time. I'm here all evening for you."

Hartnell turned away and headed towards the gap through to the stairs leading to the residential area of the Rose and Crown. These were near the back door where he had first come in that afternoon. "'Darling'," he thought to himself with a chuckle.

Room number 9 also faced the back car park of the hotel. It was three rooms along the corridor from the room Hartnell had been allocated. It was a slightly different shape than his room, though. In these older buildings, nothing is particularly uniform the way it often is in modern hotels. This was a much smaller room than Hartnell's, and it didn't benefit from built-in wardrobes, having just a small exposed rail for hanging clothes. There were the same drink-making facilities, though, and the room was painted the same colour as his.

"I can see why this room is vacant," Hartnell thought. "It's probably the last room they offer out. Or maybe the cheapest."

He placed onto the bed the photographs Ana had given him and also the photographs of the room from the official notes. He kept them distinctly separate to ensure they didn't get mixed up. Hartnell also removed from a sleeve an account given by a member of staff from the Rose and Crown, and he began to read it.

He arrived on the Monday afternoon and came into the reception. He didn't have a reservation. He was just hoping we had a room. We actually had a few spare that day, I recall. My first impression of him was that he didn't look like the kind of person who holidays in Listingbourne. He was young, tall, and unshaven, his beard almost full, and his clothes were shabby. He asked for the cheapest room and said he would like to stay for five nights. The room rate was £55 per night, and he paid the full £275 there and then in cash. We don't usually ask our guests to pay until they check out. We take a swipe of their credit cards as insurance, but as he said he didn't have a card, he offered to pay the full amount in advance. I was, of course, fine with this. He then went back to his car and gathered his belongings. I remember he didn't have much with him. He was carrying a laptop under his arm, and he had a medium-sized sports bag, which looked quite full, bulging almost. That was all he had.

I didn't see much of him during his stay. He came for breakfast on the Tuesday and the Wednesday morning, but apart from that, neither I nor the others here saw him at all. He just stayed in his room. On the Wednesday afternoon, however, I did see him. He was wearing just a pair of trainers with no socks, a pair of swimming shorts, and a blue top. He came into the bar and counted out an amount of money and put it into the pocket of his shorts. He ordered a pint of lager and went over to the fruit machine. He played on that as he drank his beer. When he was finished, he put the empty glass on the bar and said "cheers" and headed out of the front door onto the street. I saw him through the window heading towards the harbour. I never saw him again after that.

Hartnell looked onto the bed at the various images in front of him. He looked at the photographs of the body on the beach and noted again the shorts and the blue top. "So how did Hastings end up with a stab wound?" he wondered again. "He was a long way out to sea. He was struggling and was being pulled under, as the sea was quite rough. There were no other boats around, according to the captain's statement. So Hastings drowned there and then, two miles out to sea from here. Which can only lead to the conclusion that someone thrust a knife into the back of a dead body on the beach the following morning before 4 a.m., when it would have been pitch black. But why? No one could have stumbled across that body by accident at that time of night. No one would have been there. Was this an accident but someone wanted to make it look like a murder?"

The bed was covered in photographs. Hartnell decided to focus on the hotel room he was in, having given up on trying to make sense of the scene from the beach. He looked around the room and glanced back down at the pictures time after time, often picking a few up and holding them in the direction they were taken for visualisation purposes. He worked his way through all of the photographs.

The laptop computer was on the small desk, next to a wallet bulging with bank notes. A set of car keys was also there, as was a mobile phone. On the hanging rail acting as a wardrobe there were two shirts on hangers. A couple of polo shirts had been found in the drawer, along with some underwear. The laptop bag was lying on the floor of the room, the straps flailing out untidily. In the bathroom was a selection of toiletries dotted around: a toothbrush, toothpaste, deodorant. The usual suspects. Back in the main room, a coat was lying on the bed.

The inspector looked long and hard again at all of the photographs. This was the room of a man who clearly planned to return to it later that day, and yet he did not. But Hartnell wanted to know why Hastings did not return. The incident was down on record as an accident, given the fact that the cause of death was drowning and given the accounts of the people on the boat. The stab wound simply seemed to be noted yet ignored in the official report. Hartnell was more and more convinced that something had either been covered up or major procedural errors had taken place.

"He knew he was being tracked by the police. His body was found with an unexplained knife wound in it. This was no accident," he concluded.

Back down in the bar, Ana was continuing to surf the Internet in the hope of finding something she believed Roger would find interesting. She liked nothing more than lots of male attention, it seemed, and helping the nice policeman uncover a mystery would help her receive plenty of it. She had also found in the hotel archives the records of all of the phone calls Mr Hastings had made from the telephone in his room. She didn't find anything particularly interesting there, just one call to a taxi firm, but she did make a connection that was about to change the direction of Hartnell's thoughts altogether.

23

It was now around 7.30 p.m., and the spring sunshine was just beginning to lose its ability to adequately light Listingbourne. Hartnell knew that Sergeant Johnson should have landed back in London by now but thought he'd give him a chance to get home and settled before having another catch-up with him. Ana had called his mobile phone; she must have taken the number from the contact details his wife had given when booking the room. "Or maybe she hacked into the phone company's database too," Hartnell said jokingly to himself after he'd hung up.

Ana had asked him to come downstairs quickly, as she had found something very important. He wasn't so sure, given that she was seemingly overenthusiastic about everything, and so he took his time, tidying everything up first and stopping off back in his own bedroom to call his wife and speak to his children. Only then did he make his way back down to the bar to see what his new helper was so excited about.

The endearing student was pouring out a drink for a customer when Hartnell returned to the bar. He waved at her so she could see he had arrived, and he sat himself down back at the same table as before. Ana's computer was already on there. She was no doubt working from there now, treating it like a small, mobile police-incident room in which she was deemed important enough to be allowed in, and only returning to the counter each time she needed to serve a drink. Hartnell looked at the image on the screen. It was a geographical tutorial page of some kind titled "Longshore Drift". Hartnell knew all about this natural occurrence and was now curious what this might have to do with the case.

Ana ran over to him as soon as she had finished with her customer.

"I can see now why you think this whole thing is a mystery," she declared as she sat down hurriedly. "This doesn't make any sense at all, Mr Roger."

"Wow!" said Hartnell. "Slow down and start at the beginning!"

"OK. Here is a map of this area," she said as she flicked her computer image over to a map.

"Here is Listingbourne," she continued, placing her finger precisely on the screen. Hartnell nodded.

"That Hastings man fell from the boat around here, right," she continued. "I read that they were about two miles out to sea when it happened." She then moved her finger to a new spot on the map, a little away from the coast, into the expanse of blue representing the English Channel.

"Go on," said Hartnell, suddenly realising where this might be heading.

"Well, the body was found here, near Drewmouth beach," she said and now moved her finger to a third location on the map.

"As you can clearly see, Drewmouth is further west than us here at Listingbourne. Both the prevailing winds and sea currents here almost always go west to east. They both head across the Atlantic Ocean from the Americas and push east along the Channel in this direction." Ana then drew her hand from left to right across the screen.

"I also then checked the weather that day from the Met Office archives – another hack, I'm afraid, Mr Policeman – and was able to confirm that this was the case in September 2004. There was nothing untoward happening in the weather systems at this precise time. Both the currents in this area and also, therefore, the effects of longshore drift."

"Well?" asked Hartnell. "What exactly are you trying to tell me?"

"Roger, my dear," she said, "there is no way that a body fallen from a boat here could possibly end up further west along this coast. It is physically impossible. That body should have ended up much further east before being washed back to the shore."

Hartnell stood up in amazement. "Oh my God, you are right!" he exclaimed. "So simple yet so accurate. A dead body would simply float along on the current. And even if the person started swimming before he drowned, he would never have tried to swim west against the current. Until he drowned, he would already have been heading east!"

Ana was smiling as usual. "What does this mean then, Roger?" she asked.

"It means, my dear," replied Hartnell, "firstly that you are a genius. And secondly that Hastings' body was placed deliberately at that location on Drewmouth beach. Thanks to you, we've proved it could not have got there by the work of nature alone. Somebody interfered."

"Well, who?" asked Ana innocently.

"That is now the next part of this mystery," Hartnell replied.

He then proceeded to tell Ana Flavic even more about the case. He had deliberately left out the detail that the body had been found with a large knife wound in its back, for example, which he now informed his new friend about.

"Well, I can explain that too," she said excitedly.

"What!" said Hartnell loudly, causing a couple of the patrons in the bar to turn around and look at the pair.

"Look, Roger," she answered, flicking to another open browser page on her computer. This one was showing various newspaper archives.

"On that very same night, there was a large fight in the town of Drewmouth. I get the impression that as fights happen so rarely in this part of the world it attracted huge media coverage. Maybe the Hastings man was rescued by a boat that took him back to shore at Drewmouth. He ended up being involved in this big fight and was stabbed."

"Very good again, Ana," said Hartnell. "You are really good at this, and I can see a future for you in our police force! But, unfortunately, Mr Hastings did not die as a result of his knife injuries. The cause of death was drowning, remember? How do you explain that?"

Ana gave a very mischievous smile again. "You tell me, Roger. You're the policeman!"

They both laughed. To begin with, Hartnell had just wanted Ana to leave him alone. She was a bit of a pest, albeit a very attractive one, but her enthusiasm and her ability on the Internet had gradually worn him down. Right now, the fact that she had been able to piece together scientific proof that someone must have moved Hastings' body meant that he wasn't just glad to have her around, he could kiss her!

Hartnell was lost in his thoughts as Ana left him to go serve another customer. "Hastings was struggling in the water. He must have drowned nearby. So when, where, how, and who found the body, and who moved it? I'm not buying the fight in Drewmouth theory. There is no mention of any serious event at that fight. It seems there were a few punches thrown and a street brawl involving about eighteen people took place. It was the number of people involved rather than the scale of the violence that attracted so much attention. So indeed, someone may still have stuck a knife deep into the back of a dead body. But thanks to Ana's work, we now know that there was human intervention before that could have happened too."

Hartnell called Johnson. He could wait no longer. He had to update his colleague on everything he had found out so far.

"Well, we know it wasn't suicide or even a faked suicide," Hartnell informed his partner. "Everything points to a man who planned to return to his room. You also mentioned murder earlier. Actually, I don't think so anymore. He fell into the sea and was seen drowning. The post mortem clearly said he drowned. But something else tells me that this was no accident. The body was found in the wrong place. Why did it have a knife wound in it? Something is again not right here."

"I agree with you, Rodge," said Johnson. He was eating his dinner, back at home after his trip to Southern France. "This does seem way too bizarre to be how the official report concluded things. But remind me. You went to Devon because you know that Hastings' and Riley's prints were on the folder stolen at Leston's yesterday, and it is the final place those two people were in at the same time. Hastings died after that, so by default it is, right?"

"Go on," encouraged Hartnell.

"Well," replied Johnson. "Have you read Inspector Riley's comments from the case notes yet? He identified the body, didn't he? The same questions we are having right now about why there was a knife wound in Hastings' corpse despite him falling off a boat with no such wound – well, Riley must have had those same questions. What did he say at the time? How did he explain it on his notes?"

Hartnell wedged his phone between his neck and his ear as he pulled out the report given by Chief Inspector Ian Riley about the discovery of the body.

"Right, just skim-reading it now," he said.

Traced Hastings to Devon using number-plate recognition technology. Suspected he was in Listingbourne area. Heard reports of man lost overboard late on Wednesday night via local police. Investigations that night led us to believe missing man was Hastings. Checked with hotel and boat company. Confirmed it was Hastings. Body found next morning. Rushed to beach. I identified Hastings body. Saw the stab wound. Unexplained, as pathologists state that he drowned. Based on accounts of witnesses, Western Counties

Police didn't investigate stab wound. Notified authorities in Midlands. Hastings had no next of kin.

"So he just left it as unexplained?" queried Johnson. "Or left it for the local police, anyway."

"It would appear that way," replied Hartnell. "Although the local police file said a request was placed from higher up that the ownership of the case file be transferred to the Midlands Police team. As the drowning cause of death tied up fully with the witness statements, it appears no one batted an eyelid. Despite the mystery, it seemed the West Country Police transferred the file and closed their enquiry on it, leaving it to Riley and his force. It seems they then closed the file too."

"That is not very thorough," said Johnson rather obviously.

"Right then, Dave, my friend," said Hartnell. "I have another job for you. Get a good night's sleep, as we need to find Inspector Riley ASAP. You are meeting me in the Peak District tomorrow lunchtime!"

"You do know it is Saturday tomorrow, and my wife already hates both of us right now!" replied Johnson in a joking tone. "She's also very jealous that I went to France today!"

"Bring her with you, then!" replied Hartnell. "Seriously. We can drop her off somewhere when we find him, as we need to talk to him. She'll understand. She knows you're a policeman."

"OK!" said Johnson. "But I am two hours from the Peaks. You are about five."

"I have an early start then, don't I!" said Hartnell jokingly. "But we need to find this man. Armed with our new evidence, maybe he can help shed some light on the situation. We need to know exactly what went on in Devon all those years ago. And then we need to find out why his fingerprints and those of William Hastings came into contact with that folder."

"And who will you bring, Rodge?" asked Johnson. "Your wife – or your new friend, Ana!"

The pair ended their call with chuckles, and Hartnell decided not to head back downstairs to the bar for a drink or any dinner. "Perhaps I do need to stay away from Ana!" he thought. He did certainly need to catch up on some sleep, so in an attempt to clear his mind and start off fresh in the morning, he headed for bed. His night's sleep would be abruptly broken in a few short hours, however.

24

"He's alive!" shouted Inspector Hartnell as he sat bolt upright in the middle of the night in his hotel room. He'd woken himself up when a revelation hit him whilst he slept lightly.

"He faked it! He only went and bloody faked it! William Hastings didn't drown. He manufactured his own disappearance! You genius, Hartnell!"

The inspector's heart was beating fast. Everything had just suddenly fallen into place in his thoughts. It was just before 2 a.m. now on a dewy, mild Saturday morning down in Devon. He desperately wanted to call Sergeant Johnson, but he knew he couldn't ring him yet. It was way too early. Instead, he jumped out of bed and turned the lights on. He went over to the small desk in his room and picked up all the photographs of the Hastings drowning case again, frantically sifting through them for the umpteenth time. He threw a few onto the bed and studied the ones remaining in his hands even more closely, his hands trembling as he checked on the images to confirm his eureka moment. He let out a loud gasp as he looked first at a couple of pictures of Hastings' hotel room again and then at the images of the dead body found on the beach. He was right.

"I've simply got to call Johnson," he thought to himself whilst shaking his head. "I need to check that I'm not going mad. This changes absolutely everything. I need to call him now, and I don't care if his wife does shout at me!"

Somewhat gingerly and with more than a small degree of trepidation, he picked up his mobile phone and dialled his friend and colleague Sergeant Johnson, his hands still shaking.

"Roger, what's up?" asked Johnson, sounding much more alert than expected as he answered.

"I'm sorry if I woke you, Dave," Hartnell replied, talking way too fast for his own good. "I think I've figured two things out which pretty much change everything I've discovered down here to date, and the whole case in general. I'm sorry if I've woken up Laura, but I had to—"

"Calm down, Rodge," said Johnson. "It's OK. I'm still downstairs watching TV. I slept on the plane, so I'm a bit out of sync. I couldn't sleep. So slow down and tell me your thoughts."

"That's a relief of sorts, Dave," said Hartnell. "I feared Mrs J was going to terminate her friendship! Anyway, my friend, prepare to be shocked – I don't think Hastings drowned that day! I believe he set the whole thing up. I don't think he ever planned to return to that hotel room that day, and I also don't think the body found on the beach was his."

"What!" exclaimed Johnson. "Explain, mate. Because firstly all of the evidence clearly suggested that Hastings was planning to return to his room. And secondly the body found on the beach matched the clothing and description of the man who fell overboard. And which, I might add, also just happened to be identified by a senior policeman who knew him very well. I know you are my boss, so I apologise for how this may sound, but your reasoning here needs to be pretty special, Officer."

"I know it sounds strange, David," said Hartnell, sounding much less frantic already. "But I was studying this case solidly for several hours yesterday. In particular, I know the case photographs inside out, and it is in these pictures that I've just noticed the two vital major anomalies."

"OK, I'm listening, Rodge," said Johnson. He leant forward and turned his television off.

Inspector Hartnell cleared his throat and began. "Remember the hotel room and what they found in it? The laptop computer, the wallet, the clothes, the cash, the mobile phone, the car keys, and Hastings' vehicle in the car park. Everything was there. Everything that would suggest it belonged to a man who left his room with the full intention of returning. Anyone planning a suicide wouldn't just up and leave. Usually, anyone about to kill themselves would embark on a course of getting some kind of closure before they commit the act. For example, writing a note, contacting a loved one, confessing to a crime, revealing a secret, and so on. Here we had nothing. And a faked suicide? Well, no. No one leaves that amount of cash lying around if they want to go off the grid. Cards, yes; phones, yes. Abandon them, as they are all traceable. But cash is vital. So the investigation ruled that out too, leaving us to conclude that he was either murdered or this was indeed the accident it is reported to be. But actually, the proof lies in something that *wasn't* in the room. Something should have been found there, but it doesn't appear in the photographs and it's also missing from the deceased man's itinerary list. Something so simple, and so everyday an item, that the fact it was missing was completely overlooked."

"Come on, Rodge," said Johnson. "I'm on tenterhooks here, and you are going around the houses."

"I read the statement from the hotel about what Hastings had with him when he arrived," said Hartnell. "We know it wasn't in his room, and we also know it wasn't in his car, as that was found empty. And we know he didn't take it on the boat trip, as he went aboard completely empty-handed."

"What, Rodge?" said an increasingly frustrated Johnson. "*What* wasn't in his room? *What* didn't he take onto the boat? *What* didn't he leave in his car?"

"His bag," said Hartnell calmly. "There was no bag."

"A bag?" asked Johnson, sounding deflated.

"Yes," replied Hartnell. "He was carrying a very full sports bag when he arrived here at this hotel. The hotel maid's statement said the bag was bulging when he arrived. Well, that bag doesn't appear in any of the photographs of the room, nor was it found in his car or taken onto the boat. There were a few clothes left in the room, but certainly not enough to make a bag bulge."

"So what are you saying, then?" asked Johnson. "That he had put a few clothes in the bag and hid it at an unknown location to collect at a later date?"

"Correct," said Hartnell. "And left all of the other items in the room to make everyone think what had happened on the boat was an accident. It's quite brilliant, really."

"But how did he plan to get back to the shore? How could he have been sure he'd make it back onto dry land?" asked Johnson. "Even if he did deliberately fall into the water, he still drowned, surely? They were well out to sea on a coldish day in rough waters. And also, what about that corpse? Inspector Riley identified the body!"

"Well," said Hartnell, "I suspect he simply planned to swim to shore. I think he pulled this stunt as the net was closing in on him. We already know Riley was in this area and was planning to arrest him for a crime that would have put him inside for a long time. It is quite difficult to arrest someone who has drowned. But given what he was running from, I suspect Hastings believed he would be strong willed enough to swim to shore. He was a big, strong, athletic man who, if he was clever enough to hatch this elaborate plan, would have certainly been clever enough to know whether he was capable of making it back to the shore. But actually, I don't know if he made it back, and if he did, I don't know what happened to him. But what I do know is that the body found on Drewmouth beach was not William Hastings."

"Wow!" said a startled Johnson. "And why not?"

"A few reasons, really," said Hartnell. "They are all small in isolation, but put them together, and you see that it wasn't Hastings. Firstly, using the currents in the English Channel, Hastings would have swum east, not west, so he wouldn't have ended up in Drewmouth anyway. Either alive, trying to swim against the currents, or dead, drifting on them, Hastings must have headed east. Also, Hastings was wearing a blue long-sleeved top with the sleeves rolled up and a pair of swimming shorts when he fell from that boat. The pictures of the body on the beach were of a man in a blue top and a pair of shorts. The blue top in the photo is clearly short-sleeved, which looked like Hastings did on the boat, but his sleeves were rolled up, remember? This is clearly a short-sleeved top! And the shorts in the picture are boxer shorts. They were not the type a man would wear under swimming shorts, mainly because you simply wouldn't wear boxer shorts under swimming shorts! And finally, that stab wound. Ana, "The Serbian Super Sleuth," told me that on the evening Hastings disappeared there was a large fight in the town of Drewmouth. Nothing major was reported. However, the rumour mill in the town apparently soon started whispering that the press and the local police, although heavily reporting on the incident, played down its seriousness so not to affect the tranquil reputation of the town as a beautiful holiday spot. I believe you were right when you exclaimed murder yesterday, Davey boy. It's just that we thought a different person was murdered. It wasn't Hastings. He was probably twenty miles away at this point."

"Oh my God!" exclaimed Johnson. "Incredible. And impressive. But you do realise that all you've gone and done is given us more questions to answer, Rodge?"

"I know," admitted Hartnell. "Firstly, who was the man found on the beach? Secondly, who killed him?"

"And finally," said Johnson, "why did Chief Inspector Riley say the body was that of William Hastings? Did he make a mistake, or did he deliberately lie?"

"Well, it's just as well we're off to see him in a few hours, isn't it, Dave!" said Hartnell. "My wife has been able to track down exactly where he lives. I just hope he's going to be there, as I'm getting a bit tired, with all of this travelling around."

"We're no closer to solving Freddy Leston's burglary though, Rodge," said Johnson. "But I do believe that the key to this entire mystery could be Riley."

"And what of Hastings?" pondered Hartnell. "If he did survive his swim, then he properly disappeared out of public view, as I assume was his plan. There has been no trace of him on record anywhere since that day. We know the police were after him, but they never arrested him as planned, mainly because he was on record as dead."

"So we need Riley more than ever now," said Johnson. "He's been in possession of that folder. How? And how does he know Leston? Hastings also had that folder in his hands. How? And how did *he* know Leston?"

"Well then, my friend," said Hartnell joyfully. "Get yourself off that sofa, and get some more rest. Tomorrow could be yet another big day."

25

The phone was ringing in the living room belonging to retired policeman Chief Inspector Ian Riley. It was the early hours of the morning, and as usual he was struggling to sleep. He'd not slept well for more than ten years. Insomnia was the official description. He knew it was fear and guilt. He muted his TV using the remote control from the comfort of his armchair and reached over and answered the phone. He wondered who could be calling at this hour.

"Hello," he said. He was met with three seconds of heavy breathing, the caller choosing not to speak. "Hello," Riley said again. This time he got a response.

"You told me he was dead, Riley," came the response down the line. The voice was male, very deep, and cold-sounding. The man had a strong accent from the English Midlands.

"I beg your pardon," replied a confused-sounding Riley. "What do you mean? What are you on about, and who are you?"

There was a silence before the deep voice spoke again.

"William Hastings. You told me he was dead."

Riley began to panic. He now knew to whom the voice on the phone belonged.

"George?" he asked. "Is that you?"

"Yes," came a sinister-sounding response. "Been a while, hasn't it, Riley? I hope you haven't been hiding from me? If you were, you weren't exactly hard to find. But anyway, enough of that. Back to Hastings. You told me he was dead."

He … he is … is, George," Riley said, now speaking with an obvious nervous stutter. "I saw his … his dead body. I even arranged his cremation."

"So how come he just turned up and committed a burglary down south?" asked the man, speeding up his speech slightly. "He has just

151

broken into Frederick Leston's house in Arleswood, just north of London."

This time there was a long silence. Riley's mind was working overtime. "Hastings. Not dead. Burglary. Leston. It can't be! There is no way," he managed to bring himself to say.

"How ... how do you know it ... it was him?" he said, continuing to stutter.

"Never mind how I know, Riley," said the evil voice dismissively. "If this is correct, you know what this means, don't you? So you better hope that I'm wrong, hadn't you?"

There was yet another pause, but the silence was deafening for Riley. He finally plucked up the courage to speak again.

"You are wrong, George," he said with a newfound confidence and positivity in his voice. "Your information is not correct. He's been dead for years, and you know it."

"I hope so for your sake, Riley," replied the voice, sounding more and more threatening. "So I suggest you go and check a few things and hope you haven't got a big pile of shit you need to clean up."

"There is no shit to clean up," answered Riley confidently.

"Wrong, Riley," answered the man on the other end of the phone. "There is much cleaning up to do, actually, and I'll probably need to do some of it myself. I'll need to deal with Leston first. No one will ever see him again."

"Is that wise, George?" asked Riley.

"Very," snapped back the dark, deep voice on the phone, as if infuriated that his idea was being questioned. "He's served his purpose, and besides, I'm unlikely to be high up on the police's suspect list when he's reported missing, am I?"

"So then what, George?" asked Riley dismissively.

He didn't like the answer he received. "Then I'll send some boys up to yours. Just to be sure there are no leaks."

The phone then went dead. The man had hung up. Riley swallowed, his Adam's apple prominent in his throat, almost bursting through. He turned pale as he slumped down in his chair, staring into space.

26

"A nice Saturday in the Peak District, Laura," said Johnson to his wife as they headed north along the motorway. "What could be better than that?"

Laura Johnson didn't smile. She knew that she was only there because her husband felt guilty about his day trip to France the day before and that the real reason they were going was that he was still working. Still, she felt happier to be with him now and not having to spend another day on her own. She was a tall lady and a little overweight, much like her husband. At 45 years old, Laura was resigned to her role as a policeman's wife, having foregone a career of her own many years ago to be able to support her husband in his. Today her slightly reddish hair was done up nicely for this rare trip out, and she wore her best red spring jacket for the occasion too.

"I know you are just trying to be sweet, David," she said. "But I'm not stupid. Just drop me in Bakewell, and I'll do some shopping. I know you and Roger don't really want me around."

"Honey, look," said Johnson. "Roger and I just need to find this Riley guy and speak to him. It won't take long. Then I'm all yours. We can even stay up there for the night. Find a little hotel. What do you say?"

"Is Fiona coming?" asked Laura.

"I don't think so, darling. Sorry," said Johnson. "Rodge is coming straight up from Devon and not going home first."

Laura shook her head. "So I will be alone all day again. Great."

Johnson didn't answer. He knew he had to head one hundred and fifty miles north that day to meet Inspector Riley. To bring his wife with him had been a good idea of Hartnell's. He knew that Laura was getting a little fed up with the extra hours and inconvenience night-shift work was causing. They could at least spend some time together this way. They had been married for twelve years now, and Johnson knew his wife did understand the unconventional hours that a crime investigator had to work. They didn't have any children, and so Mrs Johnson spent a lot of time on her own. Although she was choosing right now not to show it, she was grateful to her husband that he had invited her on the trip.

Inspector Hartnell was also on his way to the Midlands, having given his wife the news that he wasn't heading home to her and their twin boys just yet.

"Well, OK," said Fiona Hartnell. "Me and the kids will head down to the seaside this afternoon, then."

"Stay away from fishing boats!" said Hartnell, having told his wife the full extent of his investigations and findings over the last twenty-four hours.

"So, is Ana with you?" asked Fiona sarcastically.

"What do you mean?" answered Hartnell.

"You've told me all about the things you've discovered whilst you have been in Devon," said Fiona. "And you mentioned that Ana girl five times!"

"She was a great help," said Hartnell defensively. "Are you getting jealous, honey?"

"Luckily for you, I know what your kids mean to you, Roger, darling!" replied Fiona. "I know that you're not that stupid to jeopardise being able to see them!"

Hartnell chuckled. "I can't help it if you are married to such a handsome beast, can I, dear!" he said jokingly.

"Whatever!" said Fiona dismissively. "Give my regards to Laura, won't you?"

"Of course," said Hartnell. "See you tonight."

Thirty minutes later, he pulled into a car park on the edge of the picturesque Peak District Town of Bakewell, where he had arranged to meet the Johnsons. The car park was laid with gravel and had no discernible spaces. There were just a few cars dotted around today, probably due to the weather, Hartnell assumed. A few trees lined the boundary of the car park, beyond which was a fairly wide, shallow, fast-flowing stream, in spate with all of the rain, heading towards a beautiful stone arched bridge. Beyond that Hartnell could see the town.

It was just before noon, and he had been on the road since around seven that morning. He had made good time. Unfortunately, the weather was not quite as nice as it had been on the south coast. It was dull and overcast, with intermittent heavy showers. "Laura is not going to be happy!" thought Hartnell to himself as he got out to have a quick look around.

By the time the Johnsons pulled into the empty parking space next to his car, Hartnell had returned to his vehicle to avoid another heavy downpour. With a little wave, he gestured to Laura, sitting in the passenger seat of the car on his right, to open her window, and he did the same.

"Good morning, Laura!" said a jovial-sounding Hartnell. "How are you, my dear?"

"Hello, Roger, my darling," she replied warmly. "I'm very well, thanks. How are Fiona and the boys? Didn't fancy coming for a swim, then?" she added sarcastically, motioning to the sky and the heavy rain.

Hartnell chuckled. "I think with the cost of fuel as it is these days, they decided to stay where they were and get soaked for free!"

Both Laura and David Johnson gave a little laugh.

"Actually, I think they will head to the coast today," added Hartnell. "I hope they have better weather than we have here."

"I'm going to have a little look around here, Roger," said Laura. "Do a little bit of shopping and leave you two boys to do what you need to do. I've got an umbrella and David's wallet. What could possibly go wrong!"

After a few moments the rain eased off slightly, and the trio took the opportunity to get out of their cars. Roger Hartnell and Laura Johnson embraced each other, and then the two police officers shook hands warmly.

"Good to see you, Dave," he said. "Thanks for running around for me like this. Ultimately it's my reputation with Gault that is on the line, so I'm very grateful, my friend."

"That's not a problem," replied Johnson. "I want to get to the bottom of this as much as you do. And I still think that Chief Inspector Gault is the reason I've never been promoted. I'm desperate to put something on his desk large enough that he finally takes notice. It's just a great coincidence that this 'simple' burglary is so much bigger than he thinks it is."

"I really do appreciate your support, Davey boy," said Hartnell putting his arm on his friend's shoulder. "Now, let's do this. Let's find Riley and discuss everything we need to with him. Leston, that folder,

Hastings, and the body on the beach. I'm sure he's going to shed much more light onto this case for us."

"Can we be sure we can do this and not get found out?" asked a nervous-sounding Johnson. "If Gault finds out that we are talking to and probing a retired policeman and not looking directly for our suspects, I'm sure he'll be furious."

"We'll be OK, buddy," replied Hartnell. "After all, we are trying to solve that burglary. I don't see the harm in trying to get answers from a man who may be able to help us. He's unlikely to have many contacts in the force still, or he wouldn't have tried to vanish. By that, I mean he left no forwarding details with his force. So he won't be complaining to Gault now, will he, if we push him hard? He wants nothing to do with the police."

"OK, I get it," said Johnson. "Would you like me to drive?"

"Please," replied Hartnell. "I've been on the road for several hours now."

The two policemen said their goodbyes to Laura, who opened her umbrella and headed off towards the town centre and the shops. Hartnell and Johnson then took their respective places in Johnson's car and headed off.

"So how did Fiona really find Riley?" asked Johnson. "Quite impressive."

"Well, she said it was quite easy," answered Hartnell. "She just put a few key words into Internet search engines. You can easily work things out from there. There are websites that display entries from phone directories, for example. So she found an Ian Riley living around here using that method. At that point she didn't know it was our Ian Riley, but then she found an article posted in a local newsletter about gardening. There was a letter written by a local resident, a Mr Ian Riley, a retired police officer who lives in Pulford's Farm, Farley Hill. He wrote in asking for advice on how to grow potatoes on a steep west-facing slope!"

"Don't you just love the Internet!" said Johnson with a laugh. "So how far is it from here?"

"Only a few miles," replied Hartnell, pointing at a large tree-covered hill in the near distance. "It should be just over that ridge."

"And what's the plan when we get there?" asked Johnson. "Are we simply going to knock on the door, explain who we are, and just ask to talk to him? He might not exactly be pleased when we tell him he's made a huge mistake."

"He might already know," said Hartnell. "He may have always known. For many years he has gone to great lengths to cut himself off from the world. As I always say, people who hide usually are running away *from* something. Another person maybe? A crime? Or perhaps, in this instance, a mistake? Or now we think it might have been a deliberate mistake. Even more reason for someone to lay low."

"Yes," agreed Johnson. "If he vanishes off the grid, he will never know if it is ever discovered by anyone that he failed to investigate a murder because he identified the wrong person. His reputation may be ruined, but he'll not care a bit, as he'll never know. I assume it's why he took his pension the way he did. Cash in and run before he's found out."

"It's just a shame for him that he's taken up gardening!" said Hartnell jokingly. "Or we'd never have found him either! But in answer to your question," continued the inspector, "yes, we will knock on the door and simply ask him some questions. But the line of questioning we will use to begin with is Leston's stolen folder and why his fingerprints and those of Hastings were found on it. Let's not mention anything about our suspicions over his handling of the drowning incident or how we think he deliberately identified the corpse as Hastings when it wasn't. Remember, we only had a few dark photographs to reach that conclusion. He saw the body from point-blank range, and he knew Hastings. We'll save those questions for later on."

27

The two policemen arrived in the small village of Farley Hill. The settlement consisted of about two hundred houses, mostly built using the distinctive local grey stone, centred on the tall steeple-towered seventeenth-century church. Overlooking the village on three sides were fairly sizeable green hills so typical of this part of England, the tops of which were covered in mist and cloud on this wet day. Just beyond the village, as the small lane started to climb, Hartnell instructed Johnson to pull the car over to the side of the road on a gravel lay-by.

"There it is," said Hartnell, pointing to a gate. "The entrance to Pulford's Farm."

"Looks a bit posh," observed Johnson. "I'm looking forward even more to getting my pension now!" he said jokingly.

The exterior of the premises was flanked by mature hedgerows, broken only by the five-bar gate which appeared to act as both the pedestrian and vehicular access to the land. Beyond the gate and the hedges were some reasonably well-kept lawns, about fifty meters long, flanked by the continuing hedge on the left and the driveway leading down from the gate on the right. At the end of the drive and grassed area was the building itself, clearly a former farmhouse. The building was about two hundred years old and was grand and rendered white, in a double-fronted Georgian style. Off to the right side were a couple of smaller outbuildings; the working farm they once served had long gone but the name of the farm lived on. Now this dwelling was occupied by the former police inspector Ian Riley.

"OK, let's do this," said Hartnell as he opened the door and got out. Johnson did likewise, and they crossed the road to the gate, as the rain beginning to fall steadily again.

"Do we ring, or knock, or just open the gate and walk down there?" wondered Johnson, looking at Hartnell for guidance.

"Let's just open the gate and walk up to the house," came the reply. "There is no Beware of the Dog sign, and there is no bell or buzzer here, anyway. It's what the postman must have to do!"

They opened the gate, the wooden Pulford's Farm sign in white lettering on a grey surround swinging back with the gate as the men passed through and headed towards the old farmhouse. The walk along the grey-stoned driveway seemed to last an eternity, with a few nerves jangling in both men by now. Were they about to get the answers they craved? As they approached the house, the front door opened, and there stood a man of about 65 years of age. He was of medium height, with a head of strong grey hair, and he was very pale. He was dressed very smartly in shoes, trousers, and a blue shirt but wore no tie.

"Chief Inspector Ian Riley?" asked Hartnell as he gained eye contact with the man. The man nodded and turned away back into the house, leaving the front door open, clearly as an invitation to follow him in.

"I didn't expect anyone this fast," he said.

Hartnell and Johnson looked at each other. Years of working together had enabled the colleagues to be able to read each other's facial expressions, and that skill was very useful again here. It was clear to both men that the other was thinking, "How could he know anyone was coming? Let's go with this and see how it plays out."

Letting themselves in and then shutting the front door themselves, the police officers followed Riley down a small, picture-lined corridor through into his main living room – and what a room it was. On one side was a huge open fireplace, and it was blazing away in all of its glory on this cold, wet day. On the other side of the room there was a large bookcase, full to the brim with various publications over three shelves. Two similar-sized sofas faced each other in symmetry on either side of a large rug in the centre of the room. The main jaw-dropping spectacle of the room, however, was at the far end, which was the back of the house. A huge set of patio doors revealed the most magnificent panoramic view. Right from the bottom of the back garden, a large hill sloped gently up towards the clouds, the various shades of green dotted with the occasional white fluffy clump of a sheep.

"Magnificent!" said Johnson out loud.

"Indeed. Thanks," replied Riley. "The top of that hill is more than five hundred meters above sea level, one of the highest in the entire peak district. Not that you can see the top today. You should see that view when we've had a day of snow. When this was a working farm, almost everything you can see from here belonged to this estate. Long before I came here, mind you."

"You still get to look at it, though," added Hartnell.

Riley smiled at his guests. "You really aren't what I was expecting at all," he said.

The two policemen shot each other a glance again. The expressions were still clear: "Let this run." Both men also had the same second thought. "We may not be who he was expecting."

"You know who I am, clearly," said Riley. "Please, at least tell me your names before you throw the book at me."

Thinking quickly, and not wanting to give too much away, Hartnell took the lead. "This is David, and I'm Roger," he said calmly but firmly, noticing that Riley did not then move forward to shake hands at this point, which would be the norm.

"So, Hastings," said Riley.

"Maybe we are who he was expecting, then," thought Hartnell. "But if so, how the hell did he know? Let this run for now."

"George tells me he thinks he didn't drown," Riley continued as he sat down and motioned for his guests to do likewise. "Do you care to share your thoughts on the matter, if indeed he's even bothered briefing you?"

Hartnell took the initiative again in case Johnson wasn't quite on the same wavelength as he was. He knew neither of them knew who George was, but Riley seemed to think they both did. They had to be so careful not to fully identify themselves, as they probably were not who Riley thought he was talking to at all.

"Well, I think he staged his own death when he was running away from you," said the inspector assertively. "He had hidden a bag full of clothes and probably stashed away some cash somewhere. He then left all of those items in his room to make it look like an accident. So we don't think he did die."

Riley gave out a nervous chuckle. "Is that *all* you've got?" he asked sounding somewhat bemused. "For Christ's sake, I've told you people many times that he's dead. What you just said about him trying to fake his own death may have been the case. He may have jumped in himself. Whatever. But he still ended up dead on that beach."

Johnson went to speak, but Hartnell raised his arm to stop him. He was leading this one.

"Clearly not his body, Inspector Riley," he continued with authority. "And you know it. And you knew it that morning in Devon, too, didn't you?"

Riley shook his head. "No. It was him. I knew him very well. I had more than a hundred sessions with him and did all that maths stuff with him and George. I'm guessing you did not. You probably never even met him. So, with all due respect, let me decide if it was him or not."

He delivered his words confidently, but Riley was shaking and was still pale. From all of his experience of interviewing suspects, Hartnell knew that Riley was hiding something and, more importantly, was about to crack.

"You needed him gone, didn't you, Riley?" challenged Hartnell again. "That is why you claimed that body was that of Hastings. You were under a lot of pressure yourself, and a dead Hastings relieved all of that, didn't it?"

There was sweat pouring down Riley's face. Hartnell, whom he still thought at this point had been sent there to seriously harm him, possibly even kill him, had him on the ropes, and Riley, unnecessarily nervous, caved in.

"The captain of that boat," said Riley quietly, "he told me that there was no way that Hastings could have survived in the water from where he fell. His crew saw him struggling two miles out to sea in cold, choppy seas, wearing not a lot. He would have drowned just minutes after he was last seen. The experts at the force also agreed this would have happened."

"So you claimed that body found on the beach was Hastings," said Hartnell. "You knew that unless there was closure, that is, a dead body, the Hastings case would stay open. And as you were reliably informed he'd died anyway, you used that body on the beach as the closure required. You checked that the dead man's rough description and clothing was a close enough match to Hastings. And you even arranged the cremation and all formalities, as he had no next of kin. If you burnt the body, the evidence has gone forever."

Riley took a deep breath. "So now you know why. And, as I'm sure you have been told, I never recovered mentally from the deceit and the fact that I chose not to investigate a murder. It set in motion the decision for me to quit the police force. I couldn't go on, could I?

He looked up to see Hartnell and Johnson looking at him, nodding empathetically, which he wasn't expecting.

"But really, gentlemen," he continued, "I'm curious as to why you really came. Hastings still died. There are few doubts about that, even though I lied about the identity of that body. Why does George now think he's back? He said something about a burglary in the south. He said Freddy Leston had been targeted in Arleswood, or something along those lines."

No facial expressions could possibly express what was going on in the minds of the two policemen now, as they didn't know themselves what to think. Hartnell's sharp brain leapt into gear again. He continued speaking assertively, as he felt Riley was scared of him.

"Yes, we'll go through that, Riley," he said. "Can you make us a drink though, please? We've had a long drive."

"Of course," said their host. "Anything in particular?"

"Coffee, please, I think," said Hartnell glancing at Johnson for agreement.

"Yes, coffee," said Johnson. "Milk but no sugar for us both."

Riley nodded and headed out of the room. The two policemen then got together to very quickly share their thoughts, keeping an eye on the door. Hartnell went first.

"Firstly I don't think he knows who we are. I believe he thinks we work for this George person. And we don't know who this George is. But most importantly of all, how the hell does this George know about that burglary?"

"Well," said Johnson. "I don't mean to sound flippant, but someone must have told him. We know Riley had several encounters with Hastings, and so if someone now thinks he's returned from the dead, they have let Riley know. But it also suggests that someone thinks Hastings committed the Leston burglary."

"Oh my good God!" exclaimed Hartnell, a little louder than he should have done. "His fingerprints were damn well on it! What if the answer has been staring at us in the face all along? Those prints weren't ten years old. We just assumed they were, as our computer told us that he was dead. And the Riley prints were old, so we dismissed the Hastings set as ancient too."

"Billy!" said Johnson. "Billy. William. Northern accent. Large man. Around 30 years old! William Hastings was sitting in our police station on Thursday morning!"

Hartnell's face dropped. It hit him soon after he heard Johnson say it. Other pieces then started to fall into place.

"Everything is linked," he said. "Morgan – or Hastings, I think we can say – was looking for something in Leston's house which had something to do with Riley. I don't think he found it or he would have done more to hide the folder in Burgin's."

"We know the connection between Hastings and Riley. What is the connection between Riley and Leston, then?" asked Johnson. "I think we should have looked harder at that folder when we had it. It seems there was more in there than I thought when I looked. As I said, it was just a load of mathematical stuff. Leston is a mathematician, after all, but it would have made a terrible autobiography!"

Hartnell put his finger to his mouth. He could hear footsteps. "I'll push him on Leston," he whispered.

The heavens opened for yet another time that day as Riley bought two cups of coffee into his lounge for Hartnell and Johnson. "So then, Hastings. Why does George think he's alive?" the host asked, getting straight back down to business.

"It's all to do with Leston," replied Hartnell. "What is your relationship with Frederick Leston?"

Riley looked confused. He frowned and looked at Johnson to see if there were any clues written on his face. There were none. He shuffled in his chair and looked around again. He wasn't alarmed, he was confused.

"You are asking me about Leston?" he said.

"Well, he's quite famous," said Johnson, "in certain circles."

"You know damn well I know who he is," said Riley.

"Of course," replied Johnson. "Silly me. I knew that you are more into gardening these days, so I thought you might have forgotten."

Riley didn't see the funny side. He just stared at Johnson, clearly trying to unnerve him. Before he'd made the drinks, Riley had felt he was being bullied slightly by Hartnell. Now he was determined to get on the front foot. He saw Johnson as the weaker man, a tactic no doubt ingrained into most policemen.

"Why are you, of all people, asking me if I knew Leston?" he enquired again, staring straight at Johnson. "Seems a very strange question for you two to come here and ask." He stood up and started pacing around his lounge.

Hartnell and Johnson shot each other a look. It was clear to both of them that whoever Riley thought they were meant the question of whether he knew Leston was bizarre. Had they just inadvertently blown their cover? Riley's head was also doing overtime. "If they have asked me this question, then it is clear that they have not been sent here by George at all. They don't know anything about this. They are probably private investigators or something, and I've just revealed my worst secret. My worst lies and deceit. But at least I'm not getting my head smashed in just yet. I knew they'd arrived too soon to be George's men. I should have gone with my instinct."

Riley awoke from his thoughts a very different man. "I think you should leave now, gentlemen," he said loudly, standing up and pointing to the door. His mood had clearly changed suddenly. He was no longer passive; in fact he had turned quite aggressive.

"You clearly didn't come here to beat me up for lying all those years ago, and I doubt you have the power to arrest me. I just told you a big pile of lies over the last half an hour anyway, so you can piss off—*now!*"

"I don't follow," said Hartnell politely.

"You come here to my house after a decade," Riley continued aggressively. "Who are you? Journalists? Private Investigators? Unbelievable! Now get out."

"And what shall I tell my client?" asked Hartnell as he rose to his feet, playing along.

"Tell him or her that Hastings is dead," replied an angry Riley. "He died about ten years ago in a freak boating accident off the coast of Devon. Tell them that."

He headed for the entrance hall to his large house, waving his arms at Hartnell and Johnson to urge them to exit the house immediately.

"Goodbye and get lost," he said as he ushered the men out of the door. "I knew you were just a pair of wet jobsworths. Good job I just told you a load of bullshit."

The door slammed behind Hartnell and Johnson, and they were left standing on the doorstep, getting very wet.

"Let's make a dash for the car," suggested Hartnell. "And compare thoughts in the dry."

The men made their quick dash back up the driveway leading away from the farmhouse towards the gate. The rain had made the large metal catch slippery, and it seemed to take Johnson an age to open it, even though in reality it was only a few seconds. Riley watched them run from the window of his house.

Back in the car, the police officers began to discuss their rather strange meeting with the retired inspector.

"Well, that was an interesting thirty minutes, Rodge!" said Johnson with a laugh. "I didn't even have any of my coffee! This thing just gets weirder with every new turn."

"Yes," agreed Hartnell. "We were right about that body on the beach, and as no other body was ever found nearby, we were probably right about Hastings faking his own drowning too. We need to find out who this George is. He clearly knew Riley and Hastings twelve years ago, and somehow he also knows all about the Leston burglary. And it seems that mathematics links them. And he also mentioned a session. What are sessions?"

"Yes!" exclaimed Johnson. "Remember I told you what was in that folder? It was mathematical symbols and equations and things like that."

"So," interrupted Hartnell, "if Morgan is Hastings, why did he take that folder from Leston? How did Riley touch that folder a decade ago? It's clear Riley knew Leston twelve years ago too, even though we don't know how, as our host just lost it when we asked."

"OK," replied Johnson. "What next?"

"Well, whilst I'm up here, I'm going to check in on Peter Kerrigan," said Hartnell. "He lives nearby, according to the records and from what he told us. After we hauled him in on Thursday, he would have felt uneasy and contacted home just to hear familiar, friendly voices. Someone will know where he is. He's probably there himself. He's never been in trouble before, so he'll have taken refuge in a place he feels safe. It shouldn't take long."

"And I'll get home and start brainstorming on everything," said Johnson. "We started with a tricky jigsaw puzzle, and now the puzzle keeps getting larger and larger."

Hartnell nodded. "Good idea. Right, let's go," he said from the passenger seat. "We can't really sit here any longer. It's starting to look a bit odd, us waiting in this lay-by. He is certainly still watching us from the house."

Johnson then manoeuvred the car out of the lay-by where they had been parked and began to do a three-point turn to head back in the direction they had come from earlier. Just as they were about to pull away, a large silver 4x4 off-road vehicle pulled up into the same lay-by. It was driven by a very large, completely bald man wearing a black jumper. He was around 40 years old and was alone in the vehicle. He bought his vehicle to a halt as Johnson was slowly pulling away.

"Get a good look at the man," said Hartnell. "I'm pretty sure he's the person Riley was expecting. He thought we were him. We might need to identify that man later on."

Hartnell and Johnson did indeed get a good look at the man, and Hartnell, from the hidden position on the passenger side of the car, was even able to subtly take a photograph of the man using his smartphone. The two of them then headed off back through the village and down the hill towards Bakewell to meet a no-doubt equally wet Laura Johnson.

Meanwhile, the large man got out of his enormous silver car and headed down to the front door of Pulford's Farm. He knocked on the door. A few seconds later, Chief Inspector Ian Riley opened the door with a very confused look on his face; there in front of him was a large man with a sinister-looking grin on his face.

"Yes?" asked Riley.

The big man cleared his throat and spoke with a brash London accent. "The name's Smith."

Riley stood still in the doorway. He knew this man by name. There was no point turning and running away. The end had come. "Sleep at last," he thought. Smith reached into his jacket and pulled out a handgun, pointed it at the former policeman, and pulled the trigger, firing once straight at his forehead. Inspector Ian Riley was dead.

28

Inspector Hartnell pulled his car up outside a semi-detached council house on a large estate on the southern edge of the city of Nottingham. Sergeant Johnson and his wife, Laura, had headed back south ahead of him, as planned. This would hopefully be Hartnell's last call of the day before he could head home himself and spend some quality time with Fiona and their twin boys.

The rain had by now subsided, and it was quite a pleasant afternoon. Hartnell glanced at his watch. It was just before five o'clock. "Hopefully this will take about thirty minutes, and I'll be home before eight," he thought to himself.

The inspector surveyed his surroundings. All of the houses were semi-detached, each the twin of its attached neighbour, and all had a driveway and a small front garden. This was not an affluent area. Probably only a few of the dwellings were privately owned, the rest being the property of the local authorities. The estate had been built in the late 1950s and was largely made up of dull, grey pre-fabricated buildings built to temporarily handle the post-war housing demand but still inhabited some seventy years later. There were a few children around, playing in the street, despite the presence of a few green play areas. The kids could only be about 6 to 10 years old, but they seemed happy enough. It was quite safe, as no cars could ever really get up much speed here. There were too many twists and turns in the roads and plenty of cars parked in the streets to slow down any vehicles. A slightly older youth wearing a hood concealing his face shot past Hartnell with his bike as he stepped out of his car.

"Sorry, mate," the boy shouted as he rode off around the bend.

The policeman laughed and headed across the road to the address given by Peter Kerrigan two days ago whilst under questioning at Arleswood Police station, number 23 Parkside Avenue. The front garden was extremely untidy, with the grass quite overgrown. No attempt had been made for years, it seemed, to attend to the flowers underneath the front window of the house. On the driveway was a twenty-year-old small, rusty family hatchback car that Hartnell suspected was no longer used, given that one of the wheels, the front left, was missing. There was rough patch of well-trodden-down grass between the car and the long grass of the main garden that was today acting as refuge for a seemingly abandoned and unloved small child's bike. "This family is not doing well," concluded the inspector as he reached the white front door and knocked.

He had just noticed that the paint on the door had almost all peeled off and was in desperate need of a new coat when the door was opened from within. Standing on the mat in the doorway was a small lady, around 50 years old, wearing an apron. She had a large amount of curly ginger hair covering the top, sides, and back of her head.

"Hello," said Hartnell politely and cheerfully. "I'm looking for Peter Kerrigan. Is he here?"

The lady didn't answer straight away, choosing instead to look up and down at this visitor to her house. Hartnell suspected that not too many strangers visited the house, and if they did, they probably weren't as well dressed as he was right now.

"Who are you?" the lady said eventually, in a sharp fashion, with a Northern Ireland accent.

"My name is Inspector Hartnell," said the police officer, holding up his badge so the lady could clearly read it. "And I was hoping to have a quick word with Peter, if he is in."

"Oh dear," said the lady, her voice dropping from the sharp tone she'd just used. "You had better come in, Inspector. What's he done? What has happened?"

Hartnell took the lady up on her offer and followed her into the house. He was led through a small entrance hall and into a living room, where she asked him to sit down. The room was clean and tidy, as was the passageway he'd walked through, which was a relief for him. The carpets had been vacuumed, and the tables and surfaces were all dust free and shiny. Based on what he had seen outside the house, he had been dubious as to the standard of hygiene and cleanliness inside of house.

"He's not necessarily done anything at all," said Hartnell finally, answering the lady's question. "I just want to talk to him. Are you his mother?"

"Yeah, I am," said the lady, holding out her hand. "Mary Kerrigan."

"Nice to meet you, Mrs Kerrigan," replied Hartnell with a smile as he shook her hand. "As I said, I'm Inspector Hartnell. Now, is your son here?"

"No, I'm afraid not, Inspector," replied Mary. "I haven't seen him for three days now. Are you allowed to tell me what you want to talk to him about?"

At that point a young girl of around 7 years old came into the room, dressed in a flowery orange dress, with her orange hair tied innocently in two little pony tails, one on each side of her head.

"Mummy, can I have a drink, please?" the girl asked very politely.

"Oh my," Mary said as she jumped to her feet. "Where are my manners? Inspector, can I get you a drink?"

As Hartnell had not gotten the chance to drink the last beverage he'd been offered, by Inspector Riley, he was keen. "I'd love a coffee, if it's OK," he said.

"Of course it's OK," replied Mary with a wink. "No one comes to my house and doesn't get offered a drink, Inspector!"

"Very kind of you, Mrs Kerrigan," added Hartnell.

"Come on, you," she said to her daughter, ushering her towards the kitchen. "I'll be two minutes, Inspector. "The kettle had just boiled when you arrived, anyway. And please call me Mary."

Hartnell had a good look around the small living room. On the mantelpiece above the electric fire stood a few photographs. He got out of the small arm chair he was in and walked over to look at them, immediately recognising Peter in a couple of the pictures. It appeared he was the second oldest of five children. There were four older boys and the youngest was a girl, the one who had just appeared in the living room. Mary appeared to be present on many occasions, but there was no sign of a father in any of the photographs.

Out of the corner of his eye, Hartnell could sense that someone was watching him. He turned his head to see the young girl staring at him.

"Mummy wants to know if you want milk and sugar," she asked.

"Just a drop of milk, please, little one," replied Hartnell.

"Milk, Mummy!" the girl yelled through an open doorway at the far end of the room. She turned her head back to look at Hartnell.

"Are you here to tell us where Peter is?" she asked. "Mummy is really worried about him. He's been gone for a few days now, and nobody knows where he is."

Hartnell knelt down so that he was at the eye level of the young girl. "What is your name, little one?" he asked her gently.

"Rosie Kerrigan," she answered sweetly.

"OK, Rosie," he said. "I'm afraid I don't know where Peter is. I was hoping he was here. But, my treasure, I do know that he is OK and that you don't need to worry. I have seen him recently. He was fine."

Rosie smiled at Hartnell. Behind her, her mother had appeared in the doorway, holding a cup of coffee for the inspector.

"Please, could you go and tidy your bedroom, Rosie darling?" she said to her daughter. "I need to talk to the nice man about Peter."

Without any fuss or protest, young Rosie Kerrigan did as she was told and headed out of the room. Her footsteps could be heard running up the stairs as Mary and Hartnell sat down in chairs.

"I wish I could get my kids to do that!" said Hartnell jokingly.

Mary gave a small chuckle, but Hartnell could see that her eyes were watering up slightly with tears. He knew she must have overheard what he had said to Rosie. The dilemma Hartnell now faced was what exactly he should tell his kind hostess.

"So you say you have seen Peter, Inspector," said Mary, starting to cry. "I popped to the shops on Tuesday morning, and when I came back he was gone. There was no note, but I could tell he'd taken a few things with him. I could tell something was different."

"Yes, I've seen him," said Hartnell compassionately. "Just two days ago. On Thursday morning at my police station, in fact."

Mary gasped.

"Don't worry, Mary," he said. "He looked well."

"But why was he there?" asked Mary nervously.

"Don't panic when I say this, Mary," said Hartnell. "But he was arrested in connection with a burglary."

The lady gasped again. "No, not my Peter," she said, tears running down her face.

"Look, it's OK," added Hartnell. "I let him go again. I didn't believe he had done anything wrong. I simply think he was in the wrong place at the wrong time."

Hartnell was stretching the truth a little in an attempt to calm Mary down. He hoped that his showing this empathy might make the lady more willing to help him find Peter. Mary Kerrigan didn't look much better with the news that her son had been released, however.

"I don't understand, Inspector," she said, shaking her head. "Firstly, Peter has never been in trouble before. He's not stupid, like his older brother was. And secondly, if he was then released, why hasn't he come home? He knows I'll be sick with worry."

"I can't answer that. Sorry," said Hartnell as he took a sip from his drink. "I just needed to talk to him about the sequence of events that led up to his arrest. I think he could hold the key to finding the real culprits. As I said before, I think he was in the wrong place at the wrong time. I wanted to tell him that I believe him but that we need his help further. That's all I was after today when I came here."

"You sound like you are from Southern England, Inspector," said Mary. "Are you?"

"Indeed, I am," answered Hartnell. "North London born and bred."

"So was Peter down there, then?" asked Mary.

"Yes, he was," replied Hartnell. "That is where my patch is. A small town called Arleswood in the commuter belt just north of the city."

"So what was he doing all the way down there?" asked Mary again. "Apart from heading into Nottingham, or a few trips to the extended family in Ireland, that boy never leaves here. He's very shy and quiet."

"I was hoping to ask him that," said Hartnell. "So, as he's not here, I'm going to have to ask you to think hard, Mary. Can you think of any reason why he was down south? We found him staying in a hostel with a couple of known criminals, amongst others, and we're pretty certain he didn't know any of them."

Mary jolted slightly. It was the words *known criminals* that hit her, and Hartnell noticed her cowering.

"What's wrong, dear?" he asked her sympathetically. "I think you want to tell me something, don't you?

"I'm afraid he does know criminals," she said, her face ironically devoid of tears despite the worrying thoughts now entering her head. "Well, at least one, anyway."

"Go on," encouraged an interested Hartnell.

"His older brother, Richard," she said, looking Hartnell directly in the eye. "He's in prison now for various violent misdemeanours. This estate is unforgiving, Inspector, and a tough place for young boys to grow up in. He got mixed up with the wrong crowd when he was about 10, when we first arrived from Ireland. He was bullied badly to begin with, but he soon became the main boy on this estate. He had to in order to survive. But Peter? No, Peter wasn't like his brother. He was always a good lad, shy and polite. He saw the effect that Richard's antics were having on the family – and on me, especially. I was losing my eldest son and was broken-hearted, and Peter held the rest of us together, making sure the other two boys did not get into any trouble. The temptations here on this Parkside Estate were too easy, but also the boys were protected because they were Richard Kerrigan's brothers. The youngest two boys, Mark and Harry, are now at a school in Belfast, away from here, trying to get to university. Peter succeeded in keeping his brothers out of all the shit that goes on here, Inspector. I'm so proud of them all. So you can understand why I'm upset when Peter is linked to crime, having devoted his life to keeping his family out of it. And I'm also missing him dreadfully. Usually there was just myself, Rosie, and Peter at home, and him suddenly not being here, walking out unannounced, is tearing me apart."

Hartnell was moved by the story; he offered a warm smile and placed his hand on her lower arm for comfort.

"And your husband?" he asked, noticing Mary's wedding ring. He felt confident enough that he had reached the stage in the conversation where that was a fair question to ask. "Where is he?"

"He left us," she said with a grimace. "Rosie was a tiny baby, so it was seven years ago now. He comes around every now and then, but he's a very heavy drinker. He can't remember the kids' names most of the time."

"He left you to bring up five children alone?" asked a startled Hartnell.

"Four Children. There was no Rosie back then. He left about twelve or so years ago," said Mary, the tears returning to her eyes. "But I don't blame him at all. He caught me in this very house upstairs in bed with Richard's parole officer, and it broke his heart. Richard was about seventeen and was getting into serious trouble, having recently been convicted of carjacking and joyriding in the next estate over. We didn't have much money, but we threw everything we had at getting him straightened out. James, my husband, was already suffering with the shame of Richard's antics. He was struggling at work and was already succumbing to drink. He came home early one day and me and this man were upstairs in our bedroom. Use your imagination, Inspector."

Hartnell didn't know whether to interrupt, as the story was probably irrelevant, or to let her carry on. She was in floods of tears. Maybe she hadn't spoken about this in years and was now letting it all out. He stayed silent but also gave her a sympathetic smile, understanding the strains of family life all too well.

"You know the strangest thing about it, though, Inspector," continued Mary, "is that I really don't remember much about it. I've kind of blanked it out of my memory. I dearly loved my husband, but his heavy drinking meant that we'd become very distant from each other, and so we rarely spoke. But I do know I wasn't remotely attracted to that parole officer, either. He was a vile little man. He used to come around fairly often during the day when James was at work for a chat about Richard's progress and how I could help him. About two weeks before the day James caught us, he said to me that if I had an affair with him, he could help Richard more, wipe his slate clean. He said he could get access to better help if I 'helped' him. He also said that if I refused, things would get very difficult for the whole family. He wouldn't recommend small boys like Harry and Mark growing up in an environment and family such as this. I knew exactly what he was doing, and I felt vile and physically sick. But my son was struggling, we had spent a small fortune already on trying to help him, and my youngest boys were the new light of my life. That man knew my weakness. He knew I would have done anything to help reform my son, and one day I fell for it."

"And did you try to patch it up with James?" asked Hartnell. "Did you explain that it was more or less blackmail?"

"I felt I tried every day for years," replied Mary. "We had four children who needed us, especially Richard. But the shame was too much for James. He said he could never undo what he'd seen. He felt he'd been deceived after we'd emptied our life savings together to help our son. It was no good. He was a broken man, and it was all my fault. As I said, Inspector, I don't blame him."

Hartnell tried to offer warmth to her, but he now felt very uncomfortable. He'd been in the house twenty minutes and had found nothing out about Peter at all.

"How did this affect Peter?" he asked.

"Not good," answered Mary. "He was about ten, so it hit him right at the wrong time. The other boys were six and five and didn't quite get the issues, but Peter knew all right. But we became closer. Richard distanced himself from me, but Peter and I grew closer. It's almost as if he didn't accept it."

"And what of the parole office worker?" asked Hartnell.

"Well, obviously I told him never to come around again," answered Mary. "We stopped that program, and so none of us ever saw him again. He was a horrible little man, anyway. I'm so ashamed. I didn't make a formal complaint against him, but I wish I had of done now. What would have been the point? It would have been my word against his, and this awful episode would have been dragged through the courts horribly publicly. None of us, especially James, needed that."

"It's OK," said Hartnell comfortingly. "We all have a past, Mary. And I'm sure Peter will turn up soon. As I said, I'm pretty certain he's not in any trouble; I just need his help. I'm sure there's a reason he hasn't called you these last few days."

Hartnell finished his coffee and got to his feet. "But if he does, please get him to call me. Promise him it will be OK."

"I will do, Inspector," replied Mary. "I'm not quite so worried about him anymore now that I've spoken to you."

"And also, Mary," added Hartnell, "if you come across anything that gives you a clue to where he may be, or why he went to Arleswood, please can you let me know that also?"

Mary and Hartnell said their goodbyes on the doorstep of the council house on Parkside Avenue, and the inspector headed for his car.

"Well, that was a waste of half an hour," he thought to himself as he unlocked his vehicle using the remote-controlled key fob. He could not have been more wrong.

29

I t was 7.30 on an already sunny Monday morning in Arleswood as Billy Morgan sat eating his breakfast in a small cafe. It had been four days now, and he had stayed well out of sight, despite never having left the town. He had planned everything meticulously, and pretty much all developments had proceeded as he'd expected them to. He'd known he would be tracked by the police and his enemies to Burgin's Hostel on Thursday morning. It had been a gamble, but he'd been sure the police would find him first, and he was right. He'd also predicted correctly that the local police would release him and his men pending their investigations and that they would also suspect Frederick Leston was involved somehow in the Burgin's ambush. That was confirmed to him when he listened in on the police's short-wave radio band. For most people, the signal was impossible to detect, but for a criminal mastermind and a genius, eavesdropping was simple. Mostly the police were communicating on digital signals these days, but there was still plenty of information available to him over the good old-fashioned airwaves. Something caught his ear, though, on the TV in the café as he was just finishing a cup of coffee.

"The North Midlands Police Force are this morning facing up to conducting a murder enquiry over the death of one of their own," said the smartly dressed lady on the bulletin. "Former policeman Inspector Ian Riley was found shot dead at his farm in the Peak District earlier this morning."

This was a development that Morgan had not anticipated, but he immediately knew why the retired cop had been killed. A large lump came up in the back of his throat. He knew Riley. He didn't like him at all, but he did know him, and hearing the news like that on the TV about someone he knew felt surreal. But that, of course, wasn't the source of Morgan's worried feeling.

"Havelock found out I was alive and took his revenge on Riley," he thought. "Riley must have convinced him that I was dead all those years ago, and so when I announced myself to the world the other night, it's got back to Havelock that Riley lied to him."

Morgan suddenly felt very ill at ease. This was not what he had expected at all.

"If he could kill a cop like Riley, then he wouldn't hesitate to kill a piece of scum like me, and maybe even the others," he thought as he nervously looked around the cafe, shuffling in his chair. "I need to contact the others. We are no longer safe."

He contemplated the consequences of getting in touch with his compatriots. Was it best to not contact them at all? Could his messages be tracked even though they were just two prepaid phones? Could the police track them? No. A message would not trigger anything with anyone; no one knew those numbers. The guys were probably safe, providing they didn't come back to Arleswood. But they did need to be aware of what had happened.

Were they staying silent and well hidden, not using bank cards, as instructed? Were they OK? Had Philippe cracked and headed back to France? Had Peter gotten homesick, as he'd feared he would? They would be far enough away from there, after he'd helped them onto the train on Friday, but he thought they ought to meet. The lock-ups they'd used were at Bedford Railway Station, and the last time he'd seen them they were heading north on a train that would pass through Bedford. "I'll try there," Billy decided.

Billy Morgan had one final look over his shoulder and was then head down, looking at his phone, to type a message to Phillipe and Peter.

"All has not gone to plan. Meet 8 a.m. Bedford Cemetery on Wednesday" was the simple instruction to both.

He then stood up, leaving a ten-pound note on the table to cover the bill. He put his hood up and left the café, instantly blending in with the people on the streets enjoying their weekend. Ten seconds later, another man stood up and left the establishment, following quietly and unnoticed behind Morgan. He was a small, stocky man wearing a dark baseball cap and white trainers.

30

U sually Inspector Hartnell looked forward to returning to the day shift after a week on nights, but he wasn't looking forward to the week ahead; he felt differently this Monday. The last four or so days had been like a non-stop roller coaster ride. He felt he was running on empty, and the week hadn't even started. He would have liked to use his Monday to fully reflect on everything, but today, however, he was on duty. He feared the day-to-day running of his police station would hamper his ability to fully analyse his findings. He had spent most of Sunday catching up with his family. He knew that there would be no point alienating them from his life, or he would never be able to concentrate on his police work. He had chosen to ignore the case the previous day with the hope that a fresh week and a fresh view might help him fit all the pieces together.

A final thing was troubling Hartnell. His commanding officer, Chief Inspector Gault, would no doubt be making contact with him for an update on the Leston burglary enquiries at some point during the course of the day. He didn't really have anything to say that the chief would want to hear. He hadn't found any of the men who were potentially involved, and he couldn't really tell Gault about the jaunts he and Johnson had made to France, Devon, and the English Midlands.

He had given Sergeant Johnson the day off, but in reality this meant he was working from home. It enabled at least one of them to properly concentrate on piecing together the puzzle. The investigation of a simple burglary had led them to uncovering a twelve-year-old previously investigated murder and a hoaxed suicide, with a retired policeman who had a guilty secret sitting right in the middle. But it appeared that the pivot of all of the events was the mysterious Billy Morgan. Was he once known as William Hastings? And if so, why was he now back in Arleswood pretending to be someone else? And why did this Yorkshireman, a French chef, and a shy man from Nottingham break into the home of Frederick Leston and steal something they immediately discarded? And why did they let both the police and the victim know where they were? To uncover a puzzle like that would take a clear head without the distractions of a busy police station.

Another issue not helping Hartnell was the fact that, aside from Johnson, he didn't feel he could ask his team to help him. After Gault's dressing-down and performance warning, he didn't know to what lengths the chief inspector would go to check up on him or how many of the Arleswood team would be asked to directly report back to him should Hartnell wander off course. He had been given strict instructions to investigate the burglary and find the suspects. Under no circumstances should he be down in Devon or up in the Midlands digging into events from a decade ago.

Other than his trusted friend, Sergeant Johnson, who was no doubt already a couple of hours into his investigations, Hartnell did still have some people on his side today. There were a few other experts he could freely call on. His wife, Fiona, who had found Riley so easily just using a bit of common sense and the ability to manipulate the Internet, would continue to offer her support to help her mundane day pass by. And, of course, he had his new young friend, Ana Flavic, down in Devon. Perhaps she was a little bored on this grey Monday morning and would be willing to help him.

Hartnell called Ana and asked her to work some more of her magic. She clearly was very advanced in uncovering secrets held deep within the murky bowels of the World Wide Web and knew how to extract them too. Luckily for Hartnell, she didn't work in the hotel on Mondays; she was only too pleased to help "her Roger".

"Look for a link between Peter Kerrigan and William Hastings," he suggested to her. "Plus Kerrigan and a man called Frederick Leston. In fact, take all of these names. Kerrigan, Hastings, and Leston I've already mentioned. Add to the list Phillipe Le Sac and Marcus Stone. Please find anything that links any of these men."

"Anything for you, Roger!" she jokingly told him.

Meanwhile, Fiona Hartnell, part-time secretary at a small firm of accountants, had more than enough time on her hands to spend the morning on Internet search engines for links and clues. Having dropped the twin boys off at school, Fiona was only too pleased to get involved. Usually she was bored to the point of frustration simply sitting at a desk and asking people to wait in reception or taking phone messages.

"Look for any link between Riley and a man named George from around ten years ago," he had asked her that morning as he'd kissed her and their children goodbye. "Whoever George is, they knew each other back then. I'm sure you can find where he used to live, considering you found out where he lives now. So, old neighbours, community leaders, and so on might be a good place to start, and remember he was in the police, so check lawyers, judges and, of course, other policemen from the Midlands force."

His instructions to Johnson had been even more straightforward when he'd issued them early on the previous morning. "Simply try to piece together a scenario that could link everything together that makes logical sense. This whole sequence of events has been so unusual that if you are able to do that, I'm convinced, you will have uncovered what we are looking for. Nothing else could fit!"

Hartnell was sitting alone in the corner of the main reception room of Arleswood Police Station when his thoughts were interrupted by a female voice.

"Inspector Hartnell," said PC Watton. Then "Inspector Hartnell!" she said even louder.

"Sorry, PC Watton," replied Hartnell. "I was miles away! How can I help you?"

"We've just had a strange phone call, Inspector," replied Watton. "A man simply asked if you were here. As soon as I said yes, I believe he hung up. I'm afraid he wasn't on the line long enough for us to trace anything."

Hartnell was motionless, thinking hard for a moment, a reaction misread by Watton.

"I'm sorry, sir," she said in a slightly panicked voice. "I had no time to ask him—"

Hartnell stopped her in full flow. "It's OK, PC Watton!" he said. "I know that there is not a lot you could have done differently and not much you can give me here, either. I was just trying to think whom it might be. Any guess at the man's age? Or did he have any kind of distinguishable accent?"

"Very difficult to say, sir," replied Watton. "It was not an old voice, for sure. No obvious accent either. He didn't say enough for me to pick up anything. He simply said – and I'll quote this word for word – 'Is Inspector Hartnell on duty today?' I said, 'Yes, he is', and the call went dead. That was the conversation in its entirety."

"OK, thanks," said Hartnell. "Very interesting. I'll be in the control room if you need me, PC Watton. I clearly don't know who the person was, but my gut tells me that someone will be paying me a visit today!"

He walked off with a smile on his face as his thoughts took over. It seemed someone wanted to talk to him. This kind of call had never happened to him before; his guess was that it could only be linked to his recent activities with the Leston case. Maybe someone had a confession to make! Whatever it was, it could only help him unravel this case.

Hartnell sat in the control room, away from the hustle and bustle of a working police station, but even in his quiet sanctuary he was unable to concentrate on anything other than PC Watton's phone call. His mind was considering all of the various possibilities as to who the mysterious caller might have been, so much so that he started talking out loud.

"Could it be one of the four original burglary suspects? Is it someone connected to the fight at Burgin's? Someone from the Devon police, maybe with a secret to tell me? Perhaps Inspector Riley worked out who we were and has come to connect a few more dots."

He was pleased that he had a team working on the investigation for him, as he was achieving nothing himself so far this morning.

The inspector kept looking at his watch. PC Watton, the young policewoman who often manned the front desk, had taken the phone call soon after 9 a.m. Time was ticking by painfully slowly. He had been reviewing a few files and had signed a couple of documents, but he hadn't had any calls from Johnson, Fiona, or Ana, and he still hadn't received his visitor. It was now well into mid-morning.

Meanwhile, Johnson wasn't having an enjoyable morning either. "Why Arleswood, and why now?" he thought to himself whilst looking through the Philippe Le Sac case again. "Where did he go after he walked out of here? Floregge promised to call me if he showed up back in France. The guys at the station found nothing of any interest or relevance when they translated the police notes from the Le Sac arrests in Rocheville. No link to the UK at all, but as Floregge pointed out, residents of that part of Southern France have contact with the British all the time. OK, what about Riley? Who is George? I don't know where to start, here. I can't create a logical scenario from this at all!"

Frustrated and dejected, he felt he needed a rest, and so, at just before eleven o'clock, he turned his TV on to catch the latest news headlines. It was then that he heard the bulletin about Inspector Riley. "Oh shit," he said out loud. "What have we done?"

Back at the police station, Inspector Hartnell decided that the team needed to try something different. "This isn't clever," he told himself. "There are four of us working away on this independently. If we were all in one place, I'm sure we'd be far more efficient. But one of us is four hours away in Devon. How do we do this?"

He was disappointed with himself that the answer took him so long, as it was far from rocket science. He simply needed to call Sergeant Johnson into the station. The social sergeant would no doubt be desperate for the company, bored and frustrated at home. He would ask Fiona to drop by also, and then the three of them, all in the same room, could set up a video call with Ana. "She's bound to have the technology on her machine," he thought. "But is this allowed? Can I use two unpaid civilians in this way?" He was just about to ring his colleague Sergeant Johnson when his phone rang. A bizarre feeling then entered his mind as he looked down and saw his friend's name on the phone display. It wasn't a feeling of telepathy but one where he instantly felt something was wrong. *Intuition*, he called it.

"David, my friend," he said quietly and informally, first checking around that there was no one listening. "Please tell me this is good news and that you've figured everything out."

"Roger," replied Johnson, sounding equally non-enthusiastic. "It's Riley. He's been murdered."

Hartnell sat motionless and silent in his chair in the control room, a million thoughts rushing through him all at once. There were no questions back to his friend. He quickly logged onto the Internet to check the news himself. The details were sketchy, but apparently the experts could already tell that Riley had been killed sometime between Saturday morning and Monday morning and that a few visitors had been spotted at his farmhouse on Saturday.

Neither policeman quite knew what to say, and for a good few minutes there was complete silence. In the end, Johnson spoke and confirmed to Inspector Hartnell that he was on his way in to the station. The men agreed not to contact Chief Inspector Gault or the North Midlands Police until they had got their heads together. They knew there would be some pretty serious questions for them to answer, but they would also be vital in the murder hunt.

He was now even more curious about the phone call that Police Constable Watton had taken that morning. Was it related to the Riley murder? Had the killer come to take him out too? He tried to eat his sandwich but found he had no appetite. He sat there alone with his thoughts, staring down at the desk and struggling to focus, a cheese sandwich with a solitary bite mark taken from it in his left hand. Suddenly there was a knock on the door of the control room, which woke him from his slumber. He hoped that finally he would get some answers.

"Inspector," said Watton, "sorry to bother you, sir, but we need you on the front desk."

"Do I have a visitor?" asked Hartnell slowly as he swung around on his chair to face the policewoman.

"I'm afraid nothing as exciting as that!" answered Watton. "We just need you to sign a few papers so we can process some warrants and boring things like that!"

Hartnell sighed and smiled vacantly. "OK, I'm there in two minutes!" he said and took another bite of his sandwich.

"Oh, and a courier just dropped off an important case file for you to review," added Watton.

Hartnell's eyes opened wide and his ears pricked up; he immediately sensed something was odd. He thought for a moment, running his thumb and forefinger down his chin.

"How do you know it's important?" he asked in a quizzical fashion, contorting his face slightly to show his confusion.

"The courier said it was," replied Watton, immediately realising how juvenile and innocent her comment sounded. "It was strange, as I didn't have to sign anything, and he appeared to be in no discernible uniform either. I recognised him, though, so I thought it would be OK."

Inspector Hartnell leapt out his chair and rushed past PC Watton at the door of the control room and headed for the reception area. His female colleague gallantly followed behind him, struggling to keep up. Before she could let the inspector know which documents she had been referring to, Hartnell had located them and was opening it. It was a brown A4 envelope.

"Please get me the CCTV feed from that camera," he instructed PC Watton whilst nodding his head at the camera directly above the desk, knowing that the man would now be long gone. "Even if you need to get that Mortimer kid in. I need it very urgently."

Watton looked confused. "He's just a courier delivering a report, sir," she stated.

"He was no courier, and this is no report," exclaimed Hartnell to his colleague, causing a junior officer to poke his head out of one of the interview rooms to see what the commotion was. "This is the missing piece to our puzzle," he added as he picked up the file and swiftly headed back to the control room.

A minute later, a rather glum-looking Sergeant Johnson walked through the front door of the station and exchanged pleasantries with PC Watton.

"Cheer up, Sergeant," said Watton. "The inspector's in a strange mood, so I need at least one of you normal today!"

"Did you hear the news from the Midlands this morning?" replied Johnson. "It's very sad."

"Of course," responded Watton empathetically. "Makes us all sad when a policeman takes a bullet, I guess."

"Indeed, PC Watton," replied Johnson. "And that's why I'm a bit down and probably why Inspector Hartnell is a bit strange."

Johnson headed down towards the control room, having been informed of Hartnell's whereabouts by Watton. He opened the door and saw the inspector sitting there looking at the file, his eyes barely looking up from the desk despite the interruption.

"Roger," said Johnson, trying to get Hartnell's attention.

"Hello, David," replied Hartnell, giving Johnson about half a second of eye contact before reverting back to the papers on his desk. "We might have been handed the answer to all of our prayers. This file was handed in to this station a few minutes ago. It's all about William Hastings."

"Inspector Hartnell, sir," said Johnson. "We must discuss Riley. We have to work out our next move. We have to report to the police up there. We saw him Saturday afternoon, remember. We may have seen the killer, that huge bloke with the bald head, remember? He was scared of a bloke called George. We have to tell Chief Inspector Gault."

No one said anything for what seemed an eternity. Both Sergeant Johnson and Inspector Hartnell felt their eyes drawn towards a tall man standing in the doorway of the control room, his face so angry that the blood vessels in his face looked as if they would soon rupture.

"Tell Chief Inspector Gault what?" screamed Gault from the doorway. "Tell Chief Inspector Gault just why the hell you were visiting a retired policeman on Saturday afternoon in the Peak District? And why that policeman just happens to now be dead? Is that what you wanted to tell me?"

"It was linked to the Leston case, sir," said Hartnell confidently. "We only found out a matter of minutes ago about the murder. I was about to call the Midlands boys and you about our visit, so I'm curious how you knew we were there, sir?"

"An elderly neighbour, Hartnell," said Gault with a grimace. "She thought you were acting suspiciously, and so she took your number plate. When the news of the murder came in, she contacted the police, who traced the car back to you and immediately called me."

"I assure you, sir," said Hartnell. "He was alive when we left him."

Gault flashed a look back at Inspector Hartnell. His face was bright red with anger still, but his expression had become one of disappointment. Just then, two uniformed police officers arrived at Gault's side by the door of the control room. The uniforms were different; presumably they belonged to the North Midlands Police Force.

"I think you had better accompany these gentlemen back to Nottingham, Inspector," said Gault. "The good news for you is that I no longer give a shit what you have or haven't done regarding my instructions on the Leston burglary. The bad news is, Hartnell, you are currently the only suspect in the murder of a decorated former policeman."

"Sir, you don't possibly think—" stuttered Hartnell.

"No, Inspector. For the record, I *don't* think," responded Gault, speaking slowly but clearly. "But these officers don't know yet, and so right now you will do exactly as they say. You are going on a little trip, and for once I'd love it if I'm wrong and you did do it. Now get out."

Hartnell stood up from his chair and shook his head, but he didn't say anything. He looked at Sergeant Johnson, who had remained quiet throughout the exchange with Gault. He winked at him and pressed the file into his chest.

"Read it," he said quietly under his breath, and he headed over towards Gault and the other two officers. He passed his chief inspector without so much as glancing up at him, and he disappeared out of the door, followed immediately by the two officers.

"Sergeant Johnson," said Gault condescendingly as he turned his attention to Hartnell's worried compatriot. "What are we going to do with you?"

"Sir, they can't suspect Inspector Hartnell, surely," said Johnson. "Otherwise I'd be a suspect too. We were both there, and this witness would know that. We left Riley in his house alive and well, I promise you."

"Oh, be quiet, Sergeant," said Gault with an alarmingly quick change of tone. "You know exactly why you didn't go with Hartnell and why I've kept you behind."

Johnson looked confused.

"Leston, you idiot," continued Gault. "What have you done with Leston?"

Johnson now looked even more confused and started to fight back. "What do you mean, what have I done with Leston?" he said. The cogs started ticking in Johnson's brain. If this question was being asked, then something had happened to the old man, too.

The grey matter in Gault's brain was working overtime too. He knew how to read a reaction and was immediately certain, therefore, that Johnson didn't know anything about Leston. The response had been too sincere, too genuine.

"Frederick Leston is missing," said Gault, having now calmed down a little. "His wife rang me personally to tell me. She hasn't seen him since Saturday morning. He went out to do a little grocery shopping and hasn't been back since. Strange, isn't it, Johnson, that of the various people you have been to see recently, one is now dead and another missing?"

"We last saw Leston on Thursday mid-morning," replied Johnson. "You know we suspected him—"

"You both have some serious questions to answer, Sergeant," interrupted Gault. "And everyone from the Home Secretary down seems thinks it is for the best if the two of you are kept apart."

Johnson looked blank as Gault continued. "You and I are going to have a long chat, during which you are going to tell me that Inspector Hartnell keeps asking you to disobey orders, keeps asking you to break the rules and put his fellow officers' safety in jeopardy. You are going to confirm in writing that he keeps going against standard procedures and protocols, always in sharp contrast to your judgement. And that he sent you to France in direct defiance of my orders. Yes, I know about that, Johnson. And that he dragged you to Riley's on a whim after his own pointless excursion to Devon. I think I'm going to need a new inspector soon, and if you comply, you could be in the running. One of my current team has probably just passed his sell-by date. I'd hate to have to dispense with you too, Johnson."

It was obvious to Sergeant Johnson what Gault was trying to encourage him to do here, and he didn't like the feeling he had. He couldn't betray Inspector Hartnell, surely. But he couldn't lose his job either. He'd only ever known how to be a policeman and had no other experience. He had very few formal qualifications, certainly not enough to get a job with similar earning potential. If Hartnell was removed from the force in disgrace and Johnson didn't give evidence against him, he would be complicit in the misconduct and might also be sacked. But he couldn't betray his best friend, could he?

"I know he is your close colleague, Johnson," continued the chief inspector as if reading the mind of the man in front of him. "But this could be great for your career. Imagine it: Inspector David Johnson. It sounds good, doesn't it?

Johnson took a sharp intake of breath.

"I shall be back in an hour, so stay right here, please," continued Gault. We *are* going to have that chat. Do I make myself clear, Sergeant? You are skating on very thin ice, and you should be thinking of ways to impress me."

With that, Gault swept out of the control room, turning dismissively on the balls of his feet and heading out, leaving Johnson alone in the dim room. The shocked sergeant, now unsure of his own future as well as that of his friend, sat down on the nearest chair. He knew he and Hartnell wouldn't end up with a murder charge or a kidnapping charge, as clearly they were innocent. But he was worried that Gault was trying to build a case to have Hartnell fired, and there probably was enough evidence for him to do so, especially if he himself were blackmailed into giving evidence.

PC Watton rushed into the room to check on him, having seen Hartnell and then Gault leave with the worst expressions on their faces. He merely waved her away without as much as a word. Then he was quite disappointed with himself. The gesture was a rude one towards a colleague who was also a genuine friend, but he really couldn't cope right now with worrying about such things. His thought process was completely muddled, and he needed to be alone.

Then he picked up the brown A4 envelope full of papers which Hartnell had thrust upon him. Johnson found this package very strange as there was a date-stamp on the envelope of the previous Thursday from that very town, Arleswood, and yet the package was hand-delivered to the police station approximately twenty minutes ago. The original address had been handwritten on the envelope. It was a PO box rather than an address. And whoever owned that post box has now sent the contents of this envelope to the police.

The envelope had already been opened, by Inspector Hartnell presumed Johnson. He put his hand in and withdrew the contents. Indeed, the contents were all about William Hastings. There were details of court hearings, solicitor's forms and, strangely, many pages with mathematical equations on them. Intrigued, and with strict instructions not to leave the station, Sergeant Johnson turned on a little desk lamp and began to read.

31

25 October 2001

Judge Harris asked everyone in the courtroom to stand as he addressed the foreman of the jury. "Have you reached a verdict?" he asked.

The middle-aged foreman with large, round spectacles nodded his head. "We have, Your Honour," he said.

"And do you find the defendant guilty or not guilty?" spoke the judge.

There was very little suspense in the courtroom at this time, considering the verdict was about to be read out. The courtroom was virtually empty. There wasn't a single person sitting in the public gallery, and the main benches, often full of large legal teams, had just a few occupants today.

"Guilty," uttered the foreman in a clear deep voice.

The small court fell silent momentarily. None of the two dozen or so people in the room were particularly surprised at the verdict. The defence case had been built largely around trying to prove that the police had gained their evidence illegally rather than by trying to convince the jury there was enough doubt as to the defendant's guilt. Even the defendant himself seemed quite laid back when questioned in the witness box, as if he knew he had little hope of acquittal, a fact not lost on the judge during the trial.

The elderly judge cleared his throat. "Very well," he said and turned his attention to the defendant.

"Mr Hastings. You have again acted with complete disregard for the law and shown no remorse for your victims at all. It also came to my attention over the last day or two that you simply do not have any respect for this court, or myself, or even your own legal team. Based on your previous crimes and your behaviour here, I am quite within my rights to send you to jail. You just don't seem to care what is happening to you. I won't be passing sentence today, and you are hereby ordered to return next week for sentencing. I am, however, requesting a private meeting immediately after this session with your lawyer and representatives from the Crown Prosecution Service, and also the police, to discuss my options. In the meantime, you will be escorted from this courtroom back to your detention centre and be subject to electronic tagging to ensure you respect the terms of your curfew and the rules of Marlborough House."

William Hastings broke his eye contact from the judge and lowered his head. He had just been found guilty. His crime was stealing cars, dismantling them so they effectively vanished, and selling the parts cheap for a quick cash sale. Even the prosecuting lawyers described the venture as "ingenious in its simplicity". It was difficult for the police to trace and arrest anyone when the stolen item no longer existed. He had been caught only because he had been accidentally hit by a police car out on routine patrol. As Hastings was well known to the police, this had ended his little enterprise.

He was a large man, tall and athletic and at just 18 years old, already a serial offender who had racked up several convictions for theft and public-disorder offences. This was his first offence as an official adult in the eyes of UK law, and although he could handle himself, Hastings feared prison greatly. He hadn't worn a suit or a tie this day. He didn't see the point. He'd just worn trousers and an open light-blue shirt. He fell into a daydream.

*　　*　　*

William Hastings was born in 1983 in Leeds, Yorkshire, the son of Robert Hastings and Juliet Morgan. Both parents were just 19 themselves when William was born and couldn't cope with the demands of parenting and looking after a baby at all. By the time William was 3 years old, his father had died of a heroin overdose, his mother had turned to prostitution to help feed her own drug habit, and he had been placed into foster care. Although his mother visited him daily and gave him as much love as she could, she grew ever more distant over time as her own downward spiral into the abyss took hold. She applied several times to have her son placed back into her care, her lawyers citing that looking after her son would be the catalyst to reform her lifestyle, with a young William himself making a heartfelt plea on her behalf. Unsurprisingly, the authorities declined Juliet's requests. On William's eighth birthday, he received a card from his biological mother at his foster home which simply read, "I'm so sorry, William. I'll love you forever." Later that day her body was found washed up on the banks of the River Humber Estuary in East Yorkshire, she clearly having jumped from the nearby Humber Bridge.

William Hastings never forgave the authorities for his mother's suicide, blaming many different parties for not reuniting him with Juliet permanently. From that day forward, the bright but troubled child vowed to never conform to any authority. Within a week he had been expelled from his primary school for locking the headmistress in a broom cupboard overnight – revenge, he said, for her not supporting him in his quest to live with his mother. Later that same month, he was detained by the police for starting a fire outside the council offices where he had made his plea to the welfare officers. The very next day after that, he wrote MURDERERS in large letters in red paint across the car-park sign of the same offices.

Although he was fond of his foster family, Hastings never felt loved by them, and before his ninth birthday he had been removed by social services. He was transferred to another family after he was caught stealing jewellery from his foster mother. There then followed a five-year period during which he was expelled from several schools and was in constant trouble with the police for numerous petty crimes. He was an early developer, and by the age of 14, Hastings had grown substantially and was already over six feet tall. This physical presence brought a new skill set to his armoury: aggression. He would often wander the streets of Leeds city centre late at night, as he had no family, no friends, and certainly no place he felt welcome. One night he was approached by three gang members from the Leeds underworld who mistook Hastings' dishevelled appearance and aggressive mannerisms as an attempt to intimidate and undermine them. A fight ensued, and the outnumbered Hastings was beaten badly, needing three months of hospital treatment, although he did manage to land a few blows on his attackers himself. He was interviewed by the police and was able to identify the men with the help of sketch artists.

The Leeds Police force then feared for the young Hastings. Word had got around the streets that this young delinquent had identified wanted members of a notorious criminal gang and that they would need to take this man out. The police also knew that Hastings was a loose cannon, and given his capacity for trouble, it was deemed that the best course of action would be for the teenager to leave the area. A deal was struck with social services, and William Hastings was taken eighty miles south to the city of Nottingham and was placed in a young offenders' institute there. The youth himself was only too happy to go. He had lived his entire life in Leeds, and the city could offer him nothing except painful memories. The recent physical ones now compounded the mental ones he'd had since birth. He was glad to be out.

Simply moving to a new city was never going to solve the effects of the sad early life of William Hastings. By the time he reached his mid-teens, he was an orphan who had had no proper parenting or discipline in his life at all, and he had a tendency to look for trouble to ease his boredom. Now the situation was much worse. He found himself spending twenty-four hours a day with other young offenders. But he was happier now. Firstly he was away from the hurt of Leeds, and secondly he had one other saving grace: his brain. Hastings was brilliantly clever, especially at mathematics.

Tuition at the young offenders' facility was simply designed around trying to focus the young men's brains for long enough to stimulate them into thinking that there could be more to life than crime. Most of the tutors bought in to teach were quite military in their approach, disciplined and tough, and they didn't actually have any teaching experience. Any weakness shown by the staff was immediately exploited by the boys, which simply could not be allowed to happen. Therefore, the ability to intimidate and control was valued much more highly than the actual ability to teach. The tutors had to be mentally strong and physically intimidating, or the youths would do nothing in the classes except disrupt. However, despite the lack of teaching knowledge, it was noted by several of the staff that Hastings' skills in mathematics were way beyond anything they had seen before. A few hours a week of focus in the classroom, however, was never going to be enough to keep the disillusioned and destructive Hastings out of trouble. Over the next four years he became as well known to the police in Nottingham as he had been in Leeds, culminating in this day's trial.

*　*　*

"Mr Hastings. Mr Hastings!" The judge was trying to get his attention, but William Hastings had been lost in his thoughts, head still bowed in the dock, which was clearly angering the judge further. Then Hastings looked up.

"Mr Hastings," said the judge sternly, "I put it to you that you just don't care about the rule of law. Now, please, will you look at me before I charge you with contempt of court? Eventually your behaviour will get you exactly what you deserve."

Hastings felt a strange rush of adrenalin and sadness attacking his senses simultaneously, but in the end anger won out.

"What I deserve, Your Honour?" he said loudly and aggressively. "Did I deserve for my father to die? Did I deserve for my mother to commit suicide because she was told time and time again that she couldn't love me? To be beaten to within an inch of my life for no reason, only for the police to send me away rather than hunt down and jail the culprits that I identified? Please forgive me if I appear to not care, Your Honour, but you are indeed correct. I don't give a shit. If my life has taught me one thing it is that life isn't fair, so why play by the rules? Jail me if you want, Your Honour, but that isn't going to teach me right from wrong is it? I think we both know we're past that now."

There was an awkward silence in the courtroom, and a few of the jury clearly felt moved by what they had just heard. The judge wrapped up his formalities and dismissed the court. As he'd previously stated he would, he left the room with the Crown Prosecution lawyers and Hastings' own defence team. Instead of sending Hastings back to Marlborough House, though, he requested that the guilty man remain at the court building in a waiting room, supervised by a police officer.

Just over an hour later, Hastings was escorted from his room, along a wide corridor inside Nottingham's main court complex, and through a set of large, decorative, dark wooden doors to a sizeable room. In the middle of the room there was a grand oak desk covered by a green leather rectangle, leaving a margin of about three inches of oak all the way around the edge. The walls were all wood-panelled, and hanging on the wall were framed portraits of various dignitaries and officials. Sitting behind the desk was Judge Harris, still wearing his white wig and robe, the left side of his face lit by sunlight coming in through the small window to the side of the room. Hastings also recognised in the room Mrs Catherine Wood, QC, the Crown Prosecution lawyer from his trial, and his own lawyer, the overworked and tired Mr Richard Kempster. They were both on the near side of the desk, opposite the judge. Standing to the right of the judge, behind the desk, was another person, a short, stern, and confident-looking man sporting a weak, unwelcoming smile. The judge then asked the police officer who had escorted Hastings to the room to stay, and he invited everyone to sit.

"Mr Hastings," started Judge Harris, "as I mentioned in my summary in the courtroom, I am quite within my rights to send you to jail for your crimes, not to mention for the contempt with which it seems you hold the entire justice system. That said, and you mentioned it yourself, I'm not sure that sentencing you to a custodial term would benefit society or yourself in any way. Therefore, in conjunction with the CPS and your legal team, it is agreed, in principle at this stage, that you will be placed directly into the care of the head of this region's rehabilitation team." Judge Harris opened the palm of his hand and indicated the short man now sitting to his right.

"You may ask yourself, Why am I offering this to you?" the judge continued. "Well, the answer is twofold, really. Firstly your own personal circumstances tell me and the people here gathered in this room, including the prosecution team from the Crown, that yet another extra chance should indeed be granted to you. And secondly it has become known to me and the relevant authorities, from your time at the Marlborough House Young Offenders Institute, that lurking just below the surface you keep hidden a young man who excels at arithmetic. A young man who, when properly monitored, focussed, and stimulated can show the world what is achievable. Under this man's supervision," he said, and he indicated again the short man to his right, "you will learn to harness the power of your brain as a force for good, Mr Hastings, and not your brawn as a force for bad. I firmly believe that with the required attention and training, you can help this team rehabilitate many more young offenders. You can be a great role model. I don't think you are evil. I just think that you don't have anything worth living for. You have nothing to crave to make you want this world to be a better place. Do not take this offer lightly, however, Mr Hastings. It could be a long, hard, and very uncomfortable road for you, and any non-compliance once you have started the program could lead you to a much harsher sentence than you would otherwise have received. It is a path to redemption and a route to a clean life within the system, away from criminality, under the guidance of a man who has a proven track record in reforming the lives of many young men like yourself. So, Mr Hastings. Do you accept this offer and avoid jail?"

The nervous 18-year-old looked at his lawyer, who gave him a small nod, with a very tired expression on his face.

Hastings had been grabbed internally by the judge's words about a life within the system, away from criminality. As he had gotten older he had ever wondered how this could be possible. How could he ever escape this life? He knew he could never get a job given his criminal record, and he had no family to fall back on to help him rebuild. He had always accepted that he would be a loner forever, making a small dishonest living from various unscrupulous activities like his car-theft scam. It had seemed that a proper job was never going to be his destiny. But here was a judge offering him a way out.

The large youth lifted his head, a small tear running down the side of his cheek. He knew he should be on his way to prison right now, and yet this empathetic judge had effectively saved him. He couldn't bring himself to smile. He hadn't smiled since he was just a toddler, running around in the meadow with his mother and father. He could still remember vividly the sunny days when the three of them would sit on the grass on the hills overlooking Leeds. It wasn't until he was much older that he realised that on those occasions his parents were probably injecting heroine while he ran around nearby. Still, he had never doubted their love, and they were the only happy memories he had.

"I accept," said Hastings quietly, struggling to speak properly given the way he was choking up.

"Excellent!" proclaimed Judge Harris.

The short man on the judge's right rose to his feet and walked over towards Hastings, instinctively forcing the young man to also stand. The judge cleared his throat.

"William Hastings. Please meet George Havelock."

Printed in the United States
By Bookmasters